I THINK
I LOVE
YOU

AURIANE DESOMBRE

I THINK I LOVE YOU

Underlined

Text copyright © 2021 by Auriane Desombre
Jacket art copyright © 2021 by Jeff Östberg

All rights reserved. Published in the United States by Underlined, an imprint of Random House Children's Books, a division of Penguin Random House LLC, New York.

Underlined is a registered trademark and the colophon is a trademark of Penguin Random House LLC.

Visit us on the Web! GetUnderlined.com

Educators and librarians, for a variety of teaching tools, visit us at RHTeachersLibrarians.com

Library of Congress Cataloging-in-Publication Data is available upon request.
ISBN 978-0-593-17976-5 (pbk.) — ISBN 978-0-593-17977-2 (ebook)

The text of this book is set in 11-Gamma ITC Std.
Interior design by Cathy Bobak

Printed in the United States of America
10 9 8 7 6 5 4 3 2 1
First Edition

For Jack, the funniest person I know

I THINK
I LOVE
YOU

CHAPTER ONE

Emma
· ·

I delete emails from school, unread, on principle (especially the ones they send out at the start of summer break), but I've already read this one four times. I scroll through it once more, my eye lingering on the phrases that made my heart jolt. *NYC-LA Film Festival, emerging student artists,* and my personal favorite, *fully funded trip to Los Angeles.*

The guy walking behind me huffs as I commit the cardinal New York sin, stopping in my tracks in the middle of a busy sidewalk. I ignore him, scanning the email one more time. Kate, my cousin, peers over my shoulder curiously, but I can't tear my eyes off it. I've been putzing around New York with my uncle's camera for years, but I've never shown my stuff to people who aren't related to me. This film contest is a chance for me to show it to industry professionals—people who will take my work seriously.

This could be my chance to tell the gay rom-com story of

1

my heart, the kind I've never seen on-screen before, despite the hours of my life I've spent glued to the Netflix romantic comedy section, falling in love with the idea of love even as I yearned to see myself in the stories about it. Just because the straights in Hollywood don't know how to tell my story doesn't mean it's not out there.

"Look at this." I tilt the phone screen so Kate can get a better look, and read it one more time along with her.

Dear Students,

We hope you are having a lovely summer break! Here is a wonderful opportunity from the NYC–LA Film Festival. The festival supports emerging student artists and has opened a high school division within its student contests.

The contest entry requires a fifteen-minute short film in a genre of your choice. The grand prize–winning team will receive a scholarship to be used for tuition toward an undergraduate degree related to film, and a fully funded trip to Los Angeles, where the team will attend networking events and have the option to interview for summer internships at high-profile film production companies. The winning student film will also be presented at the NYC–LA Film Festival alongside the winning entries from the undergraduate and graduate student contest divisions, and winning filmmakers and their guests will be invited to the screening.

We hope you will represent Messina High School with your fabulous work! Click here to find out more.

Best,

Jennifer Austin

Dean of Student Life

When she finishes reading, Kate smiles at me, dimples crinkling into her cheeks as her face lights up with the kind of gentle support she always gives me. "That sounds so perfect for you."

"We have to enter this contest." I stow my phone back in my tote bag. "We could make a whole short film."

Not to mention the scholarship money, which I know would go a long way in convincing my parents to let me go to film school. So far, their response has been *Choose a degree that has more return on investment,* rather than the *Yes, we support your dreams unconditionally* approach I've been hoping for.

Plus, how many high school students get to interview for internships at actual production companies? (None, if I go by the many polite emails I've gotten in response to my applications, emails inviting me to reapply when I'm in college.) If I win this competition the summer before my junior year of high school, that will definitely help me stand out.

Kate raises her eyebrows. "I'm not sure how much help I'd be. I don't know anything about film."

I twist my thick dark curls into a messy bun to get my hair off my sweat-soaked skin. It's only June, but the classic New

York summer humidity has already thickened the air. Even my strappy floral dress isn't light enough to save me.

"Let's get to Georgie's," I tell Kate. "We can talk about it in the AC."

She nods, and we jog across the street, sidestepping an overflow of trash on the opposite corner, and pull open the door to the café. The sweet, sweet cold air rushes over my skin, raising goose bumps on my arms. I breathe a sigh of relief. It smells like coffee and vanilla from the candles burning along the windowsill. None of the hot garbage stench from the street has made it inside.

I wave to Tom, who's already staked out our usual table in the corner. Kate wanders over to him. They hug awkwardly, Kate blushing at the contact with him. I watch them, forcing myself to ignore the twitch in my pulse. I want Kate to be happy, more than anything else. At least one of us might find love.

Just not me. I've been holding out for my sweeping love story, one that's exactly like the way my parents met after they'd been anonymous hall rivals all of their freshman year of college. I want the longing, the butterflies, the staying up late at night replaying our most recent kisses, all the beautiful things they had. Instead, all I have is stress about telling my parents that I'm bisexual.

That, and exactly zero suitors. At least I have a cat to get me set up for my looming spinster days.

I swallow hard against the feeling and force myself to smile as I join Myrah at the counter. She's wearing the gold eyeliner

4

I got her for her birthday, which looks incredible against her dark skin, even if the matching gold necklace clashes horribly with the puke-green apron her boss makes her wear.

"Can you believe them?" I ask Myrah. "I don't know how much more of this mutual pining I can take before they get together already."

She grimaces at me, leaning against the cash register.

"Welcome to Georgie's. How can I help you?" she asks in a deadpan.

"It's only"—I glance at my phone screen—"ten-thirty. You can't be that dead inside already."

Myrah blinks at me, her flat expression unchanged, and I laugh.

"Bet you wish you'd just worked at JCPenney with me during the year so we could have the summer off together," I say.

"If you say 'I told you so' one more time, I'll—" Myrah starts, but I hold up my phone, cutting her off. She leans over the counter to scan the email, her apron bunching at her hips.

"Is this for real?" she asks when she finishes.

"Yeah, the school just sent it," I tell her. "You would definitely get into that screenwriting course next summer if we won this."

"And if I did that, I couldn't work here anymore," she says, glaring at the coffee shop at large.

In its defense, it's the cutest coffee shop in the Village. Rows of little wooden tables line the white walls, and the arched windows are framed with plants. Plus, there's enough room

5

to maneuver without crashing into someone else's cup of tea, which is more than I can say for anywhere else in the city.

"Okay, I'm in," Myrah say. "I think we should— So, an iced tea for you?" she adds loudly as her boss walks by.

I stifle a giggle and take the drink she passes me, and then make my way over to Kate and Tom. Setting it on the table between us, I slide into the empty chair next to Kate.

"Where's Matt?" I ask. We agreed to meet here this morning to offer Myrah moral support during her shift, but now I want to get everyone on board for the movie.

Tom shrugs. "He should be here soon. Why?"

I slide my phone over so he can read the email. As he scans my screen, I round on Kate.

"You could do costume design," I tell her. I've always admired her work. Her focus has been on body positivity in design ever since she got serious about fashion, and her clothes always look amazing. "Besides, it's a trip to LA. Look, you can even bring a plus-one."

I fish through my bag for my notebook, and turn to a fresh page to start scribbling down roles. At the top, I write in bold lettering *Untitled Rom-Com of My Heart.*

Making a rom-com that acknowledges that there are bi girls in the world feels like the perfect start to my film career. I write my name next to *director,* give Myrah the screenwriter title, and list the rest of our squad down the page.

"Maybe you should wait until people agree to work on it with you before you start assigning roles," Kate says as she scans the page over my shoulder.

I nudge her out of the way. "You all better do it with me."

Tom is already nodding. He's the biggest movie nerd in our group (aside from me, of course).

"Put me down for director of photography," he says. Dimples dig into his cheeks, which are scuffed red at his insistence on shaving even though he doesn't really need to. "I need a cinematography reel for college applications."

I scribble that into my notebook and look expectantly at Kate, tapping my pen next to her name.

Kate fidgets in her seat. "I don't know, guys. I'm working at the teen center this summer, so I'll be busy. And you were all in TV Production together, and I know nothing about cameras. You don't need me."

I scoff. "I always need you. Plus, think how great being a costume designer for a movie at a film festival would look on your college apps. And this would definitely help me get into NYU." A smile tugs at the corner of her lips, so I keep going. "And again, I cannot emphasize this enough, but if we win, we get to go to LA. For free. To be part of a super-professional film festival."

"And interview for internships," Tom adds. "And get college money."

I glance over at him. The excitement shining in his eyes mirrors mine. He needs this as much as I do.

His smile wins Kate over. "Fine, you win. I'll design your costumes."

I squeal and throw my arms around her shoulders. "You're the best."

This is true. Despite her constant rants that the brands she loves never carry cute clothes in her size, her love of fashion has made her the best-dressed person I know. Even now, in the thick of summer when absolutely no one ever looks cute, she's made her sunny-yellow-sundress-and-flower-hair-accessory combo truly stunning. Her fashionable touch will make the movie special.

She digs her sketchbook out of her bag and opens it on the table. The door swings open, and Matt walks in. After a pause at the counter, where Myrah gives him the same dead-inside greeting she treated me to, he joins us.

"How are you drinking hot coffee?" I ask, glancing at his steaming mug. "I sweated my body weight off on the walk over."

"Thanks for that image," he says as he raises his mug to his lips.

"You're welcome," I say primly. "Read this."

Matt leans across the table to read the email. The strong scent of his overapplied body spray prickles my nose as he nudges me out of the way to finish reading. "Emma, the deadline is three weeks away. You know I want to help you, but we can't make a whole movie in three weeks. That's too much work."

"The student entry only has to be, like, fifteen minutes long," I protest. "We can put together fifteen minutes of footage, easy."

Matt winces, his eyes fixed on the screen to avoid meeting my gaze.

"Come on," I say, nudging his shoulder. "It'll be fun. We hang out all the damn time anyway; we might as well do something useful. And everyone else is already in, so you basically have to."

Matt, heavily outnumbered, sighs. "Fine."

I breathe a sigh of relief. Making this movie is the first step into the film industry. I can't imagine anyone I'd rather take that step with than this bunch of awesome nerds. Thinking about it makes my heart light up with warmth.

It's moments like these when I'm truly grateful that Sophia Kingsley, Tom's best friend, moved away to Paris. Now that she's been gone for a whole year, I'm finally free to do the things I love alongside the people I love, without her hanging around and making everything awkward.

"What can I do to help?" Matt asks.

He was in TV Production too, but unlike Tom and me, he's not looking to work in film. It was the only elective that fit into his AP-laden schedule.

"You can be in charge of snacks," I say.

"As long as I get a fancy title for the credits."

"Chief Officer in Charge of Sustenance and Morale," I tell him.

"And making sure I don't faint," Kate adds as she rips open a granola bar. She has mild syncope, and her mom is always filling her bag with snacks so she doesn't pass out.

"All we need now is an idea," Tom says.

I nod. "I want to make this a gay rom-com."

I live for the cheesiness of rom-coms, for the size of the

love stories they portray, blown up to fill a whole movie with the depth of the romance. I've seen every rom-com I've come across, even the bad ones, and I've loved every single one of them. Especially the bad ones.

"I love that idea," Kate says quickly.

The warmth returns to my heart. Ever since I came out to the group as bi two years ago, she's tried her best to find little ways to be supportive. Especially since I haven't told my parents yet, or anyone in our family except her.

"I think it could be sweet and funny," I say. "We don't see a lot of gay representation in the rom-com sphere, and it would mean a lot to people."

Me being the people in this scenario.

Myrah joins us, bearing a croissant on a plate.

"I think that's for someone else," I tell her.

"I know," she says. "But I wanted to talk to you guys. How's the movie going?"

I show her the notebook. "We're thinking a gay rom-com."

Myrah grins. "Sounds good. I'll write about whatever you want, but only if you find me a date for Kate's dance."

The teen center that hired Kate is planning a summer fling dance for its campers, and even though we all privately agree that it sounds as lame as shit because most of the campers are in the eleven-to-twelve age group, Kate is organizing it, so we all have to go.

"I would do that either way," I say. "But what about Colin?"

She swallows, her gaze dropping to her fingers as she traces the rim of the croissant plate. "I broke up with him."

"Oh, I'm sorry." I lean over the back of my chair to hug her waist. Colin was her sixth relationship in the two years we've been in high school, so we're all familiar with the Myrah breakup routine. Especially Myrah.

"It's fine," she says. "We were only together for, like, a month. He was barely my boyfriend."

"What happened?" Kate asks, getting up to wrap her arm around Myrah's shoulders.

"We didn't want the same things," Myrah says. "I don't know. I'm not that sad about it per se. It would be nice to date someone long enough to call it a relationship. I'm sick of this short-term dating cycle I'm stuck in."

She swallows, and Kate tightens her grip on Myrah's shoulders. Matt wraps her in a hug. He's the best hugger in the squad—despite his tendency to lean into the body spray too hard—on account of his broad shoulders. She buries her head in his chest for a moment, and her shoulders shudder. It's impossible to tell if that's from crying or from struggling to not inhale Matt's cologne.

"You'll find someone," I say, but the words feel hollow on my tongue. I know how useless they feel when I'm the one hearing them, when Kate tries to comfort me in moments when my yearning for my own great love story takes over.

"Everyone has their own path," Tom says. "Finding love doesn't mean it'll last forever."

The corners of his lips turn down as he speaks, and my lips twist in sympathy as I realize he's thinking about Kendra Lyman, his first girlfriend, who cheated on him at homecoming with Chris Doyle after she and Tom had been together for almost two years. It took us a week to get Tom out of his room after that. He hasn't dated anyone since.

Though he sure has been making eyes at Kate a lot.

"Whatever," Myrah mumbles. She lifts herself from Matt's chest and rubs her eyes with the heels of her hands. Her mascara smudges. "Let's focus on this movie. I can write you a rom-com."

We back away from the huddle we've formed around Myrah, returning to our original seats. Myrah drags an empty chair over from a nearby table and shoves it between Matt and me. Tom scoots his chair closer to Kate, who's sitting on my other side, and traces the outline of one of the fashion designs in her open sketchbook.

"This is so cool," he says, looking up to meet her eyes.

I don't need to glance at Kate's face to know that it's glowing red.

"Thanks," she says. "But you're the one who's going to make the movie. Your stuff is always so impressive."

I watch them out of the corner of my eye, not bothering to hide my smile. I might be nauseous with envy, but I can't help smiling at the way they look at each other.

Even if their little romantic moment means I'm left sitting here alone, twiddling my thumbs.

"Aaaall byyyy myyyseeeeelf," I sing under my breath. Myrah hears me and glances up at Tom and Kate. She snorts, but Kate doesn't get it.

"What's up?" she asks, shifting in her seat to face me.

I smile at her. "Nothing. Go back to flirting."

"Wh—" Kate blushes, her cheeks turning a steep red. "I wasn't—"

Before I can answer, the door swings open again. I glance over at the movement, not expecting to see anyone we know. The whole squad is already here.

So when I spot a sleek crop of blond hair, my heart ices over.

Sophia Kingsley is standing in the doorway.

I stare at her, my brain blanking as white static panic noise fills my ears.

She left. She was gone. The day she moved to Paris factors as one of the top four days of my life because it meant the end of awkward silences and transparent attempts to distance myself from her so people would stop shipping us just because we're the only two out-at-school gay girls in our grade.

Why is she back?

The rest of the group freezes around me, and I can feel their collective shock. Kate's eyes grow wide, Matt inhales sharply, and Myrah's jaw drops.

Tom screeches and shoves past me to bounce across the room and throw his arms around her.

"You're here," he says, his voice breaking with excitement. "You're back."

She hugs him, her grip tight around his shoulders. "I'm back."

Matt and Myrah jump out of their seats to join the lovefest. They pile into a giant group hug, their surprise and enthusiasm pouring out of their traitorous mouths. I turn to Kate, whose face turns red when she sees my expression.

"Why is she back?" I ask.

"Let's go ask her," she says.

I grab her wrist to stop her from moving toward them. "Kate, you know how I feel about her."

"What has she ever done that was so bad?" Kate folds her arms across her chest.

I slump down, my spine digging into the back of my rickety chair. Sure, Sophia's constant anti-love rants rub me the wrong way. But the truth is, Sophia has never done anything so terrible to me. When I came out as bi, I could tell that Sophia was everyone's first thought. Like, just because I'm bi and she's a lesbian, everyone assumed we'd end up together.

I hate the assumption more than I hate her. So I keep her at arm's length.

"Well?" Kate says.

I shrug. Shaking her head at me, she gets up to join the rest of the squad, and wriggles into their group hug.

I pointedly cross my legs away from the group as they make their way back to the table. Then I fold my arms and stare at Sophia with what I like to think is a cool, aloof expression.

She's taller than when she left, so she towers over me even more. At least she's built like a twig—I could totally take her in a fight. She's wearing thin dangly earrings, skinny jeans, a flowy French blouse, and what I'm pretty sure is an actual *beret* pinned to her head. She looks like Paris vomited onto her.

Sophia looks me and my basic blue floral dress up and

down. I shrink under her gaze. She comes with a healthy side of overconfident *I came out to my parents years ago and they still love me* vibe that rattles my nerves every time I see her. The sleek new Parisian haircut she's sporting doesn't help either.

Before either of us can say anything, Tom turns to Sophia with a giant smile on his face.

"Hey, we're making a movie. What do you want to do?"

And just like that, Sophia, avowed relationship-hater, pops my happy gay rom-com-making bubble. It'll destroy the movie if she's on set, dragging us all down with her horrible love-is-stupid vibes.

"Direct, obviously," Sophia says. "I learned loads about film while I was in France. We could do something really artsy and cool."

I wrinkle my nose. Artsy is the last thing I want for my rom-com.

"I'm the director," I say. "It was my idea in the first place, so you can't fight me on it."

At least she respects dibs. "Fine. I'll be the screenwriter."

"Myrah's already writing it."

"I'll act, then," Sophia says flatly.

I swallow. I'm out of excuses.

"That's perfect," Tom says.

"We needed an actress," Kate says, pursing her lips at me. "You chose the perfect day to come back, Soph."

I turn away from Sophia, looking back down at my notebook, but my mind stays stuck on her. Now that she's back, she'll ruin everything. How am I supposed to win this contest with a sweet love story when she complained all of freshman year about love? She spent the whole time shitting on Tom for being in a relationship, and teasing me whenever I mentioned a favorite rom-com. I can't have that kind of energy on my set.

"How did you even know we were here?" I mutter.

"I called Tom's, and his dad told me," she says. Her shoulders slump forward, and for a moment I feel bad.

But then I remember that she's already threatening my movie, and I'm going to end up a single mess who never gets to go to LA. And die alone with Lady Catulet and all her future kittens.

Damn. Even in my wildest fantasies, my cat's love life is more exciting than mine.

And with Little Miss France on my set, it's gonna stay that way forever.

CHAPTER TWO

SOPHIA

· ·

Tom nudges me as soon as I sit down. "Why didn't you tell me you were coming back?"

I flinch. When I left Dad's tacky new apartment this morning, he beamed at me over his cup of coffee. "Your friends must be so excited to see you again, Sausage," he said, using my childhood nickname, the one that has stuck since I was four and was much shorter and stockier and sausage-like than I am now. The nickname made me think of our summer trips to Coney Island when I was in elementary school, my parents each taking me by one hand so they could swing me forward. I'd tumble forward, screeching with laughter, and whenever I fell, Dad would ask, "You okay, Sausage?" while Mom dug through her purse for princess Band-Aids.

Of course, my family is totally gone now. The divorce made sure of that.

"They can't wait," I said, and I let the front door of his

brand-new apartment—the one he got without me—slam shut before he could ask me any more questions.

Now, though, I wish I'd told Dad the truth. I didn't tell anyone I was coming back. It wasn't a conscious decision. I kept opening our group chat, ready to tell them I'd be back after the school year ended, but then I'd see all the messages they sent each other all day. They'd talk about moments I wasn't there for, quip at each other with inside jokes I'd missed, and make weekend plans I couldn't join. When I scrolled back up to count, I found only four texts from me, lost in a sea of messages among them. How was I supposed to chime in out of the blue to announce I was coming back?

So now I do the only thing I can. I smile at Tom, and I lie. "I wanted to surprise you."

He flashes his teeth, but it looks like the movement strains his cheek muscles. "I missed you. We didn't hear from you much."

I swallow. "I was so wrapped up in Paris. It's pretty great over there."

If lying alone in my bedroom with a shitty brokenhearted playlist counts as great, that is.

"What, too cool for us now?" Tom asks. He's still smiling, but his voice wobbles and his thick eyebrows knit together, contradiction written all over his face.

I laugh, pretending I don't hear how upset he is. "Of course not, *mon ami.*"

I shift in my seat to examine the leafy green plants lining the windowsill. Anything is better than looking at the skeptical hurt darkening Tom's eyes.

It's a short-lived relief, though. As soon as Myrah's boss is done shooing her away from us back to her post by the cash register, the litany of Paris questions descends again. Only Emma, who barely shoots me a glance before scurrying after Myrah, doesn't seem to care.

That suits me just fine. This is awkward enough without throwing Emma into the mix. Everyone always expects me to be with her, and the way she goes on about rom-coms, I worry that she expects it herself. I'm not about to throw myself into a relationship with anyone, though. I've seen where that road leads, and I want nothing to do with it. The awkward silences we share whenever the two of us end up alone together, which I've made sure is rarely, are more than enough relationship with Emma for me. It's a good thing that she left to hang out with Myrah by the register as soon as I sat down.

"Did you meet any cute French girls?" Matt asks.

I take a deep breath, which is meant to clear my head but which only serves to remind me that teen boys, as a group, really need to learn to stop using cologne as a replacement for deodorant. Reason number 2,347,683 why I love being a lesbian.

Matt and Tom stare at me, waiting for an answer, and I yearn for the floor to swallow me whole. When the floor fails me, I toss my hair instead.

"Bien sûr," I say with a coy smile. Saying it feels like a betrayal to Julianne, but I make myself keep it light. They don't want to hear about the messy French flirtation that I ran away from as soon as it could've turned into something real, and I don't want to tell them about it.

I keep my fake confidence up throughout their question-ing. I roll my *r*'s as though this French accent sounds natural against my lips, even as it slashes my throat. But no matter how much I try, I'll always be the one who was gone for the whole year; who missed out on all the inside jokes and movie nights; who didn't answer their messages and lay around in Paris, in-haling the warm-bread smell from the bakery across the street and wishing the smell comforted me as much as it felt like it should.

I tug at the collar of my blouse. I wore it because it makes me look French, but it's been squeezing against my throat all morning.

"And how was your mom's wedding?" Kate asks, leaning over Tom's lanky frame to meet my eye.

"We saw the pictures," Tom says. Accusation flashes in his voice.

I bite my lip, and flinch at the waxy taste of my matte lipstick. "Yeah. Sorry I didn't keep more in touch. I was so wrapped up in it all."

I keep my tone as level as I can. How much fun can they have expected me to have in France? I was only there because my parents got divorced. It wasn't exactly the romantic vaca-tion they all seem to want it to be.

"Well, tell us about it now, then," Tom says.

I wrinkle my nose at the memory of Mom in a flowery white dress, the symbolism of which is somewhat ruined when one's daughter is stuck in the bridal party, wearing a puffy blue monstrosity. Especially when that daughter used to think she

20

had the perfect family, tied together by her parents' perfect love for each other and for her.

It was always just the three of us, going on weekend trips around the city. Every winter, we'd go ice-skating exactly one time, and then fifteen minutes in, after we'd all fallen over each other at least three times, we'd remember that no one in our special little trio had the balance necessary to skate. We'd give up and get hot chocolate, and judge the other skaters as if we were commentators at the Olympics, rather than a bunch of clumsy idiots who'd barely lasted five seconds on the ice. Mom and Dad would both do silly voices and get some newscaster banter going that always made me snort hot chocolate out my nose.

Then they got divorced and tore all that apart, and my mom abandoned me in Brooklyn so she could go live her best romantic life in Paris, because apparently her best life doesn't include me. She only tore me away from my life here long enough to make me watch her pledge to love someone for the rest of her life. And those vows aren't quite as impressive if they're made barely a year after the bride has just finished shredding the same pledge she made to another man.

And then she packed me right away again, so she could enjoy that newlywed life without the bother of having me around, a constant reminder of the life we used to share.

"Did you make any cool new French friends?" Kate asks.

Her tone is friendly, but I can hear what lies underneath. *What new friends did you make that were so cool that you didn't talk to us for months?* But it's not like I can tell them about

Julianne, even though we agreed that we should be *friends*. Not that she wanted much to do with me or my friendship after she got a new girlfriend. Yet another way that romance found to ruin my life.

I glance down at my phone, as if thinking about her is enough to conjure a text from her, but the screen stays dark.

When I don't answer, Tom sighs, turning to Kate. "How's dance prep going?"

She beams, and the tips of her ears grow pink when she meets his eye. It's hard to tell how Kate really feels about you, because she's so lovely to everyone, but maybe she likes Tom back after all. The thought makes me shudder. The last thing I need is to spend the rest of the year dealing with a couple. I already had enough of that with Julianne and her new girlfriend making out all over our *lycée* and snubbing my offers to hang out. I can't lose Tom to a new romance too.

"It's going pretty good," she says, the earlier tension dissolving from her tone when she looks at Tom. "We're still trying to work out a theme, but we have the DJ and the food all set."

"Maybe we can use it for a scene in the movie," Tom says. "Really showcase your design skills."

I perk up. I wasn't just trying to pull rank on Emma with my cinema talk earlier. I got really into movies while I was in France. Plus, this competition could be more than a huge professional opportunity. It could be my way back into the group.

"Do we have a script yet?" I ask, leaning toward the group. "I was thinking it could be really fun to do something more avant-garde. That kind of thing always does really well at festivals, and—"

"Oh, I think Emma wanted to do a rom-com," Matt says.

I glance over at Emma, who's giggling by the counter with Myrah. Her whole face lights up when she laughs.

"A rom-com?" I ask. I can't think of anything I would want to do less. "For a festival?"

"I think it sounds sweet," Kate says softly.

I bite my lip. Two seconds in, and my one plan to win back my friends is already shooting me in the foot. I can't make a whole movie singing the praises of romance right after the awful time I had in Paris. I just can't.

"That never does well at festivals," I say with a dismissive wave of my hand. "We should have a brainstorming meeting and talk about it."

"Great idea," Kate, always the peacemaker, says brightly. She waves to Emma, who exchanges glances with Myrah before making her way to us.

"When can we have a brainstorming meeting with all of us?" Kate asks. "To talk about the movie."

"Myrah gets off work at four," Emma tells her. "We could start writing after that?"

"We need to settle on an idea before we start writing," I point out.

Emma glances down at me, her dark eyes flashing. "We already have an idea. We're doing a rom-com."

I purse my lips. "I don't know if that's the best idea for a festival."

"Excuse me?" Emma's arched eyebrows knit together.

I want to flinch under her gaze, but I force myself to stay cool. I cross my legs, my knee knocking against the bottom of the table.

"More cinematic, artsier pieces tend to do really well at festivals," I say. "If we did something like that, we could have a real chance."

"We have a real chance with a rom-com," Emma says, her tone unchanging.

"We can talk about it at the meeting," Kate says before I can argue.

I nod, and Emma sets her mouth into a firm line. I look away from her, twisting my fingers around a strand of short hair. If they do a rom-com, there'll be no room for me in this movie, and I'll lose my in. I'll lose my friends. I already spent the past year totally alone after I lost my only friend to the clutches of romance. I can't lose these guys too.

Emma turns away to tell Myrah about the meeting, leaving me to smile awkwardly at the rest of the squad to cover for the painful silence that follows.

Untitled <u>Rom-Com</u> of My Heart

Taken from the notebook of Emma Hansen

Director—Emma Hansen

Director of Photography—Thomas Levine

Screenwriter—Myrah Evans

Costume Designer—Katerina Perez

Chief Officer in Charge of Sustenance and Morale—Matthew Jeffers

Idea: A gay rom-com!!!! We need this!!!

Notes:

What tropes?

All of them—definitely there will be only one bed at some point.

Can Lady Catulet have a part?

No, she would ruin everything.

Would Georgie's let us shoot there?

Myrah's boss is a meanie, but maybe? Worth asking!

Teen Center?

Parks—which ones are we allowed to shoot in without a permit?

Thrift stores for costume pieces.

Cast: Sophia Kingsley

CHAPTER THREE

Emma
· ·

When I picked the library across from the coffee shop as our meeting space, I didn't realize how much I would want to shout for the entire meeting. We're only ten minutes into the meeting, and my blood is boiling.

"There's nothing wrong with a rom-com," I say heatedly, for what feels like the billionth time. I keep my voice low, since we're at a crowded row of tables between the dimly lit stacks. The guy sitting next to me has already shot me several dirty looks.

"I'm not saying there is," Sophia huffs, even though that sure sounds like what she's saying. "I was thinking that it would be cool if, instead of a rom-com, we do something a bit more dramatic. If we push the boundaries of our subject matter a little more, we could really—"

"We're doing a gay rom-com," I say, folding my arms across my chest. "That's nonnegotiable."

"Who died and put you in charge?" Sophia mutters.

I gape at her. Where is this coming from?

"No one had to die. I'm the one who found out about the contest. This whole thing was my idea."

"Well, I'm the one who spent a year hanging out in the *birthplace of cinema.*" She tugs at the bottom of her blouse. "A good leader knows how to use her assets, Madame La Directrice."

I bite the tip of my tongue, hard, to keep myself from rolling my eyes.

"Maybe we can compromise," Kate says quickly. "Did you learn any French when you were away?"

"*Où sont les toilettes?*" Sophia says, her accent so prim and proper that it makes me want to rip her tongue out of her mouth.

"Where's the bathroom?" The corners of my lips rise as seventh-grade foreign-language class comes back to me. "Classy."

Sophia glances down at me. "*Tu me fais chier.*"

"What does that mean?" Kate asks, a strain winding through her tone despite her obvious efforts to keep it light.

"Literally, 'You make me shit,'" Sophia mumbles.

Kate's face freezes in shock, but I'm struggling not to laugh. Sophia is the enemy here, I remind myself. She's trying to take away my rom-com.

Still, she's kind of funny.

"It means 'You annoy me.' Whoever came up with it must've known you," she adds, meeting my eye.

A high-pitched giggle seeps into my voice despite my best efforts to squash it. "I think you're confusing me with Activia."

Myrah sighs. "I don't think we're getting anything done here."

"And the librarian is about twelve seconds away from shushing us again," Kate adds, glancing over her shoulder in her constant fear of getting in trouble.

"Why don't we each take some time apart to come up with more fleshed-out ideas?" I say. "Then we meet up and decide as a group. It's a team effort."

This is the perfect plan. There's no way Sophia will be able to come up with a plot. All her "ideas" so far are just words masked with French superiority and the insistence that "that's what does well at festivals."

I have ideas already. Ones I'm passionate about. That's what does well at festivals.

Now I just have to convince the rest of the group.

I glare at Myrah and Kate, my arms folded across my chest. They have the audacity to sit there, perched on the end of my bed, chatting about the day as if my life hasn't been utterly ruined.

I say as much, and Myrah tsks at me. "You're such a drama queen."

I purse my lips as I lean across the bed to drag my cat onto my lap. The only one here who hasn't forsaken me. I'm sitting cross-legged in the middle of my plush purple duvet, and I dump her onto my thighs. She paws at the hem of my dress, and I can't help but smile at her little bean feet. "What do you think, Lady Catulet?"

She meows, and I kiss the top of her head. Turning to the two traitors, I smirk. "She agrees with me."

"Funny how she always does that," Myrah says.

I glare at them again, narrowing my eyes as far as I can without closing them completely. My vision becomes a blur of eyelashes.

"That's because I'm always right," I say. "I don't want Sophia dragging us all down."

Kate and Myrah exchange glances. Myrah swings her legs around so that they're stretched out on the bed in front of her. There's not much room to sit in here. I'm operating with New York City apartment sizes, so my bed takes up most of the space, and the rest of it is always a clutter of books, DVDs, and clean laundry I haven't gotten around to folding yet because I'm still suffering from JCPenney-induced folding nightmares. It always looks like a hurricane exploded through my closet, so we end up in a pile on my mattress, the eye of the laundry storm.

"How is she dragging us all down again?" Myrah asks. She shakes her legs out against the mattress.

"She's going to ruin my cute rom-com with her angsty French *I know all about cinema* bullshit."

I slouch, staring gloomily at the fading *Clueless* poster my mom got me for my fourteenth birthday. The poster lines the wall opposite my bed, and I have fairy lights strung above it because I told myself they would make the messiness of my room look homier. I always forget to buy batteries for them, though, so it ends up looking like I thought it would be cute to decorate my walls with weird bits of wire.

At least I have cute floral throw pillows, or else this room would be a full disaster zone.

"It'll all be okay," Kate says. She stretches across the bed to rub a comforting slow circle on my back.

I give her a sly grin.

"Anyway, Tom seemed into your designs," I say with a smile. I can't help myself, even if it makes the zit breaking out on my chin ache. This is a real-life rom-com waiting to happen.

"Funny," Myrah says, playing along. "I didn't realize Tom was so into costuming."

"He's been helping me with some of my ideas," Kate says, her voice so low, she barely squeaks out the words.

I scoot toward them to needle her further. Lady Catulet yowls at the movement, and jumps off my lap to dart under the bed. Her tail pokes out from under the edge of the blanket.

"I can't believe Kate finally has boy drama," Myrah practically coos with excitement.

"I do not have boy drama," Kate protests. "I just—"

I'm not about to let her try to convince us that nonsense is true, so I cut her off. "Like a boy, but you're too shy to tell him how you feel? Just like he's too shy, for that matter? That sounds like boy drama to me."

Placated by the calm, Lady Catulet leaps to me and pads

around on my lap to make a comfy bed of my thighs. I stroke her head while keeping eye contact with Kate like a James Bond villain, and the cat purrs into my palm. "Doesn't it, Lady Catulet?"

She meows again, and Myrah rolls her eyes.

"Stop using your cat for validation. Did you train her or something?"

I smirk. "She knows wisdom when she hears it."

"I'm glad someone else finally has the boy drama," Myrah says, lifting her body up on her palms so she can cross her legs underneath her before dropping down. "Speaking of which, I have this new coworker who's super dreamy-looking." She pauses, wrinkling her nose. "So much so that I just used the word *dreamy* in casual conversation."

"What?" I lean over, flop onto my stomach, and cross my legs behind me. Lady Catulet squirms to escape my arm, so I lift it to let her dart away. "You *just* broke up with Colin."

"I know," Myrah says with a shrug. "But I told you, I'm not so cut up about it. We were only together for a month; it's not like I've lost the greatest love of my life."

I inhale, the smell of the pine tree candle flickering on my cluttered nightstand washing over me. "What's his name?"

"Peter," Myrah says. Her face lights up when she says his name, and I sigh wistfully. If it won't happen for me, at least I get to watch my friends fall in love, to marvel at the way it lights them up from the inside out. "His first day was today, and I swear to God, I think I melted when he rolled up his sleeves to figure out how the latte machine works. That *arm hair*." She wiggles her eyebrows at Kate, who blushes.

"Oooh, when's the wedding?" I ask. Myrah shoves me, and I topple over, grabbing Lady Catulet so she doesn't fall off the bed as I collide with the mattress.

Kate throws her arms around Myrah's neck and pulls her into her chest. They're pretty cute, the two of them, mooning over their boys and falling over each other in love.

And I guess it's totally fine that I'm sitting on the outside, watching them. I have Lady Catulet. I hug her to my chest, and she claws at me to get away.

Or not.

"Look at you guys," I say. "You're so cute, with your Peters and your Toms."

They break out of their hug. Myrah's all blushy-smiley, but Kate buries her face in her hands.

"This is why we need to make a rom-com," I say, gesturing to the two of them. "This means so much to all of us, this whole love thing. We could make something so special. Please don't let Sophia ruin everything."

Her pretentious French garbage would never get me to LA, no matter what she thinks does well at festivals.

Myrah stares at me. "You'd hate any idea she has, on principle, just because it's not a rom-com."

"Look, apparently she's been sent back from France specifically to ruin my life," I say.

Myrah turns to Kate. "See? Drama queen."

I sigh. "Doesn't make her any less annoying," Or any less of a life-ruiner. For me and my movie, and for Kate and her budding new romance with Tom.

"You were both being annoying at the meeting," Myrah argues.

I gape at her. "Excuse me?"

Myrah throws her hands up. "I'm just saying. Neither of you were listening to the other or were willing to compromise—or consider that one of us might also have ideas. You bickered the whole time like an old married couple."

I cringe. We don't bicker like a married couple. I rightfully pointed out all the flaws and stupidities in her ideas, in an effort to help her fix herself, and she argued with me because she has no introspection or taste. I don't see why she has to be part of the movie in the first place.

I guess she can be pretty funny. And, objectively, some people might find her attractive, with her graceful curls and high cheekbones. If they haven't had their eyes checked in a few years.

But that's it. She brings nothing else to the table.

"Well. I'm not about to stop fighting her. So. Guess we have to kick her out of the movie," I say, shrugging. "She basically excused herself when she went to Paris and stopped answering all your messages. And then didn't even tell anyone she was coming back. Or are we looking past that now?"

Kate examines her fingernails, her typical response to potential conflict. Myrah laughs.

"Good luck convincing Tom to ditch her," she says with a side-eye at Kate.

And then, I swear, Kate's face gets even redder.

"You love him," I screech, pointing to her pink cheeks. "We have to make this happen."

Even though Sophia waltzed back into our lives, apparently with a new ambition to ruin my dreams, it doesn't mean I can't still save today by getting Kate a boy. At least one of us should get to be happy.

Kate's face is positively fuchsia. "Nothing's going to happen. I'm sure he's not into me like that."

Myrah and I make eye contact, and then we burst out laughing. I double over, wheezing. My stomach aches, but I can't stop. Myrah wipes tears from the corners of her eyes.

"*He's not into me like that*," she wheezes. "Kate, you're too much sometimes."

"He's—" Kate starts, but I cut her off before she can try to argue.

It's not that I don't want to listen to her. It's just that she's so blatantly wrong, it's honestly not even worth giving her the time to make the point.

"We'll have to prod them along," I say to Myrah. "Seeing as they're both completely incapable on their own."

Kate opens her mouth to argue again, but Myrah plows through her attempt at speech.

"How are we supposed to do that?" Myrah asks, gesturing to Kate's face. "Neither of them can talk about this stuff without turning purple."

"I'm n-not . . . ," Kate sputters, but even she can't argue against that. The evidence is all over her face. And reaching for her collarbones now. She falls silent, drawing her knees toward her chest, and Myrah pushes her shoulder affection-ately.

"We'll have to help somehow," I say, brain whirling. How are we supposed to get the world's two shyest people together without their incapacity to face their feelings getting in the way?

"I can't believe you're a matchmaker now," Myrah says. "After this, you have to help me with Peter."

I catch sight of Kate's face, which has faded closer to its original light brown as her eyes have drifted off into a day-dream, and smile at Myrah. "I can't help it," I say. "Look how cute she is."

I nudge Kate. She refocuses on us. "What?"

"Nothing," I say, as sweetly as I can. "Go back to daydream-ing about Tom."

"I'm not . . . ," she starts again, but there's no arguing. Kate has no poker face, no control over her tone, and fifty thousand tells. The poor thing can't lie. "One day, you'll regret your teas-ing, Emma Hansen."

"Doubt it."

"We still need a plan," Myrah says.

I chew on my lower lip, casting my eyes around the mess in my room, as though this disaster zone holds the answers to romance.

Given that we're in my bedroom, and I'm an avowed spinster already working on my cat collection, it feels un-likely that I'll be the one to figure this whole romance thing out. But then I remember the dance Kate's been working so hard on, the one she's already cajoled us all into attending with her.

It's cliché, but the dance could work.

In fact, the dance is all I can think about for the rest of the evening. And even as an avowed romantic, this is not like me. The thought of a dance normally sends me tumbling down an anxiety spiral, in which I picture the hundreds of ways I could meet the love of my life even though I know nothing will happen and I'll end the night crushingly disappointed. But tonight, the thought of the dance has me hopeful. Maybe love can win after all.

Just not for me.

The thought consumes me so much, I'm only half listening to our family HGTV marathon.

Oh yeah. My parents and I are really cool.

We're piled onto the overstuffed couch in our living room, which, like the rest of the house, is much tidier than my room. Dad is a total neat freak, which I suppose is for the best when our apartment doesn't give us much room to work with. We have a coffee table between the couch and the TV, kept at the perfect distance to prop up our feet while we watch, and he always keeps a vase of fresh sunflowers on it.

We're halfway through our second episode of *House Hunters: International,* and Dad is cursing at the screen. Because not only do we watch things like *House Hunters: International* on a regular basis, but we also get really into it. So into it that my middle-aged father is scoffing at the floor plan of the Parisian apartment this girl is looking to buy.

"You can't have an easy commute to the center of the city at that price," he roars. I pat his shoulder in solidarity.

I'm normally swearing about the buyers' choices right alongside him, but tonight I'm only vaguely aware of the apartment the Realtor is walking her through. My mind is on the dance, and on Kate, and on Sophia, and how I can get Kate with Tom before Sophia talks him out of the real-life rom-com I'm setting up for them. She hung out with him after the meeting this afternoon, and I just know she spent the whole time trying to win him over to her side.

I have no idea how anyone could think that love is so terrible. My romanticism is my mom's fault, probably. I grew up finishing my homework at double speed so we could watch a new romantic comedy together, and I fell in love with the idea of love as I watched it written large across my television screen.

The fact that I'm not out to my parents only makes me love the on-screen romance even more. It's a safe place, a place to escape into a world where love is not only possible but guaranteed, for everyone.

Whenever I see couples at school, holding hands in the hallway or making out by lockers, I melt. Even though I wish I had someone to intertwine fingers with in the halls or text before class, I don't get how anyone could look at two people in love and not fall a little bit in love with their love. Even couples who make out in the middle of a busy street are kind of adorable.

With any luck, I'll be smiling at Kate and Tom any day now. As long as this dance thing works.

"Oh, sure, of course she's choosing her home based on the view," Dad says, his tone dripping with disdain. He leans down on the couch to rest his feet on the edge of the coffee table, using his toes to nudge aside the unopened book on European art that Mom displays there. "Who cares if you don't have a functioning kitchen. As long as you can gaze upon the Eiffel Tower while you starve to death, it'll all be fucking worth it."

Mom puts on her best stern face. "We talked about your word choices during family movie night."

"It's fucking okay, Mom," I say.

"Don't you use that language with me, young lady," she scolds, but given that she's still laughing, her comment loses its bite. Lady Catulet, who was asleep on her stomach, stirs at the movement, and pads at Mom's shirt with her tiny feet. "Family TV night is sacred space."

I sigh, turning to the TV screen. This is why I can't have love the way Kate and Tom can. I mean, sure, I'm dying to be in a relationship, but how can I threaten this? Most of the girls in my grade hate their moms right now. I love hanging out with mine, even if she has been known to say things like "It's LG-BTQIAP now? What's next? QRSTUV?" while my dad chuckles in the background.

It's not that they're homophobic per se; they do support gay rights. But some of their views are pretty outdated, and they aren't exactly bending over backward to educate themselves.

I can't risk our relationship. I can't risk things changing.

I definitely can't risk family HGTV night. Not when this girl in Paris is about to blow all her savings on an apartment with a bathroom that looks semi-functional at best, and my dad is about to throw the remote at the TV.

Mom wraps her arm around my shoulders when the show cuts to commercial, squeezing me closer to her.

"How was your day?" she asks.

I groan. "Sophia Kingsbitch came back from France today and started a campaign to ruin my idea for that film competition."

Mom clicks her tongue. "If you're going to swear, at least be clever about it."

That's my mom. Doesn't matter what I do, as long as it's funny.

Actually, that explains a lot about my worldview, now that I think of it.

"Who's that again?" Dad asks. He pushes his glasses up his nose. He only wears them when we watch TV, even though his doctor says he needs them all the time.

"That annoying girl Tom is friends with," I say. "Speaking of Tom, he's about to be Kate's boyfriend."

Dad chuckles. "Can't wait to see the look on Eduardo's face when he finds out his daughter is dating."

"Natalie will be pleased," Mom says. "She worries Kate is too shy to go after what she wants."

I swallow. Maybe I shouldn't have said anything. Teasing Kate about Tom is one thing, but if the details of my plan get back to her, it would fall apart. And Mom tells Aunt Natalie everything.

"It's a secret for now," I say. "Kate is definitely too shy to go after what she wants, so I have to go get it for her."

39

Mom rubs my shoulder before disentangling herself from me to lean against a pillow. I turn to look at her. We've switched off all the lights for movie night, so she's only lit up by the glow of the TV screen. "Don't be so focused on others that you don't take care of yourself."

"Believe me," I say with a laugh, "a lack of self-focus isn't a problem I have."

"Don't get so wrapped up in Kate finding someone that you forget to look for yourself," Mom says, nudging me. "You have to put yourself out there too."

A weak chuckle escapes my lips, and I rub my palms against my knees. "Yeah."

What else am I supposed to do? I can't exactly tell her that she's the reason why I'm not looking for love, because I can't guarantee who I'll find it with, and it might not be the boy they expect. It's easier to focus on Kate's love life instead.

Besides, it's not like anyone I know is measuring up to the great romantic love story I'm holding out for. My rom-com collection is better than anything I've found in the real world. And my laptop screen is a way safer place to watch love play out than in my own life, especially when my parents don't even know the half of who I could love.

With that in mind, I reach for my phone; my pulse drums in my fingertips as I type. If the closest I can get to happiness is through Kate, I'll take that any day of the week. She deserves a life made in the model of the happiest of romantic comedies.

I just have to pray that my plan works.

CHAPTER FOUR

SOPHIA

. . . .

I understand that lying on the couch with a brand-new teal IKEA pillow balanced on my face doesn't exactly communicate mental wellness, but it still surprises me when Dad walks into the room and immediately asks what's wrong.

"Nothing," I say without moving the pillow. My voice is muffled, but I leave the pillow there. I like it there.

Dad bends down to pat my leg awkwardly, and I tilt my head so I can see him.

"You don't look like nothing's wrong." He's looking down at me with the mail dangling from his fingers.

"Your new place is . . . nice," I say, looking around the apartment. It's a two bedroom, like we had before I left, back when I still had a functional family, but nothing else about it is the same. It's all new furniture, most of it from IKEA. I'm pretty sure I've seen this exact square coffee table in a million other apartments. The gray couch is cute-ish, I guess, but the hard

41

pillows are making my back sore, and he got an armchair in the exact same design, which is way too matchy-matchy.

"I like it too," Dad says, not quite picking up on my tone as he looks around the little living room. I follow his gaze, wishing I could find any semblance of personality in the arrangements, but it looks like he re-created an IKEA showroom. The only sign that someone lives here is the mail he drops on the coffee table.

"The apartments in Paris are so much sunnier," I say with another sigh, eyeing the one little rectangle window in the living room, which is half-blocked by the window AC unit. The window is facing the wrong way too, so that it gets too much light in the morning, and none at all in the afternoon. At least the AC is on full blast, chasing away the late-afternoon heat. It's nice to be out of the beating sunshine.

Dad reaches for the remote and flicks the TV on. "Sorry this isn't living up to your grand Parisian expectations."

I force a laugh. "They have all these nice big windows."

We watch the news for a moment, though I don't pay attention. Hearing the news in English is throwing me off.

"Do you have any plans tonight?" Dad asks as a commercial break starts.

"I might go over to Tom's."

"That would be a good idea," Dad says. He doesn't take his eyes off the TV. "I'm going to be out tonight."

"Working?" I ask. He and Mom always used to alternate when they had to work late at their respective banks. But now that they're divorced, I end up alone whenever he has to work.

"Actually," Dad says, staring hard at the TV even though it's only an ad, "I have a date."

I choke on my own spit. Coughing, I sputter, "A *d-date*? You can't have a *date.*"

Dad finally looks directly at me, his bushy eyebrows raised. "What? Your mother gets remarried, and I can't have a date?"

"I don't know who told her she could get remarried," I mutter to myself, but Dad doesn't hear me. I look up at him. "Fine. Have a good date."

He grins, patting my leg again. "Thanks, kiddo. I get it. It must be hard."

I sigh. He doesn't get it at all. If he did, if he knew that his stupid divorce and his stupid date were sentencing me to a lifetime of solitude, he wouldn't be going out in the first place. Plus, how can either of them possibly date or fall in love or get married again after what our family went through? Can't they see that love is a myth?

"No," I say, as light as a breeze. "Of course not. I'm going to Tom's, and you're going on a date. Everything is totally normal."

I swing my legs off the couch and trudge to my bedroom—also full of generic IKEA crap—to get my shoes.

A school year isn't that long, in the grand scheme of things, but it feels like it's been eighty thousand millennia since I sat here, on Tom's beanbag chair, playing video games. Even the

43

controllers, which are the exact same ones I have at home, feel unfamiliar under my fingers.

I never thought I'd feel out of place in Tom's room, even though it's the antithesis of mine. His walls are covered in nerd posters, ranging from *Doctor Who* to, my personal favorite, an original *Star Wars* poster from the seventies. His TV is pushed up against the wall opposite his bed, and the space between his bed and the TV is covered in beanbag chairs and pillows. It's like the whole place has been designed with group video game sessions in mind. Which it probably was.

My old room, on the other hand, had plants on every possible surface, so that it smelled fresh every time I walked in. There wasn't much on the walls, except for this painting of a sunset I found at a street fair, so the whole space felt perfectly peaceful. At least, it used to. Now, at Dad's new place, I just have the IKEA bedframe he picked out for me, a nightstand where I charge my phone, and a closet, where all the clothes I got in Paris are neatly stored.

But even though I love Tom's place, and have always seen it as a second home, I feel awkward here now. It's like I don't belong anymore, like I've changed so much that I can't possibly exist under the same watchful eye of a vintage Luke Skywalker poster.

It's probably why Matt is beating me so handily right now. I never used to let him do that, but here I am, living my worst nightmare.

I force myself to focus, because I'm not about to lose at video games today on top of everything else. I lean back so I can get a better view of the TV in Tom's room, which is perched precariously on a rickety stand whose shelves are stuffed with video games and old DVDs.

I squint at the screen as I swivel Darth Vader around to find another base. On-screen Darth Vader runs forward, under my control, and cuts down three oncoming rebel fighters with a swing of his lightsaber. I smirk at Matt. Rebel scum.

"Damn." Matt drops his controller into his lap as the screen flashes with my last-minute victory.

He hands the controller off to Tom. *Star Wars Battlefront* is a two-man game, which means we have to alternate. Tom settles into Matt's spot and picks Darth Vader as his character.

I frown. He knows that's my favorite, and he never used to pick it out from under me before. Now he doesn't even notice the look I throw his way. Instead he's absently fiddling with the volume control on the remote.

My spine bends as I slump over, glowering at the too-bright TV screen. I can't believe they adjusted to me being gone so quickly. My spot at our café table, in our group chats, during our video games—it's like they swept over every place I once filled, and now there's no room left for me.

Tom isn't even playing as well as he usually does. He lets me take over half the bases in about thirty seconds. I glance over at him, and his eyes are blank, his fingers idle and slow over the control buttons.

"What's with you?" I ask, more sharply than I intended.

Tom's face reddens. "Oh, um, nothing. I was . . . thinking. . . ."

He mumbles, swallowing half his words before I can hear them, but I snatch a mention of Kate's name, and my stomach drops. Is he still harping on this ridiculous crush?

45

"You okay?" I ask, praying my Kate theory isn't right. I might be re-branding myself as the Parisian One, but I refuse to let romance be part of my image. Especially because all Paris did for me was prove beyond a shadow of a doubt that love. Just. Isn't. Real.

Tom gives a half shrug, so I let the issue die there. He, however, does not.

"It's Kate," he says after a moment.

"Are you in love with her?" Matt asks, his eyes all alight and eager like this would somehow be good news. I cringe at the sight. Don't people realize how ridiculous they look when they let love take over like that?

Tom tosses the controller between his palms. "Is it that obvious?"

"I've been back for two seconds, and I knew," I say, making a face.

"Oh, you hate the idea of anyone being in a relationship," Matt says.

I swallow. How could I not? My parents said *I love you,* and then they said *I'll love you forever* in front of all their friends and family, and then they fell apart and took me down with them.

And then I tried to escape the pain of my home life by throwing myself into school, making new friends, just like everyone said I should. I met Julianne and I gravitated to her instantly, with her mass of ginger hair and the richness of her laugh. She went out of her way to help me find a home in Paris by bringing me to all her local haunts. And like an idiot, I thought we were friends.

Then she ruined everything. We were four months in, leaning over a candlelit table at our favorite restaurant, when she told me. *I love you.*

I hadn't told her about my parents' divorce—I hadn't told anyone in Paris yet—but I did that night. I told her I didn't believe in love, that I couldn't return those feelings, but that I loved our friendship.

She stopped hanging out with me after she got a new girlfriend, even though we'd agreed we could still be friends. I guess the new girl had a problem with us hanging out. So I was back to being alone.

"Because relationships are stupid," I tell Matt flatly. "In France, they don't go on about it like this, and it's so much better."

"I thought it was the city of love," Tom says.

This is true, but he doesn't need to know that. "That's such a tourist thing."

Matt shoots me a look. "Back to Kate and Tom."

"She's such a beautiful person," Tom says. Wonder washes over his voice, his eyes not seeing us. I flinch away from him. When my parents were still together, I used to think it was adorable when they said stuff like that, but it brought nothing but pain.

So I say the only thing I can think of. "Gross."

Tom blinks, and for a moment I feel bad. "Will you help me, though?"

I stare at him. Why would he ask me? Have I not made it clear enough how disgusting I find all of this?

"I don't see why you'd want me to," I say. "I didn't spend my time in France developing my moves."

"You certainly developed your style," Tom says, leaning over to give my scarf a tug. "I wish you'd . . ."

He trails off, his eyes flashing like he didn't mean to say anything, and I look away. I wish he'd been part of all the changes I underwent too. It's not my fault I was dragged to France. But I certainly don't want to talk about it, so I pretend I didn't hear.

"Thanks," I say, touching my fingertips to the scarf like I think he had complimented me. "Parisian women dress so well. I had to step up my game when I was there."

"I think New York women dress fine," Tom says without looking at me.

I swallow, turning back to the screen.

"He thinks Kate dresses fine," Matt says with a teasing grin. I can't tell if he's trying to smooth over the awkwardness between us, or if he doesn't notice it.

"She does," Tom says defensively, and Matt laughs.

I slump lower into the beanbag chair, letting my spine lose its shape as I sink into the cushiony blob. Tom's innocent smile lights up his face at Matt's mention of Kate, and my gut twinges. I want to help him. He should look that happy all the time. But love never has a happy ending, only happy beginnings that lead to long, soul-ripping, heart-crushing defeats on all sides. No matter how good relationships feel at first, they never end well. I've seen the heartbreaks to prove it.

"So how do we do this?" Matt says, clapping his hands together.

My phone buzzes in my pocket. I whip it out to see a new
group chat, one started by Emma. She's included Matt, Myrah,
and me. I blink at the glow from my screen, which feels harsh
in the dim room, as I read her text.

*EMMA: we need to get kate and tom together already. I'm sick
of seeing them moon at each other. I'm thinking the dance could be
a great opportunity! Are you guys down to help?*

I repress a groan. For one, I don't want Tom to ask what's
upsetting me. And more importantly, I want nothing to do
with this matchmaking business.

SOPHIA: not me . . . I'm not much of a matchmaker

Matt shoots me a look behind Tom's back, and I shrug at
him. My phone vibrates again, and I look down, my heart rate
picking up.

EMMA: Seriously? You don't want Tom to be happy?

I frown. I do want Tom to be happy. I also know that a relationship isn't the way to get him there. But I still have to convince the group to be on my side with my idea for the movie.
I can't let this tiff with Emma grow. I don't want to jeopardize
my place in the friend group. It already feels like it's teetering
enough as it is. I grit my teeth as I type, forcing myself to keep
the tone polite.

*SOPHIA: I'm just not really the romantic type. Matchmaking
isn't my strong suit. . . .*

"Do you mind?" Tom asks, folding his arms across his chest.
"I'm slaughtering you over here. Pay attention."

I pick up my controller again, and swerve my character to catch up to Tom's. Out of the corner of my eye, I keep tabs on my phone screen. The phone is vibrating against the carpeted floor with missiles of Emma's anger.

EMMA: *If we're not all working together, this plan will fall apart! Are you sure??*

I pick up my phone again, then drop it. I am sure.

EMMA: *Fine. Matt, Myrah? You in?*

My phone buzzes as they both agree and ask for their parts in her plan. I keep staring hard at the TV screen so Tom won't catch on. Their texts quickly bury mine, like I was never part of the chat in the first place.

I knew this would happen. I told my parents this would happen. They made me leave, and the world moved on without me. No matter how many silk scarves I wrap around myself or accents I put on, I'll never be able to worm my way back in.

We finish the round. I lose aggressively.

"You okay?" Tom asks, glancing at me. "I don't normally beat you quite that much."

"You don't normally beat me at all," I say, faking a yawn. "I think I'm still on Paris time. I should head home."

I push myself off the beanbag chair and shove my phone into my bag. Tom stares after me. He has dark eyes, but they normally come off so light and playful. Now, though, I feel every inch of their darkness in his gaze.

"Already?" he asks.

"Sorry. I guess Paris is having a hard time letting me go," I say, stretching my lips into another yawn to smooth over the awkwardness of my obvious lie.

Tom nods, and before I leave, we throw our arms around each other in the world's stiffest hug.

I trudge down the street. The sun set ages ago, so the heat has cooled enough that it's actually pleasant out. A warm breeze wraps around my skin as I make my way down to the subway. It's approximately ten billion degrees on the platform, give or take. I can barely inhale as I sweat, waiting for the train. The subway car itself is ice-cold, but I welcome the shivers that take over my body.

When I get to my dad's brand-new, empty apartment, I order Chinese takeout and spend the night eating dumplings by myself on the couch. *Bienvenue chez les Ch'tis* plays on the TV. It's one of my favorite French movies, even though it's pure silly comedy, because most of the jokes rely on language play. No matter how many times I rewatch it, there are always new jokes I get this time around because my French has gotten better since the last time I watched.

The movie ends too soon, and I quickly switch over to a random channel so that I'm not alone in the apartment with the sound of my chewing to keep me company. When I'm done eating, and my stomach is so full, I could burst right there, I fall asleep on the couch, waiting for Dad to come home from his date, a rerun filling the space around me with empty noise.

We agreed to meet in the park this time, so that we don't have to be so mindful of the library rules. This was a huge mistake. I dab my forehead with the little scarf I untied from my neck because it's way too hot for accessories, but I still feel like a puddle.

No one else appears to be faring any better. Tom's curly hair is matted down with sweat, and Myrah has apparently given up and has been lying in the grass for the last ten minutes without saying anything. Emma's polka-dotted sundress is kind of cute, but the corners of her mouth have been turned down ever since we unfurled our picnic blanket in the shadiest spot we could find in our corner of Prospect Park. I can't believe my mom sent me to New York just in time for peak summer misery.

"Okay, so I had a really cute idea for a rom-com," Emma says, at the same time that I say, "So I was thinking, for the artsy film—"

I catch her eye, and we exchange sheepish smiles. I wave at her to go on.

"So, I was thinking that we could have a gay rom-com, like I said before," Emma says, glancing at me.

I shrink under her gaze, losing focus as she keeps plowing through her pitch. By *like I said before,* she means before I came back and ruined everything. She's basically confirming all my worst fears with one sideways glance. Tears sting my eyes, but I blink them away.

"That's so cute," Myrah sighs when Emma finishes.

"It's not bad," I say, trying to cover for the fact that I totally missed the rest of her idea. "But I still think it would be stronger if we did something more artistic."

"What's wrong with the idea?" Emma says.

I cringe internally. I have no idea what she said. "It's just a bit tropey," I say quickly. That's probably true. I mean, it's a rom-com. They're all full of the same stupid tropes that would never work in real life.

Emma's face falls as she glances down at her paper. "I like that, though."

"I liked it too," Tom says. "Maybe if we mix in some of what I was thinking with—"

"Careful, Tom," Emma says grumpily. "Sophia feeds on crushing the souls of others. Don't give her too much to work with."

Well, I'm not about to take that lying down.

"Spoken like a woman scorned," I say. "Are you in love with me?"

Tom chuckles, and I breathe a sigh of relief.

"Sorry, hon," I add, winking at Emma. "I don't do relationships."

"Much to the relief of women everywhere," Emma mutters. "Anyway, you're against love in all its forms, right?"

"Hey, I love Tom," I say, reaching across the picnic blanket to do one of those one-armed hugs across his bony shoulders.

Emma gasps, taking in so much air at once that I worry her lungs will burst. "Are you . . . acknowledging your feelings about someone other than yourself?" she asks. Turning to Kate, she adds in a mock whisper, "It's evolving."

My face flushes. Emma and I used to keep each other at arms' length, and now that I've gotten to know her better, I miss those days.

Kate clearly does too, because she blurts out, "We came up with a theme for the dance."

"Congrats," Tom says, his tone almost matching hers with nervous jitters. Our fighting is throwing everything off. "What is it?"

"A masked ball," Kate says with a grin.

"Do I have to wear a mask?" I ask.

"Oh, *you* most certainly do," Emma says, shaking her head as she gives my face a once-over.

I tilt my head to give her my best angle, sticking out my chin. I spent many a bored hour in Paris taking selfies in front of la tour Eiffel, and I know this angle makes my collarbones and jawline jut out so that I look sharp and fierce, no matter how I feel inside.

"But my face is so beautiful," I say, batting my eyelashes at her.

"Your face inspired the theme."

"So, the movie," Kate says, her tone veering into desperation.

I tear my eyes away from the depths of Emma's dark ones, heat flooding my already over-warm face. I have to get ahold of myself. If I keep arguing, soon the whole group will turn away from me, just like Emma has. But there's something about her that makes it impossible for me to stop arguing. I mean, the girl is obsessed with rom-coms. It's so naïve. It would be adorable if it weren't so annoying.

"What's your idea, then?" Emma asks, turning to me with her arms folded.

I glance down at my notebook. The words blur in front of me. My throat is as dry as hell.

"I need more time with it," I say, struggling to swallow. Emma smirks, and I square my shoulders. She can't win here, even if I can't bring myself to share my idea yet.

"Artsier ideas take longer to come up with," I say. I feel bad a moment later. We've been arguing too much today. I throw in a smile, but it feels like more of a smirk.

Emma doesn't even bother to hide her eye roll.

I THINK I LOVE YOU
  By Myrah Evans
  Directed by Emma Hansen
  EXT: Park — Day

ANDIE (16) is walking down the park path. JEN (16)
bikes in the opposite direction.

They both have headphones in. They don't notice
other.

Until Andie moves to cross the street, and Jen has
to swerve her bike out of the way. She FALLS.

                    ANDIE
            I'm so sorry! Are you okay?

Jen is pinned under her bike. Andie offers her
hand, and Jen takes it. Lets Andie pull her up.

                    JEN
                  Thanks.

                    ANDIE
      It was my fault to begin with. Though you should
                probably have a helmet.

                    JEN
      I didn't think anyone would try to kill me today.

Andie laughs. Instead of getting back on the bike,
Jen walks it so she can stay with Andie.

CHAPTER FIVE

Emma

. . . .

I dance my mug to the dirty dish bin. I'm not normally in favor of dancing in public, but Myrah convinced her boss to put her on playlist duty for her shifts, and she has the best taste in late nineties pop. Plus, tonight is *the night*. After Myrah's shift ends, which should be any second now, we're going to get ready for the dance together, and as much as it's against my nature to look forward to a party—least of all a teen center summer camp party taking place in the basement of said teen center—I'm ready to burst at the thought of our plan.

This is going to be like *10 Things I Hate About You*, where everything works out at the dance. Except hopefully without the heartbreak or the side-plot punching. It's my very own real-life rom-com, and I might not be at its center, but I still get to make it happen. That'll have to be good enough for now.

My mug safely deposited in the bin—unlike the last one, which died a tragic death when I dropped it on the floor—

I make my way back to our table. Sophia, mercifully, didn't join us today. She and Tom are off doing who knows what. She's probably trying to sabotage my plan before it even starts. I still can't believe she refused to help.

Kate is busy with the dance, obviously, but Matt agreed right away to hang around waiting for Myrah with me. At least I still have one friend.

He smiles at me when I slide into the seat opposite him.

"I wanted to ask you about tonight," he says, his voice so quiet, I can barely hear him over the chatter at the table next to us. "About the dance."

I look up at him, ready to review our matchmaking plan, when I notice that he's twining and untwining his fingers on the table in front of him, eyes downcast like he's nervous.

My heart drops. He's not . . .

He can't . . .

I know I want a relationship, but . . .

I've never seen him as more than a friend.

Not that he's not a great guy. But this isn't the sweeping romance story I've read about. It's not the enduring love my parents found. This is *Matt*.

I've never thought of him this way.

"Wanna review the plan?" I ask quickly. Maybe if I give him another idea for a topic of conversation, I can change his mind.

"No. I wanted to ask if you'd like to go to—"

I inhale sharply, looking around the coffee shop in a frenzy, for anything to cut him off. If he finishes his sentence and I have to turn him down, things will be weird between us.

"Myrah," I half shout, a wave of relief washing over me as she ditches the register to head toward us, untying her apron as she does.

"We have to go get ready," I say to Matt when Myrah reaches us, and I pull her arm to guide her away. "But good luck tonight."

"Thanks." His whole body has stiffened, but I pretend not to notice. Instead I wrap my arm around Myrah and drag her out of the coffee shop, away from Matt.

Myrah pulls herself out of my grasp when we hit the humidity outdoors, and my hands instantly clam over with sweat. "What were you and Matt talking about?"

I groan. "Let's talk about anything but that."

Her eyes widen, and I know I've made a mistake. I should've made something up. Myrah might call me a drama queen, but she's the one who can't handle not being in on a secret.

"He looked like he was about to pass out. What did you do to him?"

"What did *I* . . ." My jaw falls open in protest. "More like what did *he* do to *me*. He was totally about to ask me out!"

Myrah laughs. "Oh. Is that all?"

"Is that all?" I wheeze. "Is that all? How can you be so flippant about this?"

She flounces ahead of me, leading the way to the subway. I trudge after her, glaring at the back of her head.

"He's been into you for ages," she says over her shoulder as we jog down the subway steps.

"And no one said anything?" The betrayals just keep coming with this band of idiots.

We barrel through the turnstiles. Sweat is already trickling down my back.

Myrah sighs, folding her arms. "He never said anything. It was just a vibe. I thought you were picking up on it too."

I kick at the grimy subway ground with my toe. My white sneakers scuff.

"I thought you were dying to be in a relationship," Myrah says, smirking at me.

"Yeah, but, I mean, it's Matt," I mutter.

It doesn't wipe the smirk off Myrah's face. Not even the strong smell of pee in our subway car does that.

By the time we get to Kate's apartment, my heart has become a ticking time bomb. The anticipation of this plan has my heart racing so hard, I'm low-key worried it's going to damage my rib cage. Not even Kate's bedroom—where every surface is covered in neatly organized makeup collections and color-ful fabric patterns, and which is usually my happy place, since my own room is such an incessant disaster—can calm me right now.

This matchmaking plan has to work, and now not only is Sophia refusing to participate, but Matt is out there some-where plotting to ask me out. Everything is falling apart before the plan has even started.

"Are you guys excited?" Kate asks.

I let Myrah gush, not quite trusting myself to open my mouth. Kate and Myrah start digging into makeup kits and swapping compliments on their dresses, but I hang back. I have no idea how I'm supposed to face the rest of the group after what Matt pulled.

As if she can read my thoughts, Myrah meets my eye in the mirror. "Wanna tell Kate about Matt?"

I let myself go limp, and fall sideways onto Kate's bed. I roll across her lacy bedcover to bury my face in her mound of pillows.

Kate whirls around, the dress she's holding up in front of her swaying around her knees. "What did he do?"

"He tried to ask me out," I mumble.

Kate's jaw drops in shock, but Myrah snorts, shaking her head.

"Don't tell me you didn't know either," she says. "C'mon. I thought we all knew."

"Well, no one told me," I say. "I don't know what to do."

"You should be honest," Kate says as she zips herself into her dress. "Tell him how you feel."

I shake my head. "Nah. I'm gonna stick to my plan to interrupt him every time he tries to talk and never let him get a word in edgewise."

"Sounds healthy," Myrah says, laughing as she turns to the mirror propped up on Kate's dresser to adjust the straps on her dress as she pulls it on. "Definitely a long-term solution." She pauses, checking her makeup. "I hope Peter shows up tonight."

We spent the week leaving flyers in conspicuous places, and finally caught him looking at one. Myrah, never one to back down from making the first move, told him she'd be there and hoped he would be too.

"I'm sure he will," I tell her.

She bites her lower lip, smudging an indent into her lipstick. "I hope we get to dance."

Kate hands her a tissue to fix her lipstick, and Myrah dabs at her lower lip. They both look amazing. Kate has on a dress she designed herself. She spent hours sewing every afternoon all month, and she couldn't look more fabulous in the dress's gentle curves and soft blue color. Myrah is wearing a flowing red dress that makes her look sophisticated, like she's heading to the Oscars instead of a basement.

"I'm sure you guys will," I tell Myrah. Winking at Kate, I add, "I think you're going to have fun at this dance."

"I think so too," Kate says. Her voice is so bubbly, it would spill over if you poured it into a glass. But then she picks up on my tone, and her voice cracks. "Wait, what do you mean?"

I shrug, exchanging a coy look with Myrah. Kate turns to the mascara with horror dawning in her eyes.

"What are you going to do?" she asks, her voice spiking.

"Nothing," I say, the same teasing innocence lining my tone.

My own answer makes my gut churn with anxiety. What if nothing happens?

After all, Sophia is a rogue agent here. She could be anywhere. And she'll be masked, so I might not even recognize her. I'm completely powerless to keep her at bay.

What if she ruins everything?

When we get to the teen center, I start letting go of my fears. The dance is perfect for our matchmaking purposes.

For starters, it's not in a basement at all. Myrah and I exchange confused glances as Kate leads us to the elevator.

"I told you a million times, it's on the roof," she says as she hits the top button.

"Yeah, but I thought you were kidding," I say. Rooftop access in New York doesn't exactly come cheap. But the elevator takes us all the way to the top, Manhattan real estate prices be damned.

She laughs, pushing us out of the elevator. The roof door has been propped open. When we step outside, my jaw drops.

It's not a tall building, but it's close enough to a little park that it counts as having a view. Tall plants line the edge of the roof on one side, and someone (probably Kate) has draped them in fairy lights. Colorful lanterns are strung above the dance floor, and flickering candles light each table. The breeze makes the light smell of lilacs float over to us from the tables. Music strums from the DJ stand.

Talk about rom-coms. This scene is straight out of a teen movie.

I whirl on Kate.

"You did this?"

She straps her mask to her face, grinning. "I told you it wouldn't be lame."

I glance around at the masked guests. Most of them look like they've freshly graduated from middle school, so basically fetuses, but there's a smattering of upperclassmen gathered around a few of the tables. Kate's fellow teen coworkers must've also dragged their friends out.

I don't even care if these babies are still in middle school. This is the perfect setting to finally get Kate with Tom.

I scan the crowd for the boys, and spot them leaning precariously over the railing to get a better look at a pigeon strutting on a windowsill. I breathe a sigh of relief when I see that Tom is wearing his mask.

The whole plan hinges on it, after all.

As per the plan, Matt is posted by the snack table. It's set up next to the photo station, which is decked out with a cheesy red-carpet backdrop, and a line of couples strings around it, waiting for their turn to pose. I let my eyes linger on them for a moment. I wish I had someone to line up with.

Someone other than my cousin, that is.

When Tom makes his way over to us, Myrah pokes me in the shoulder. Tonight isn't about me and my tragic singledom. It's about getting Kate into Tom's arms. I need to focus.

"Oh, Emma," Myrah says, her voice too stage-whispery. "I need to, um . . ."

"Discuss the private matter?" I ask.

Myrah nods. "Yes. The private matter."

"What?" Kate says.

"Sorry. We have to discuss a private matter," I say, before scurrying away with Myrah so that Kate and Tom are left alone. We exchange smiles as we leave them together. The plan is officially in motion. I can practically feel the love in the air.

We join the photo booth line, standing behind a cheerleading squad as they plan their pose. It hurts my hamstrings just listening to them talk. I turn away, scanning the dance crowd.

Myrah cranes her neck right alongside me. "Do you see Peter?"

I laugh, in love with the glow in her eyes. "You've got it so bad."

She nudges me, blushing. "Shut up."

We turn to our mission. Myrah gestures to Kate and Tom, who are awkwardly swaying near enough to the crowd that they could be dancing, but far enough away for plausible deniability. Kate's dress sways around her knees as she spins, and she keeps her eyes carefully trained on its hem. Tom, meanwhile, is taking great interest in the slowly darkening sky.

Thank God we came up with this plan, because this is painful to watch.

"All right, you're up," I tell Myrah.

I point her toward Kate and Tom, grinning in spite of my nerves. It feels like I'm already directing our rom-com movie, except this is way better because it's real. It's my cousin's heart on the line. And if my directing works, her heart will be so happy by the end of the night.

Myrah lowers her mask onto her face and, giving me a thumbs-up, makes her way toward them. She grabs Tom's arm, and I see her gesturing toward the dance floor. He protests for a moment, looking to Kate, but Myrah is all bubbly energy, and before he can stop her, she's dragging him away until they've disappeared into the crowd. Kate stands alone.

Perfect.

I join Matt at the snack table and hand him the decoy mask.

It's the same one that Tom has on. Matt purses his lips at me as he straps it to his face.

"This better work."

I take a step back to give him a once-over. In the dim twilight, with his entire face covered by the mask, he could totally be Tom. They don't have the same hairstyle, but Matt made sure to muss his hair up so that, in the dark, it could almost be Tom's curly look. Between that, the mask, and their matching jackets, the disguise works.

I brush lint off his shoulder, then immediately regret it when he catches my eye and lingers and makes it a Moment™.

I force a cough, breaking the tension immediately.

"Okay, *Tom*," I say, shuffling so Matt is facing Kate. "Go get her."

Matt shakes his head at me. He's fidgeting with his sleeve, shaking out his hands. "Who talked me into this? I can't imitate Tom."

I don't have time to calm him down. Kate will find the real Tom any second. I grab him by the shoulders and give him a little push.

Okay, a big push.

I watch him go, and scan the room for the real Tom. He's at the other end of the roof, trying to get away from Myrah. She's dancing circles around him, though.

Matt reaches Kate, and the two of them start dancing. I'm not about to sit on the sidelines without being able to hear if my plan is working. Keeping my mask carefully strapped to my face so Kate won't recognize me in the crowd, I make my way across the dance floor until I find a spot close enough that I can make out what they're saying over the pounding music.

"You look so beautiful," Matt says, deepening his voice to sound like Tom, and I know that Kate is blushing under her mask.

I tilt over to see Kate's lips move, and I'm sure she's stuttering out some type of thanks.

"You're such a beautiful person," Matt says. In his faux-Tom voice, the words carry, and I can just hear him over the music.

I *aww* to myself, but cut it short when I see Myrah waving at me frantically from across the room. I turn around to spot Tom making his way through the crowd. Coming right for us.

I swirl frantically and signal to Matt. He doesn't see.

"Do you want to go out with me sometime?" Matt says to Kate.

This is it, the moment we rehearsed, but Tom is moments away from reaching us and blowing the whole operation. Holding my breath, I dash toward Matt.

"Tom," I say, grabbing his wrist and yanking, "come with me."

I drag him away, ignoring Kate's protests.

"What the hell?" Matt asks, tearing off the mask. I grab it from his hand, ignoring him as he presses on. "I was asking her out."

"Tom was on the way," I say, scanning the crowd for Myrah. It'll be super suspicious if Tom reaches Kate now, before we have time to finish our plan, and Kate says yes to a date Tom knows he didn't suggest.

He reaches her, and my hands fall to my side as I watch, helpless to stop my plan from unraveling. There's nothing I can do.

But then Kate does the most unexpected thing in the world. She takes Tom's hands and pulls him toward her, until their lips are moments away, until she presses her mouth to his.

Until they're kissing.

Kissing!

KISSING!

And with that, my heart finally bursts. The plan worked. My real-life rom-com, unfolding for my cousin under my direction. And I'm happy about that. I am.

I just wish it could work for me too, someday.

Swallowing down that horrible queasy jealous feeling, I spin on my heel to beam at Matt. This isn't a moment for me to sop in my own angst or give in to tears. This is a moment to celebrate.

"We did it," I squeal, hitting him on the shoulder with Tom's mask.

I want to run toward them, but I guess I shouldn't interrupt their kiss.

Their first kiss!

But then I realize I'm alone with Matt, and he must realize it too, because he sidesteps in front of me and tucks a stray strand of my hair behind my ear. I look everywhere but at his face.

"I wanted to ask you, earlier," Matt says, his words low and gentle. It turns my knees to Jell-O, and not in the good way. "I really like you. I'd say we make pretty good partners in crime," he adds, gesturing to Tom and Kate, who are now swaying, hands clasped, in slow circles on the dance floor. "Would you want to maybe go—"

My stomach flips in on itself. I can't let him finish, because there's no way I can say yes to a date with Matt. He doesn't make my heart race, or give me butterflies. I can't picture myself holding his hand, let alone kissing him. And most importantly, this is not the big romantic moment I've spent my life waiting for. This is too ordinary, and I can't settle for this.

"Oh, Matt," I say, cutting him off, keeping my tone as balanced and kind as I can. "You're great, but I really, *really* think we're such good friends, and I don't want to ruin our friendship. I don't think going on a date is a good idea. I see us as friends and I love our friendship, and I don't want to do anything to jeopardize it."

I take a deep breath, trying not to think about how many times I just said the word *friend*.

"Sure," Matt says. "I hear you. I thought, since we're such great friends and we know each other so well, and we have such nice chemistry, that this could work out. I think we should give it a shot. Why don't we?"

He keeps going, but I'm not listening. Blood is pounding too hard in my ears for me to make out his words. I can see his lips moving, simultaneously looking like they're in slow motion yet moving too fast for me to understand. I already turned him down once, and he's still pressing me. Heat rushes over my face, and the blush extends down my arms, rolling through my whole body.

"I don't think we would be a good match—" I force myself to say, but he keeps rolling right over me. I tear my mask off my face, hoping that he'll see the stress written all over me and take pity on the girl he supposedly likes, but he keeps right on going. There are too many words in his declaration. It's not romantic, not like Billy Crystal's speech at the end of *When Harry Met Sally* . . . This is so many words that they've stopped meaning anything.

"Hey, guys," a familiar voice says from behind me, and I whirl around to see Sophia towering above me. I gape at her. Even though we've spent the week arguing about our movie, I've never been so happy to see her face. Which, I admit, looks quite lovely tonight. Her dress is a gorgeous strapless number, and she's brushed glitter over her collarbones. If I weren't furious with her for jeopardizing my movie and almost ruining my matchmaking plan, I'd say she's almost beautiful.

She nods toward the dancers. "As the two resident gays of this squad, maybe we should have a dance?"

I stare at her. The last person I want to dance with right now is Sophia, and I'm sure she has absolutely no desire to dance with me. Especially when the music has just changed from a rousing pop song to a slow number that's chased everyone but the couples off the dance floor. Why is she asking?

But then I glance back at Matt. If I say no to Sophia, I have to stay here and keep listening to him insist that we should go out even though I've already said no. Twice.

In spite of my better judgment, I take Sophia's outstretched hand. "Okay, but only for the gay rights," I say, and, laughing, she leads me onto the dance floor.

CHAPTER SIX

SOPHIA

When I walked up to Emma, the music playing couldn't have been catchier. Now that she's said yes to dancing with me, the universe has decided it would be a great time for a slow song about looking deeply into your lover's eyes or some such garbage. I almost regret asking her.

But I saw the panicked look on her face when Matt wouldn't stop talking, and I had to help. She looked so *anxious* with Matt's incessant asking out. No one deserves to be on the receiving end of a man's romantic attentions for so long after making it clear that she isn't interested. At some point, it's disrespectful of boundaries. Reason number 4,948,127 why I love being a lesbian.

Not that I want to be stuck here dancing with Emma. But this is about more than Emma. This is about standing up for women.

"Sorry about Matt," I say, glancing at him over her shoulder as we reach the dance floor. "I figured he was never going to shut up."

"Oh, you heard. That explains it." Emma laughs. "I was wondering why you wanted me to dance."

"I thought you were all about the gay representation," I say. She rolls her eyes at me, but she's still grinning.

We sway around each other, our hands hanging out our sides. Matt is still watching us, though, so this march to the death by awkwardness must continue. He looks like he's about to start walking toward us, so I take Emma's hands and spin her deeper into the crowd. She stares up at me, our eyes meeting, and for one soft second, the dance melts away and I can't look away from her eyes. They're deep brown, and they're alight with laughter. I can't believe I've never noticed the lightness in them before. They even have little smile wrinkles at the corners, like her love for life, her ability to laugh at anything, is written over every inch of her face.

We're safely nestled in the heart of the crowd, and I can't see Matt anymore. I look down at Emma. She's wearing a flowy dress that spins outward when she twirls, and she's let her wavy mess of dark hair fall around her face. If I didn't know better, I'd call it gorgeous. Instead I'm painfully aware that we've been dancing without saying anything for way too long. We've been staring into each other's eyes like this dance is something more than a rescue mission, which of course it isn't.

Emma must realize this at the same time I do, because she blinks and looks down at her feet, which aren't moving in rhythm with the music at all.

"Why did you say no to Matt?" I ask, desperate to fill the silence between us. "I thought you were love's greatest champion or something."

"I am, but . . ." Emma sighs. "Matt's not the one."

I glance over at him. He's a nice enough guy, but he's going to grow up to post shirtless bathroom mirror selfies on his Tinder profile, and it shows.

"Yeah, I get that," I say softly. She raises her eyebrows at the kindness in my tone, and I quickly laugh to cover it. Can't have her thinking we're about to become friends or something. "There's no such thing as *the one* anyway."

Emma stops swaying, glaring up at me. The fierceness in her eyes is painfully at odds with her tiny frame and stature. "Why are you always putting love down like that?"

"I think people put too much trust in the concept."

She turns away from me. "That's such bullshit."

"It's not," I say, bristling. Who is she to say that to me? "You're obsessed with the idea of love, but you've never even been on a date. What makes you think it's real?"

Emma looks down. "Tonight is supposed to be about Kate and Tom, and celebrating love. Maybe I should go find them. Thanks for saving me from Matt."

Before I can say anything else, she turns away from me and weaves quickly across the dance floor until she's gone. I linger in the crowd, but without Emma, I'm an idiot standing here by herself, reminded once again how alone I truly am.

Taking a deep breath, I force myself to snap out of it and scan the rooftop for the others. It's hard to see anything through the hazy crowd, which has spread out from the thick of the dance floor to take over the whole space as people start to seek out the snack table and the bathroom.

I spot the group clustered in a dark corner by the railing. Myrah and Emma are squealing over Kate and Tom, as if their getting together is a good decision and not the first step down the path toward inevitable heartbreak. Even Matt is beaming at them.

Emma's face falls when she sees me approaching.

"I thought I made my feelings clear," she says, all the usual tension back in her tone. "We're here to celebrate Kate and Tom, and if you can't do that, then—"

"Too bad you're not in charge of my life, then," I say. I tuck my hands into the folds of my dress under my sweater. "I'm here to congratulate Tom."

I reach over to squeeze his shoulder. His arm is wrapped around Kate's waist, and he has a vaguely shocked look in his eyes, like he can't believe this is happening.

"You're next," Kate says to Emma. Her whole face, nestled on Tom's chest, is aglow, like she's a little night-light illuminating the outline of his heart. It's honestly disgusting. I wonder how people can say stuff like that all the time, *You'll be next to fall in love,* and don't hear it as deeply threatening.

Emma looks down, laughing through her nose. "Nah."

"Of course not," I say with a little laugh. If she's so ready to go back to arguing, fine. I can do that. "Poor Emma. Never to be married, never to have a career."

Emma's face crumples.

"What?" she asks, whirling to me.

I take a step backward. The fierceness of her gaze is that intense.

"I mean—" I say, but she doesn't let me finish.

"Just because you're a miserable old crone who's determined to suck the love out of everyone's life doesn't mean you have to drag us all down with you," she snaps.

It's lucky the music is still pounding so loudly, or this fight would've become very public by now. As it is, the people milling by the snack table have glanced our way and decided to mill a little closer, as if they're dying to figure out what we're fighting about.

I stare at her. The rest of the group's eyes bore into me, and then their gazes flit between me and Emma. Tom has wrapped himself around Kate, as if shielding her.

"I'm not dragging them down," I say, gesturing to Tom. "I'm trying to save them. If you're too naïve to see that, it's not my problem."

Emma scoffs. "If you really think that, there's no way I'm letting you work on my movie. That's gonna be a celebration of love."

"Fine," I say, folding my arms. But then I remember how she kicked me out of our group for her stupid matchmaking plan, and how I had to come here alone, and how even after I tried to save her, I ended up alone in the middle of the dance floor. So I shake my head at her. "I'll make my own movie. I didn't spend a year in France for nothing. I mean, *Les Intouchables, Amélie, Les Choristes*. I can handle making a movie without you."

76

She gapes at me. "Fine."

"Great."

"Fantastic."

"May the best man win."

"I'm not stressed about it."

And with that, she turns and storms away. After a few steps, she scuttles back to grab Kate and Myrah by the wrists.

"Obviously, you guys are my crew," she says with a glare at me. Kate, with an apologetic glance at Tom, lets herself be tugged away.

I'm left to stand there, out of breath as if I'd run a marathon, with Tom and Matt staring at me. I watch Emma and her little group disappear through the door. I'm dreading the moment I have to face Tom and Matt. I turn to them slowly.

"What the hell?" Matt says.

Tom lacks the aggressive streak to say the same, but his eyes do it for him.

"How could she say that stuff to me?" I ask. "You have to see how—"

"All I'm seeing is that this insane fight you two keep pushing is going to drive the rest of the group apart," Tom says. "This contest means a lot to me. And to Emma. Now we have to compete against each other when we could've been supporting each other."

I stare at my shoes, flats I picked out because I'm already the second-tallest in this group after Matt. These guys are the ones who forgot all about me after I went to France. Besides, it's not my fault. Emma's the one who keeps booting me out of the group's activities. What am I supposed to do, let her?

There's no good option. If I drive the group apart, they'll never forgive me, and I'll still end up alone. It leaves a lump in my throat the size of the ocean I let grow between us.

"Sorry," I mumble. "I . . . didn't want to not be in the movie with you guys."

If I don't do this film contest, I drift even further from my friends, *and* I lose the opportunity to make a movie after I realized in Paris how much movies mean to me. This is my last chance to get something film-related on my college apps, to try film out before I get to college and have to commit one way or another. I owe it to myself to try.

Tom's eyes soften. "It's okay. We'll make a kick-ass movie about . . . What was it you wanted to do?"

My mind flashes to the darkness of my Paris bedroom. "I want to do something a bit more artistic. That's more in the French style, so I know more about it. That kind of artistry always does better at festivals. Let's roam around the city with a camera for a while and let it inspire us."

Tom purses his lips as he considers it. "Sounds good. I like more artsy stuff than Emma anyway, and you're right, that could do better at a festival than a rom-com."

We turn to Matt for his thoughts, and that's when I notice that his whole face is clouded over.

"What's wrong?" Tom asks.

"Emma turned me down," he says, kicking at the ground.

"Oh, I'm so sorry," Tom says, reaching over to rest his hand on Matt's shoulder.

I raise my eyebrows in fake surprise. I can't have him know

that I overheard everything and asked Emma to dance as a rescue, or he'd kill me.

"Any schemes to help me out, Mr. Romantic Genius?" Matt asks, turning to Tom with a snort.

"Tom is the romantic genius now?" I ask.

"Hey, he has a date tomorrow," Matt says.

"Yeah," I say, drawing out the syllable, "and he's so painfully shy that Kate Perez kissed him first. Kate. Perez."

Tom slaps my shoulder in response, and I grip it with one hand, squealing in fake pain. He snorts at me, shaking his head.

"Besides," I say, turning to Matt, "Emma? Really?"

"Hey, she's nice," Tom says.

I roll my eyes. She wasn't so nice when she started this insane fight with me about the film genre and kicked me off the movie team.

"Seriously, guys, what do I do?" Matt says. He looks over his shoulder at the doors leading to the elevator, but Kate is already gone. "Like, no offense, Tom, but your date wouldn't be happening without me, so it's your turn to help me out now."

Tom looks up, frowning. "What do you mean?"

Matt outlines the whole matchmaking plan, and Tom's face falls apart.

"She only wanted me because of shit you said to her?" he says, gasping.

His eyes well up, and I could murder Matt right here and now for making Tom Levine cry. Instead of apologizing or explaining himself, Matt claps his hands together.

"So what's the scheme for me?"

I shake my head at him. How can he be this obtuse? "There is no scheme. You asked, and she said no. I'm sorry it's not what you were hoping for, but you have to respect that."

Tom stares at me. "Did you just . . . give good relationship advice?"

"When it comes to stopping relationships from happening, I've got great moves."

"Your 'move' is to get over it," Matt says. "Come on. We helped Tom; now help me."

I grit my teeth together, then exhale through them as I force my jaw muscles to relax.

"That was totally different," I say, reminding myself not to bite his head off. "They were both clearly in love and needed help doing something about it."

"So?" Matt snaps.

"So," I say, "we can't trick Emma into dating you when she's already said no. You have to respect the lady's wishes. Or, I say 'lady,' but—"

"Right," Matt says, scoffing.

"I'm sorry," Tom says, giving Matt a look drenched in way more sympathy than Matt deserves. "Sophia's right. But it'll be fine. We'll find you someone else. Someone who sees how great you are."

"Yeah," Matt spits.

I can tell he's hurt, but it's hard to feel bad for him when his pain comes with a thick layer of anger. If Kate rejected him, Tom would never turn to that kind of bitter fury.

"Sorry," Tom says again, and Matt shakes his head in response.

"If it were you, I'd help you in an instant," Matt says, gesturing to the dance still raging behind us. "In fact, I just did."

I twist my heel against the floor, edging away from him. I've claimed him for my film crew, and he's been in this friend group forever. He's always been the one we turn to for help, whether it's for homework or when my parents told me they were getting divorced. But he was always so sweet to Emma too, and now that she's refused to give in to what he wants, he has completely changed.

I swallow, avoiding eye contact with him as Tom offers another reassurance. He's on my film crew and in my friend group, and I'll have to be more careful around him.

Tom pulls his phone out of his pocket, and his face lights up. "It's Kate." The light drains when he looks up at me. "Should I tell her? About what Matt and Emma did?"

I tilt my head to one side in thought, then shake it. It could be easy to stop the relationship from moving any further, to rescue Tom from disaster, but I can't be the one who makes that happen now that he's already with Kate. I never wanted his puppy-dog eyes to droop like they are now. "No. I'm sure Matt didn't say anything that wasn't true."

He steps away from us to answer Kate's call. I watch him go, with an odd pang. Emma might've been the one who kicked me off her movie, but I'm the one who forced the group apart. As Tom walks away, the distance between us feels suddenly insurmountable. So much for working my way back into the squad. Instead I've fractured it forever. And they'll never forgive me for it.

I swing open the door to Dad's new apartment, and kick off my shoes as I let it shut behind me. "Dad?" My voice shakes as I call out, and I realize how close I am to tears. I force myself to swallow before I call again. "Dad?"

My voice echoes through the apartment. Shoes in hand, I walk through the living room. The lights in the kitchen are on too, but it's empty except for a note on the white countertop, in which my dad has let me know that he's working late.

I nod at it a few times as I read, then turn to my room to put my shoes away. They land with a thud on the floor of my closet. I stare at them for a moment, then slam the closet door shut.

Dad has offered to take me to Target to find wall decorations, but I can't be bothered. What's the point? This place will never feel like home, no matter how many tacky pillows and posters I put up. The room stays bare, except for my bed, nightstand, and a pile of books in the corner that don't have a shelf to call home.

"I wanted to talk to you," I say to the empty apartment. "I'm making a movie. The dance was garbage. I think all my friends hate me."

I walk back into the living room. The silence weighs a million pounds, so I keep talking, even though it's not making me feel any better, only a little crazy.

"Should I call Mom?" I glance at my phone, and 11:18 blinks at me. Which means it's 5:18 a.m. in France, and Mom will definitely yell at me if I wake her with nothing important to say.

And I don't have anything important to say. This loneliness is hardly news. I plop myself down on the couch, flick on the TV, and settle against the pillows so that I'm lying sideways, facing the TV screen as I watch an old French favorite, calling it research for the movie, when really I'm letting it numb me over.

CHAPTER SEVEN

Emma

Myrah's footfall lands heavily against the floor as she follows Kate and me off the roof. I can practically feel the anger steaming off her shoulders as the elevator doors slide open and we file in.

"What was that?" Myrah asks, throwing an arm behind her, gesturing toward the door where we left Tom, Matt, and the devil. Music thrums from the rooftop, but the elevator doors close again, cutting us off from the rest of the party.

"Did you hear how she was talking to me? And she's ruining my movie. This is important to me. I want to go to LA." I pause.

The truth is, it is important to me for even more than the opportunity to break into the film industry, as huge as that is. This is my chance to tell my story to an actual audience. "And, I love rom-coms, and I never get to see myself in them. Every time I watch one, I'm reminded that every movie I love is explicitly not for me. I want to change that, and Sophia's stealing my chance."

I take a deep breath when I finish talking. Though I never acknowledge it to the group like this, being bi is important to me. If I want to celebrate that, who is Sophia to stop me?

Besides, Sophia knows—everyone knows—how I feel about love, and how much I want to find my own great love story. Who is she to say I'll never find it? Who is Myrah to stop me from being angry?

"What she said was mean, but splitting the groups over it was a little harsh," Kate says. Next to her, Myrah's seething.

"I don't get why I even have to ask," I huff. "You guys are my friends, and she's being horrible to me."

"It's not like you were so eager to listen to her ideas for the movie. You guys have both been arguing about it nonstop since she got back," Myrah says. I open my mouth to point out that the whole thing was my idea, but she keeps going. "And you're the one who split Kate and Tom into opposing groups over it right after they got together."

She stares me down, knowing the point has hit. The matchmaking plan meant as much to me as the outcome does to Kate, after all. I turn to Kate, eyes downcast, as we file out of the elevator, across the lobby, and into the warm night air.

"Kate, I'm so sorry," I say. "I didn't mean to ruin your night. I'm so happy for you and Tom."

I reach over to pull her into a hug, and Myrah, after an eye roll, wraps her arms around both of us. I muffle a sob, and she pulls back to catch my eye.

"You know that what Sophia said about you not finding love isn't true, right?" Myrah says, her arms still holding me. "I'm sure even she doesn't believe it. You've both been saying a lot of shit to each other lately."

I sniffle, staring at the ground. Sophia was, as always, a jerk, but maybe she wasn't so wrong.

"And," Myrah adds, nudging me, "it totally put a damper on the night I had my first dance with Peter."

I turn to her in surprise. "He showed up? You didn't say anything."

"Yeah, well, that's what happens when you turn our romantic evening into a fight."

I try to ignore the twinge in my gut at the word *our.* The two of them had a romantic evening, but all I did was watch other people take the first steps toward falling in love. The closest I got to romance was dancing with Sophia, and after the way things have been going this week, she's the last person I ever want to date.

We pull each other into another group hug.

"It was so romantic," Myrah sighs. "A slow song came on and he didn't stop or anything. He held my hand the whole time. I think this might be it."

I squeeze her shoulder. "I hope it works out."

"And?" Myrah asks primly.

"And I'm sorry I ruined your night with the fighting."

"Thank you," Myrah says. "So can we put the two groups together again?"

I grimace. I might be sorry I ruined their romantic evenings, but I'm not down to sacrifice my movie. It's my shot to get to LA and break into the industry, not just as a filmmaker but as a bi girl too.

Kate looks at my face, and I know from the way she smiles at me that she gets it. "I don't want you to have to change your idea. Tom and I can handle a little competition between us."

I beam at her. "Okay. So are you guys down for the gay rom-com?"

They both nod, though Myrah throws in another eye roll for good measure.

"Let's brainstorm on the way home," I say.

As soon as we slide onto the bright orange subway seats, I fish my notebook out of my purse so that Myrah and I can start outlining the story, with me telling her the shots I want to include, while Kate does costume sketches.

I swing open my front door in relief. It feels good to be home, and away from everything that's happened tonight.

As soon as I step inside, though, that relief drains away.

My parents are sitting on the couch, and both of them lean toward me as soon as I walk in. They're watching TV, which has bathed the semi-dark room with flickering light, and they look cozy under their mounds of throw blankets. Mom sits up so eagerly when I walk in, she's perched on the edge of the couch cushion. She looks like she could slip off at any moment. I can tell they have a thousand questions hanging on their lips. I have a feeling I don't want to answer any of them.

I take a cautious step forward, which Lady Catulet takes as invitation to wrap herself around my leg.

"How was the dance?" Mom asks. She leans over Dad's legs to grab the remote from the coffee table, and mutes the TV. The now silent news anchors keep mouthing words at each other.

"Kate totally has a boyfriend now," I say, beaming. Hopefully this news will be enough to keep their attention off me and my lack of a love life.

I pick up Lady Catulet, kick my heels off by the door, and carry her over to join my parents on the couch. She paws at my arm like she wants to be let down, but she's purring, because cats make no sense.

"Tom Levine?" Mom asks.

I nod. "He asked her out at the dance. They have their first date next weekend."

I leave out the specifics of the part I played in getting them together. I don't want to risk it getting back to Kate. She'd let something like that bother her, even though the plan changes nothing about the feelings Tom already had for her. I'm not going to let knowledge of the existence of the plan ruin its outcome.

"That's wonderful," Mom says. Her fingers twitch toward her cell phone on the coffee table, probably because she's dying to call Aunt Natalie and gossip about her niece. She must decide to wait until Kate's had a chance to talk to her, though, because she returns her gaze to me.

"What about you?" she asks.

"What about me?" I lean back to hit the light switch, and

the room is washed in too-bright light. I pull a corner of the throw blanket over my legs, and Lady Catulet paws at the tassels on its edge.

Mom reaches over to poke me in the leg. "Any cute boys in your sights?"

"Have you seen the ones in my grade?" I ask. "There's not exactly a wide selection."

This is objectively true, which almost makes me feel better about the fact that I'm only talking about the boys to hide my sexuality from my parents.

Almost.

I scroll through the NYC–LA Film Festival website. Again. My laptop is balanced on my knees because Kate has taken over the coffee shop table with her costume sketches. I should focus on our application submission. Instead my mouse hovers over the "prizes" link for a moment as I try to talk myself out of opening the page again.

I click the link anyway.

THE GRAND PRIZE WINNER OF THE HIGH SCHOOL STUDENT COMPETITION DIVISION WILL RECEIVE:

Scholarship for the pursuit of a BA or BFA in a film-related major.

For more information on scholarships and tuition assistance,

click here.

A fully funded trip to Los Angeles, which will include:

• VIP access badges to the NYC–LA Film Festival Student Screening

• Access badges for the NYC–LA Film Festival Screening

• Invitations for the NYC–LA Film Festival Gala, which will welcome professionals from across the film industry

Internship interviews with production companies and for film set positions.

For a complete list of participating employers, click here.

I reread the list for what feels like the bajillionth time. I'm supposed to be officially registering our team—now whittled down to Kate, Myrah, and me—for the contest. Once I do, I'll get an invitation to the student competition mixer here in New York, where I'll have to pitch my idea to everyone in the audience.

The thought of standing up in front of so many people—some of whom will be film industry people—makes my stomach squirm. What if they think I'm a fake?

After scrolling through the list of prizes again (which does nothing to help my flip-flopping nerves), I click on the list of companies I could interview with if I win.

And holy shit. I have to win.

These companies are all *big deals*. Some of the internship opportunities are at the big studios, but even the smaller companies all have first-look deals and their names in the credits of huge movies. Putting any one of these on my resume would make my college applications breeze through film school admissions. Plus, with experience like that, I could get even better internships once I'm in film school. This could help me graduate with a job. Winning this competition goes so far beyond this year. It could shape my whole career.

My head spins at the thought, and I backtrack to the main competition page. I can't think about all the possibilities right now. I have to focus on making the best movie I can, so I can open that door for myself.

I catch sight of the tuition page in the website navigation, and my gut twinges. I'm not the only one who cares about film. This competition and these prizes mean the world to Tom too, but now only one of us can have them.

After forcing myself to inhale, I hold my breath for a few seconds and then let the air escape through my teeth. This was supposed to be my dream coming true, and Sophia tore it all apart.

Technically—*technically*—I had a role in splitting the groups up. But what choice did I have? She was going to take my gay rom-com away from me. And given how my love life is going (aka nowhere), this gay rom-com is all I have.

I click through the website, and when I get to the registration page, I fill out the entrance form. My fingertips tremble above the keyboard. Once I'm done filling it in, I scan the form again to fix all my typos.

PROJECT TITLE: I Think I Love You
  DIRECTOR: Emma Hansen
  WRITER: Myrah Evans
  DIRECTOR OF PHOTOGRAPHY: Emma Hansen
  TEAM MEMBERS: Katerina Perez (Costume Designer)
  LOGLINE: When Stacey (Myrah Evans) meets Amber (Katerina Perez), she's forced to question everything she thought she knew about love—in the best way possible.

Myrah and I agreed to keep the logline vague for now. We can always update it once we have the full script hammered out. It's more important to get our names into the contest now, so that we can get our invitation to the mixer in time to get a shot at the Most Anticipated Film award. And from there to the top-ten screening. The winning prize. LA. Film school.

Hopefully.

I take a deep breath, and I hit submit.

Our team is officially in the contest.

I lean in my seat, staring at the confirmation page. It's really happening. Before I can celebrate for too long, the door swings open and Tom walks in, Matt trailing behind him.

"I'm pretty sure we won Georgie's in the split," I tell them, but I'm smiling. My issue isn't with them. As long as Sophia's not here, breathing down my neck with her artsy bullshit, I have no problem.

Tom crosses past me to kiss Kate, and my smile grows even wider.

"We have to meet to go over the movie," he says, and my face drops. That means Sophia will be here after all.

She walks in a moment later, her own smile falling when she sees me.

"Couldn't we have met literally anywhere else?" she grumbles, pushing past me to get to the empty table next to us. Tom and Matt settle next to her.

"This is a good place, and Myrah gives us her discount on snacks, so there," Tom says. "Plus, it's big enough for our equipment."

They brought their camera with them. Sophia fiddles with

the buttons, zooming in and out on a tea mug as she records her practice footage.

"It's a big city and a small camera," I say, glaring into her lens. "I'm sure you could find somewhere else to put it."

"I have a great suggestion for where I could put it," Sophia mutters.

"Well, it's minuscule, so I don't see why it shouldn't fit in your heart," I snap.

Myrah, who's just joined us for her break, groans. "Will you two ever give it a rest?"

"Oh, come on." Sophia gestures toward me. "Don't cut us off so that she gets the last word."

"Why not?" I lean over so I can see her around Myrah, who's stepped between us. "It saves you the trouble of racking that tiny little brain of yours."

"All right, that's enough." Kate holds up her hands.

"If this lot would let me get a word in edgewise—" Sophia waves at the others without breaking our eye contact.

"That is enough," Tom says. "Please go get us snacks and leave us alone."

Sophia pushes away from us with a huff, and her boots clomp all the way to the counter. Myrah raises an eyebrow at me.

"We would like snacks too, please," she says. "Go make nice."

I stare at her. "Are you serious?"

Judging by the look in her eye, she is, so I get up and join Sophia in line. We face pointedly away from each other as the three people ahead of us slowly make their orders. I glance back at the group, determined not to make eye contact with Sophia. They're all huddled over the table, deep in conversation.

"Do you think they're talking shit about us?" Sophia asks, her eyes trained in the same direction.

I meet her eyes. They're the color of dog poop. If dog poop were deep and rich with hazel undertones. "You, maybe."

"I'm not the one who split the groups," she shoots back. "We can find the footage on the camera. I left it on. See who they really blame for all this."

We shake on it, but by the time we get back to our table, snacks in hand, the SD card has been wiped. I take a giant bite of the banana bread I got for myself, glaring at Sophia. I don't need any spy footage to tell me who's to blame. Everything was fine before she came back from France and stomped all over my life with her thick-heeled boots.

And everything will be fine again, just as soon as I win this film competition once and for all.

Partial Deleted Audio Footage from SD Card 3

MYRAH: Well, we have to do something.

KATE: Doesn't this feel . . . extreme?

MYRAH: No.

MATT: I don't like it.

TOM: If they each think the other has a crush on them . . .

MYRAH: They'd be nicer to each other.

KATE: Nice enough for us to get the groups back together?

MATT: I still don't like it.

MYRAH: No one else has a better idea. We're doing it.

CHAPTER EIGHT

SOPHIA

· ·

"That is *not* going to be our logline," Tom says for the sixth time. We're only in the first half hour of our meeting, so it's not exactly going great.

"Why not?" Matt protests. "If we're going to go for an artsy French thing, we might as well lean in to it."

"We can be artsy without being pretentious," Tom says, pushing his glasses back up his nose.

I groan, flopping onto Tom's bed to stare at his ceiling. It still has faded outline stains from the glow-in-the-dark stars he had stuck up there when we were kids.

"I don't see what's so pretentious about it," Matt says. He's sitting on the floor, the laptop balanced across his thighs. "'A girl seeks to find her soul in—' Okay, yeah, I hear it now."

I snort a laugh, covering for the discomfort I still feel around Matt after the way he treated Emma at the dance, and force myself to agree. "Fine. It's not the best."

"It would probably help if we had a stronger story line in place," Tom says, clicking his pen.

I sigh. Given that it's my fault that the groups are split, this comment feels directed at me. I'm the one who felt strongly enough about doing this project to divide the group, after all. But I have no ideas.

"You know what would be cool?" I say, sitting up. "What if we pitch it as an improvisation project? *A girl explores herself as she explores the city in a semi-improvised discussion of self.*"

"Yeah, 'cause that's not pretentious at all," Tom mutters.

Matt nods along, though. "I think that could totally work. Festivals like a bit of pretension."

Tom rolls his eyes but waves a hand at Matt. "All right. Type it in."

Matt's fingers fly over the keyboard as I repeat what I said so he can take it down.

"All right. I'm ready to go," he says.

Tom and I leap off the bed to join Matt on the floor, crowding him on either side so we can see the screen as he submits our entry. I twist my fingers together as the confirmation page loads, and then I start when it pops up on the screen. *Your entry into the NYC-LA Film Festival High School Student Competition is confirmed.* And there it is. Just like that, we're making a movie.

The afternoon confirms my disgust in love. I agreed to accompany Tom and Matt when they meet up with Kate at the teen center, as I was promised dinner after her shift ends. This, I realize as soon as I look up at them, was a massive mistake.

Tom joins Kate on her chair at reception. They're so intertwined, it's a miracle they're not expecting a child from this position alone. Kate's head rests on Tom's shoulder, his arm is wrapped around her shoulders, her foot is permanently tucked around his ankle, and their lips touch so often, they're going to fuse together any second.

I mean. Seriously. This is a place for youths.

I grimace at them, wrinkling my nose. "Can you two please chill?"

They kiss again, the nauseating smack of their lips drowning out my words. They're even louder than the rain pattering steadily against the window opposite Kate's desk. At least there's no one else in the lobby to see this, though I can't believe Kate would act this way at work. I thought she liked her job.

I clear my throat, as loudly and as drawn-out as I can make it. Kate turns to look at me, but she doesn't raise her head from Tom's shoulder.

"It's our first official day as a couple," she says, her voice oozing with . . . ick. What is it about love that makes people act so dopey?

"In France, they would never treat love like this," I say loftily. "They treat it way more reverently."

This is another load of bullshit. When Julianne started dating she-who-shall-not-be-named (who was, for the record, way shorter than me), there wasn't a locker at school they didn't

98

press up against at some point to make out. And the number of tourists who think it's cute to go at it by the Eiffel Tower is horrific.

Tom pulls Kate closer. A feat I did not think possible. Even Matt moves away from the reception counter, wandering into the waiting area.

"Thanks for coming to meet me, sweetums," Kate says. I swear she shoots me a look as she does, like she's being so over-the-top to taunt me.

"Of course, my sweet honey flower," Tom says. He leans over and bops her nose with his. She giggles, her ears turning pink like she's embarrassed, even though she's contributing as much as Tom is to this display.

"Matt, do you perchance have a fork?" I ask, glancing at the grossness across from me. "I need to use it."

"No," he mumbles from the plush red armchair he's sunk into.

"Damn," I mutter. "I need to stab my eyeballs out."

I shoot Tom a pointed look. He's never been this ridiculous before. I don't know what's come over him. He shrugs at me, wrapping his arms tighter around Kate's waist.

"She can't handle our looooooove," Kate says, her voice dripping with cutesy *blech* as she reaches up to graze a finger-tip against Tom's chin.

And that does it. I swing my legs around on the stool and get up.

"I'm out," I say, lifting my hands in surrender. "Come get me when we're ready for dinner."

I storm away from reception. As I retreat, I see Kate and Tom exchange triumphant smiles, and my stomach twists. Were they trying to drive me away on purpose? Why would they do that? They were the ones who asked me to come in the first place.

I speed up as I maneuver my way into the multipurpose room. The soles of my shoes squeak against the floor, which has muddy rainwater tracked across it. It lessens the drama of my exit a bit, so I throw my shoulders back to compensate as I stride away.

As soon as I pass the foosball and air hockey tables, I have no idea where to go. The bravado of the moment shrivels into my chest. But I'm not about to turn away. For one, that would be embarrassing. And for another, I have no interest in a round of nausea before dinner because this band of *connards* doesn't know how to keep it in their pants for longer than two seconds.

After rounding the bookcase separating the play area from the quiet study section, I sink to the floor, letting my legs stretch out in front of me. I'll just wait here until the sight of Kate and Tom's nestling leaves my mind, and then I'll join them again when they're ready to go to dinner.

I'm about to get up and head over to them, when I hear footsteps padding down the other side of the bookshelves. I duck down behind the books as the footsteps come a little closer.

"Yeah, she's got it bad for Sophia."

Who has it bad for me? I straighten in surprise, and I hit my head against a book jutting too far out of the shelf. Ow.

Wincing, I knead the spot with my fingers and slowly turn around, straining to hear more.

Through the spaces between the books, I see Myrah and Kate standing in the middle of the rec room. Myrah leans against the foosball table, absently spinning one of the handles.

I frown. Wasn't Kate just at reception? What powers forced her to untangle herself from Tom so soon? Is her shift even over?

Before I can question it further, Kate speaks up.

"Are you sure?" she asks, crossing her arms. "Lately she seems to . . . well, kinda hate her."

"Yeah," Myrah says. She's whispering, but the room is so empty and silent, I can hear her anyway. "I swear. She's totally in love with Sophia."

I groan internally. Everywhere I turn, there's more drama. Is it so much to ask to go through high school with no crushes and no kissing and, while I'm wishing for stuff, no summer reading?

Still I lean forward, my forehead pressed against the books now. I don't want Kate and Myrah to spot me and stop talking before I find out who they're talking about. Who could possibly be in love with me?

Whoever it is, I need to know so I can stay away from them. Getting involved in this kind of thing only leads to mascara-laden tearstains on your pillows, if the state of my pillowcases in Paris were anything to go by.

"Are we talking about the same Emma?" Kate says.

My stomach drops. There's only one Emma I know. And

there is absolutely no way she's in love with me. No. Fucking. Way. This can't be true.

It can't be. What about all the stuff she said to me at the dance? Not to mention all the arguments we've had since.

I'm leaning so far forward in my straining to hear, I'm sure the book spine will leave a mark on my forehead. But I can't help it. I can't let a single word they say slip past me.

"Yes," Myrah says, so eagerly that her voice breaks out of its whisper. She looks around but by some miracle doesn't see me. She pulls Kate closer. "She talks about it all the time. She didn't want to tell you while you were focusing on getting with Tom."

"But . . ." Kate shakes her head, evidently as confused as I am. "Then why . . ."

I swallow, my heart racing. None of this feels like it can possibly be true. But it's coming from Kate and Myrah. They must be misinformed. But how could they be? They're Emma's closest friends.

"She's too proud to admit she likes her," Myrah says.

My throat itches, and I swallow down a cough. I cross my fingers, praying they'll say more, but Myrah shrugs, leading Kate out of the room toward reception. I stare at the spot where they were standing, shell-shocked. For a moment, I'm frozen. My muscles are all tensed, and I can't relax them. I can't even take a breath. All I can do is try not to fall apart.

I peel myself away from the books, falling backward onto the hardwood. How am I supposed to interact with Emma now? How am I supposed to make a competing movie? Maybe I shouldn't have split the groups. But she kicked me out!

Wincing, I push myself off the floor. I have no idea how to respond to this. Every cell in my body wants to call this a lie and move on with my life. I can't imagine anything I want less than the specter of love looming over me. But the news is coming from Myrah and Kate. It has to be true.

It makes my stomach twist, as though my gut has turned itself inside out. Love works for no one. Not for my parents, and certainly not for me and Emma. I have to squash this before it goes any further.

"What am I going to do?" I mutter as I round the bookshelf.

"Are you talking to yourself?"

I jump. Emma's standing on the other side of the shelf, hands on her hips.

"No."

I sigh. I miss the days when Emma and I rarely talked. Since I've gotten back, we've been fighting about the movie, and now this bombshell?

I want to be kind to her. Not that I return her feelings. But I know she *loves* me, so being mean to her feels . . . well, mean. Emma, this girl I've been either ignoring or fighting, is a human person with human emotions. Who knew?

"The others wanted me to come get you," she says, her tone flat. "Tom says he's sorry, and to come back. We're about ready to head to dinner."

I beam at her, flashing all my teeth. "Awesome. Thank you so much. I'll be right there."

She shrugs. "Do whatever you want. I didn't want to come get you anyway."

She turns away and stalks down the hall, her ponytail swinging behind her as she walks.

I didn't want to come get you anyway. There's gotta be a double meaning there. What it is, I'm not sure, but there's gotta be.

CHAPTER NINE

Emma

. . . .

Sophia's footsteps echo behind me, but I don't look back until I've reached reception. I linger by the front door, hoping they all get the hint. The sooner we leave for dinner, the sooner it's over and we can all go home.

Sophia leans against the wall opposite me, looking straight at me. There's a weird question lingering in her eyes that I can't decipher.

"What are you looking at?" I ask, an edge in my voice.

"Nothing," she says, her eyes darting away from mine.

I knead my palm with my fingers. Kate, Tom, and Myrah are exchanging glances, and one of them stifles a giggle. Matt's looking away from them pointedly. The hairs on the back of my neck rise as my skin prickles with self-consciousness. What joke are they all laughing about that I'm not in on? Am I the butt of it?

"Are we ready for dinner?" I ask to cover the awkwardness.

Kate nods, grabbing her bag from under the reception desk, and we all troop out of the teen center.

"How've you been doing lately?" Sophia asks, falling into step next to me as we make our way down the sidewalk. Her voice is thick with gentleness. The way she's talking to me, you'd think I was a five-year-old calming down from a temper tantrum.

I have no idea how to respond to that tone, so I stick with turning away from her to look at Tom. That's when I notice that his whole face is contorting with suppressed laughter. I glance over at Kate, whose crinkled eyes and deep dimples give away the smile she's trying to hide behind her hand.

"Seriously, are you doing okay?" Sophia asks, the same weirdly sympathetic smile stuck to her face. Why is she treating me like someone's died?

Myrah stuffs her knuckles into her mouth, and my blood boils over. As soon as we get to the restaurant, a sushi place a block down from the teen center that Kate recommended, I drop my bag onto a chair without bothering to sit.

"I'm going to the bathroom."

Kate elbows Myrah, who straightens out her face. But I'm still standing, and I'm pissed that Kate is involved in whatever bullshit Sophia came up with. Might as well commit to storming off.

Before anyone can say anything else, I half run toward the restrooms. Out of the corner of my eye, I think I see Tom and Matt following me, so I pick up the pace. There's only one bathroom, and I lock myself in before either of them can reach me.

I take a few deep breaths, trying to steady my racing heart. I don't know how to address this weird vibe that's suddenly taken over the group. But I can't hide in here forever. Maybe by the time I get to the table, they'll have sorted themselves out and my heart will have stopped stuttering.

I quietly crack the door open, but Tom and Matt are standing outside. I move to shut the door. I'm not ready to face them right away.

"Do you see her?" Tom asks.

I stop myself from closing the door all the way, instead leaning closer to the sliver of a gap between the door and the frame. Are they talking about me?

There's a long pause, followed by a thump. Did Tom just hit Matt? That can't be right. Matt is shorter than Tom, but he's got way more muscle mass. He always wins whenever we get into an argument about who in the group would win in a fight.

Besides, why would they be fighting?

What is going on with these people today?

"Uh," Matt says with a groan. "No."

"Sophia's so embarrassed," Tom says. "Do you think Emma figured it out?"

Figured what out? I hold my breath, desperate to hear more, but here's another pause. I can hear them scuffling, but I can't see what's going on without revealing myself.

"Figured what out?" Matt says. There's something off about his tone, like he's reading lines from a play.

"About Sophia," Tom says.

I strain to hear everything. My whole body is pressed against the door, and I have to tighten my grip on the doorknob to keep it from flying open. Still, I press harder, as if that will help me hear them better.

"Sophia's totally in love with Emma," Tom says in response to Matt's silence.

I exhale.

What?

They have to be talking about a different Sophia.

Of course, the only other Sophia at our school is a freshman, and she's already dating Jason Longman.

It has to be her. Our Sophia.

Blood pounds in my ears. That can't be true.

But Tom's no liar.

Still. He has to be somehow misinformed. Or talking about freshman Sophia. Maybe she finally figured out that Jason Longman is a total sleazebag.

"She's been talking about it nonstop since she got back from Paris," Tom says.

Well. That narrows it down.

My chest reverberates with this information, but my brain hasn't processed it yet.

Because . . . Sophia? In love? With me?

Yeah, not exactly the most logical combination of words.

Holding my breath so that I don't miss anything (and, let's be real, because I'm a little bit in shock; and also because this bathroom smells so strongly of air freshener that it's making my head spin), I keep listening, praying that they'll drop more details.

"Really?" Matt says, voicing my feelings. "That doesn't sound . . . accurate."

Right on, Matt.

I look down, and realize my hands are trembling. What is happening?

"She's doing her best to hide it," Tom says.

This must be why she was so nice to me today. Why she rescued me from Matt and asked me to dance. As much as I hate to admit it, this makes sense.

"I don't see her," Matt says. "Let's go back to the table."

They walk away. I let the door open, and I tumble out of the bathroom. How can any of this be true?

Coming from Tom, how could it not be? Sophia tells him everything.

But she's always going on and on about how terrible love is. I thought she was a run-of-the-mill cynic, determined to squash other people's joy. Could there be more to her than that? Could all the bitterness be a front for something more?

If she's in love herself, it must be.

I can't believe I was so wrong about her.

I can't believe I'm admitting I was wrong about something. Even if it is just to myself.

When I get to the table, I give her a small smile. Her eyes light up as she returns it. We're seated at opposite ends of the table, and I spend the whole meal wondering if I should say something to her. But what? Apologize for fighting? That would come out of nowhere, and the stubborn streak in me won't stop reminding me that she totally fought back.

But every time I glance across the table, her eyes dart away, like she was just looking at me. Cheeks reddening, I turn to my miso soup. I look up a second later, and she's a moment too slow in looking away. Our eyes catch, and we're both smiling when we return to our food.

Maybe Sophia's not so bad after all.

CHAPTER TEN

SOPHIA

· ·

Tom said to meet at Georgie's at noon, I'm sure of it, but I've been here for ten minutes already, and no one's showed. Not even Myrah is here yet, and she's paid to be here.

I pull my phone out of my pocket to text Tom, but before I can hit send, the door opens and Emma comes in, fanning herself with one hand.

"Hey," I say, half rising out of my chair. She stops to order before walking haltingly over to me, and sits across from me at the table. I nod at my fingertips, unsure what to say.

"They said noon, right?" Emma says after a long pause.

I nod, grasping for conversation. "Yeah, definitely. I don't know where they are. It's not like Tom to be late."

Inwardly I cringe. *It's not like Tom to be late?* I sound like a complete moron.

"Yeah, Kate is the most punctual person I know," Emma says. "And Myrah's literally paid to be here."

"That's what I was thinking," I say, too loudly. I shrink into my seat, and silence falls over us once again. I pick at my short fingernails, and each tiny scritch is deafening, the longer I don't say anything. One of Myrah's coworkers brings a mug of tea and drops it off in front of Emma.

"So, I, uh—" I start, at the same time that Emma says, "Well, what do—"

We laugh, and then fall silent again. Emma gestures for me to go on. I was about to apologize for all the fights we had about the movie, but the wind has left my lungs. I nod to her instead.

"How's your movie going?" she asks.

I shrug. I don't want to admit that it's going badly. She's still the enemy when it comes to the film competition. Besides, what if she suggests reuniting the groups as a peace offering? I might not have any idea where to take my film, but that doesn't mean I want to return to the world of rom-coms and disgustingness.

"Fine," I say with a shrug. "How's the rom-com?"

"Wow, did you just say that without a trace of disdain?" Emma says with a smile. "I'm impressed."

"Thank you, thank you," I say, laughing as I give a tiny bow over the table. She giggles.

"So, what got you into film, anyway?" I ask, straightening. If we're going to be stuck here alone together, might as well make conversation.

"My family and I are really into watching stuff together," she says. "And things have been kind of weird with—"

She cuts herself off, flushing, but I nod. I know she's not out to her parents yet. I know what that can do.

"So, anyway, I guess it's nice to have something that still bonds us. A thing we can all escape into," she says.

I raise my eyebrows. "Yeah, I get that. When I was in Paris . . ." It's my turn to trail off. Emma looks up at me, a question in her eyes, but I ignore it. "An escape is nice sometimes."

She holds my gaze, smiling sheepishly, and I can tell she's thinking the same thing I am. Us? Something in common? After the week we've had, who would've guessed?

She drops her gaze, tucking a strand of hair behind her ear. "Yeah."

She reaches across the table, and my heart jolts for a second. Is she going for my hand? Our fingers brush against each other, but she only grabs a sugar packet from the container between us and rips it open, dumps its contents into her tea.

"You don't hold back," I say when she reaches for another.

She laughs. "I think of it more as sweet milk with an herbal aftertaste than actual tea."

I snort, shaking my head. "Honestly, you're living your life right. So, aside from rom-coms . . . favorite movie?"

"*Ever After,*" she says immediately.

"That's a rom-com," I object. "I mean, a really good one, I'll give you that, but *still.*"

"Did you just compliment my taste?" she asks, laying a fingertip against her chest.

I shake my head. "Absolutely not. When I said *really good,* what I meant was 'mediocre at best.'"

"How dare you," she says flatly, and for a moment I worry I've gone too far and we've veered back into arguing, but then she breaks, smiling.

"Sorry," I say, throwing my hands up. "I guess I just have better taste than you."

"You just hate fun," Emma says, her tone teasing. "We should watch it together sometime. I'll prove how wrong you are."

I freeze. Did she just ask me on a date?

Surely not.

All I wanted was to get through this forced interaction with as little awkward silence as possible, and now she's asking me to *watch a movie with her*?

Before I can stutter out an awkward response, Emma goes on. "All of us. I've been meaning to make Myrah watch. She's never seen it. Can you believe that?"

"It's must-watch cinema," I say quickly, ready to move past my own internal awkwardness. My face falls when I realize what I've just said.

"Hah," Emma says, pointing at me. "You admit it."

I throw my hands up in defeat. "Fine. It has its moments."

The door opens again, and Kate trails in, hand in hand with Tom.

"You guys sure took your sweet time," I say to them, starting away from Emma. For some reason, I feel caught. We weren't doing anything, I remind myself, but heat floods my cheeks anyway.

"What are you talking about?" Tom asks, glancing at his phone. "We're ten minutes early."

"We said noon," Emma says, frowning.

"No, we didn't," Tom says.

Before this can devolve into a full on yes-we-did, no-we-didn't situation, Myrah walks in, tying her tragic green apron around her waist, and settles the debate.

Emma and I exchange glances, and I shrug. Guess I was wrong.

I fiddle with the camera lens, nodding at it like I know what I'm doing. After all this blustering talk of France and cinema and splitting the groups, I can't admit to Tom and Matt on our first day of shooting that I have no idea how cinematography works.

As I suggested, we're spending our first day roaming the city and "letting it inspire us." This is, of course, another load of bullshit. I've spent the day frantically racking my brain for an idea—any idea. All I know is that I don't want to make a rom-com. Those are garbage pieces of propaganda that force the idea onto all of us that love is somehow real. I can't condone that messaging. Especially now that I know Emma is in love with me. I can't seem like I'm encouraging her.

At least I couldn't have asked for a better day to hide behind the city as I desperately claw around for an idea. It's hot, but the humidity has momentarily left us alone, and there's a clear breeze that ruffles my blue skirt every time I take a step. It's nice, even though there are sweat stains lining my T-shirt where I had to hold the camera bag on our walk down.

"Let's get some shots of the Flatiron," I say as we walk out of Madison Square Park, where I got some black-and-white footage of the puppies frolicking in the dog run.

"Can these be in color?" Tom asks, slumping behind me.

"Sure," I say. "We can always edit it out later if we need black-and-white to fit the mood better."

I mean, I can't, because I know less about editing than I do about cinematography, but I'm sure someone could.

"Why does this have to be so depressing anyway?" Tom asks.

"For the art, Thomas. There's nothing artistically profound about a bunch of teenagers skipping around the city all day. We're looking for the message under it all."

Matt, who's trailing behind us, scoffs at this. "There can be happy messages."

"Not in meaningful art," I insist. "Haven't you ever seen a French film?"

"No," Tom and Matt say at the same time.

"Well, all the good ones are as depressing as shit," I tell them, pointing ahead. "Let's set up here."

We've reached the little triangle of sidewalk directly beneath the pointy end of the Flatiron. It's congested with tourists holding up their phones to snap photos. I sidestep a couple taking turns posing in front of the building, and set down the tripod and mount the camera onto it.

It's early evening, so the sun is casting a pink glow along

the right side of the building. I switch the camera on and pan across the building, praying that I have the color settings right so we can capture this look. It could be a metaphor for hope.

At the thought, an idea bursts open. I turn to Tom and Matt, beaming. "This should be about seeing the city through brand-new eyes. So our character isn't just exploring the city; she's exploring it for the first time ever."

"Like someone who's just moved here?" Tom asks.

"Or someone coming back after a long time," I murmur, turning to the camera. "And seeing how different everything is now. But then some things," I say, adjusting the lens so that the corner of the building seems to loom over us with its golden glow, "never change."

Tom nods. "That sounds fine. Are we going to have a script? Please?"

"I think it could be fun to improvise it still," I say. "Keep the camera rolling and see how the story goes before we set anything down on paper. We can let what we see define the story. That's what cinema is supposed to be about anyway."

Even though I'm making this all up as I go, the excitement building in my voice is genuine. I have no idea where this movie is going, and that's intoxicating in the weirdest way. It could go anywhere, like here and now with this sunset against the Flatiron and the smell of hot sugar coming from the nearby Nuts4Nuts cart, so heavy in the air that it's practically visible in the shot.

This is everything I hoped making a movie would feel like.

I switch the camera to playback mode so I can show the boys everything we've got already. We started in Central Park with some sweeping shots of leafy trees and fresh lawns, framed by imposing tall buildings on all sides. As we walked down, I kept making us stop to film the cars shooting by, even though we were all sweating in the noon sun. Now the sound of their tires crackle through the camera's internal mic. When I finally caved and let us get on the subway, I got a fantastic shot of the train sliding down the dark tunnel and toward the station, its glimmering headlights taunting us with its slow pace. The city is coming alive under my shaky direction.

"See? This is going to be fine. We should start introducing the character, though." I look up at them. "Which one of you wants to act?"

Both of their fingers fly to the sides of their noses. "Not it."

I grin. "Fine. I'll do it."

I hit record again and glance at the shot, mentally placing myself to the left of the building, on the opposite side of the pink sunset hues splashing across it, before stepping into the frame. I stare at the building, keenly aware of the camera's eye on my back, and cross my feet under me. I want my posture to look pensive. I stare up at the building I've seen a thousand times, as if I'm seeing it for the first time. Its architecture is pretty impressive, with its lacy Renaissance style and odd curvy triangle shape.

I'm stuck staring at it while the camera stares at me, and it's all making my head spin with unwanted thoughts about how I don't feel at home here anymore, even though this is my home,

118

and the building is looming over me so high that it might fall and crush me, and I can't quite catch my breath.

I stumble backward, and cover by reaching out my arms, like I just tripped on my own shoes. I turn around to face the camera. "And cut."

"Very pensive," Tom says, switching the camera off.

I grin. "Thanks. Let's get some shots of me walking through the park. We can get some close-ups. I didn't put on lipstick this red for nothing."

I walk back to the camera, the heels of my boots clapping against the sidewalk with every step. Before I can unscrew the camera from the tripod, though, I notice another group weaving through the crowds with a camera, and my heart sinks.

"What are you guys doing here?" I ask as Kate, Myrah, and Emma wave at us.

Kate points to the camera in Emma's hands. "Same thing you guys are, I think."

I stare at the camera. It's much nicer than ours. It's massive, and it has a big swirly lens. Ours is closer to fancy-home-video than professional-film-festival.

"Where did you get that?"

Emma smirks. "What, intimidated?"

"No," I say. My tone screams *yes.*

"My uncle is a cinematographer," she says, lifting her palm for Kate to high-five. The resounding slapping sound might as well be a punch in the face. "He let us borrow it."

"He made us take out insurance, though," Kate says.

I huff. "We didn't feel the need to rely on overpriced equipment. The art speaks for itself."

Emma laughs, but her thin arms are shaking from the weight of the camera. "Okay, Home Video."

She turns to set the camera gently onto its tripod. She's cradling the lens like it's a baby who still can't support its own head.

Kate, meanwhile, wanders over to Tom to rest her head on his shoulder. I wrinkle my nose at the sight.

"How's your script coming?" Kate asks.

He moves out of the way so she can look at our camera, and she leans over to scroll through our playback footage.

"Hey, she's the enemy," I protest, at the same time that Emma says, "Stop fraternizing with the enemy."

We look at each other, and my cheeks grow hot when our eyes meet. I can't help it. Is she still in love with me? Will she read into this moment?

Tom stretches, leaving Kate to peruse our footage.

"Katerina," Emma whines.

"Fine, I'll stop looking," Kate says, stepping away from the camera.

"Okay. You guys need to go work somewhere else," I say, pointing down the street. I can't focus with Emma and her feelings around. "We can't work right next to each other, and we were here first, so we have dibs."

"Fine, but we should have a movie night later," Kate says. "I'm sick of us being apart all the time."

She meets Matt's eye, and he looks away.

"I'm down," he says. At least, that's what his words are. His tone says something closer to *I'd rather discover the taste of my own intestines.* I shoot him a questioning look, and he shrugs.

"I'll be there," I say with a glance at Emma. "But only if I can pick the movie."

"Oh, of course," Emma says, shaking her head. She's trying to be snarky, but her tone lacks its usual bite. She's smiling too gently for that. "Heaven forbid you try to make someone else happy for once."

A silence falls over the group, and I realize everyone's waiting for me to fire a comeback. I chew on my tongue, the expanding silence crawling up my spine. I can't stop thinking about the look on her face at the dance. How my words made her features crumble. I don't want to make her feel like that again.

"Fine," I say instead. "You pick the movie."

"Fool," Emma says, shaking her head at me. "We're watching *Notting Hill* and then having an in-depth conversation about why it's one of the best rom-coms of all time."

"No, we're not," Myrah says. "We should go to an outdoor movie before it gets too hot to be any fun."

"Fine," Matt grumbles. He returns to the camera. After clicking around for a few moments, he gasps. "What the hell?"

I run to him, my heeled boots clacking against the pavement. "What?"

"Everything is gone."

I shove him out of the way and frantically maneuver around the camera settings. The playback is empty.

My brain feels as blank as the SD card has apparently become. I turn the camera off and on, I close the flip screen and open it again, I smash all the buttons one by one and then two by two, but to no avail.

"We spent the whole day shooting," I say, my eyes widening at the little screen. "We had some good stuff. What happened?"

Tom is beside me now, tapping away at the buttons, but everything is completely gone. I take a shaky breath, stepping away from them. This movie has to be perfect. How am I supposed to create a full short film in two weeks if I've lost all my footage? My chances of winning this thing are circling the drain, about to disappear with all the shots I got today.

Emma's face twists. "I'm so sorry. We'll leave so you guys can get back to work."

I nod, distracted by my own disasters, but she catches my eye, and the stress melts out of my shoulders for a moment. I lose myself in her eyes, noticing again how they dance with laughter. I force myself to drop my gaze.

"Are you in love?"

Dad smiles down at me. I answer his question with what I like to think is a soul-crushing glare. I'm in my usual spot on the couch—which is to say, I'm lying on it and taking up all the room, covered in pillows. I've been lying here for almost an hour, breathing in the heavy silence of the empty apartment. I didn't expect him to come home before I left for movie night.

"Forgive me for asking," he says, throwing his hands up. "A teenage girl in love. Ridiculous notion."

"Why would you even think that?"

I can feel the teenage angst rising up in me, but being aware of it doesn't make it any easier to stop it from coloring my tone. Especially because his question makes Emma's dimpled face spring, unbidden, to my mind.

"You've spent a lot of time hugging that pillow and staring forlornly at the ceiling," Dad says with a chuckle.

He crosses the living room to settle on the armchair, and bends over to take his shoes off. Under the shiny black exterior of what he calls his "work straitjacket" outfit, he's wearing purple polka-dotted socks. I got him these particular socks three birthdays ago.

"That's because of all the summer catch-up work I have to do," I say.

"Ah, of course," Dad says, but his tone is the one you use with little kids when you're playing along with some three-year-old's harebrained scheme. "Everyone knows how homework strikes at the heart of every hormone-addled teen. Just fills you with passion and despair, huh?"

"I am *not* in love," I say. Because I'm not. Emma might be, but that doesn't mean I am. I'm concerned for her well-being after finding out that she's been having all these feelings. That's all.

He shakes his head at me, and kicks his shoes off to rest

his feet on the coffee table. "There wouldn't be anything wrong with it if you were," he says. "Sure no girl's caught your eye?"

His tone is always cautious when we get into the specifics of my dating life, or lack thereof, like he wants me to know that he's okay with me being gay. It's colored his voice since I came out in eighth grade. It's as corny as hell. It always makes me smile. Even now, when he's accusing me of something as horrendous as *being in love*.

"No girl has caught my eye," I say firmly.

Emma's smile pops into my mind again, but I banish the image from my thoughts. Of all the girls at Messina High, she's definitely not the one who's caught my eye. Because no one's caught my eye. If anything, I've caught her eye. But that doesn't mean anything to me.

"Soph?" Dad says.

My eyes snap up to meet his. "Yes?"

He runs a hand over his face. "You're so not in love, you're daydreaming the second I mention a girl, and you can't hear what your old man is telling you?"

Groaning, I roll my body around so that my face is buried in the pillows. "I'm not in love."

Still chuckling, he gets up, shoes in hand, and heads to his room. I'm left to breathe through the pillows and try not to panic. I can't help it. Emma's gotten to me. Not because I'm in love with her or anything. I'm not. I just hate thinking about her pining after me. It's an ego boost, sure, but I can't stand the thought of her upset, of anything dimming the life that shines out of her, in everything from the high-pitched sound of her laugh to the glow of her face.

Dad comes back in, rocking polka-dotted pajama bottoms and a *Star Wars* T-shirt. He looks at me, still half-buried under a stack of pillows, and laughs again.

"Yep, I remember those days."

"I have no idea what you're talking about," I say. My voice is muffled because of the pillows, but I power through. "I know you can't be talking about the love thing again, because I made it clear I'm not in love."

Dad switches on the light before sitting on the edge of the couch, squashing one of my toes. I twitch it out of his way.

"I don't mean to pry," he says softly, patting my knee.

"There's nothing to pry about," I mutter. I tilt myself onto my side for breathing and speaking enhancement.

"Well, I guess there's plenty of time." Dad moves to get up.

"It's not like that," I blurt. "I'm not going to be falling in love, *ever.*"

Dad lands down on the couch, frowning. "And why do you say that?"

I fix him with a look, and he swallows.

"Just because it didn't work with your mom and me—"

"Just because it's never worked for anyone ever," I interrupt.

Dad sighs, and launches into his lecture. It's the only one he's ever given me, about how I shouldn't let my parents' divorce ruin my life.

"Don't give up on love just because the two people who

raised you couldn't figure it out," Dad says. "Your mom found it with someone else, and I'm sure I will too. If I ever figure out how to stop being such a dork."

I roll my eyes.

"Don't let this harden you," he says, his gaze softening.

I wince at his words. Is that how everyone sees me, as some hard, uncaring rock of a person? Is that why Emma won't tell me how she feels, and why Kate and Myrah think I'd be so mean to her if she did, and why Tom and Matt were so mad at the prospect of working with me on the film when I split the groups? That's so unfair. Just because someone doesn't want to be in a relationship, that doesn't make them uncaring. I care about things. I love my friends; I'm excited about this movie. I'm not hardened.

"Okay. I'll go fall in love," I say, swinging my legs off the couch. "I have a movie night to get to. Maybe it'll happen there."

After all, an unwelcome little voice whispers, *Emma will be there.*

I stab my earrings in as I walk out of the apartment, nodding goodbye to my dad. Talking to him about this stuff is all well and good, but he's such a doofus that I have a hard time taking his advice seriously. And, I mean, what does he know about being a teen girl in not-love?

A thousand years ago when something was on my mind, I crowd-sourced solutions with my parents. When I almost failed chemistry, Dad helped me with homework while Mom spent hours online looking for a better tutor. When I didn't make the soccer team in middle school, Dad made me mint tea and Mom made a list of clubs I could join instead. And the time I tore my dress before the eighth-grade dance, where I so badly wanted to impress my first ever crush, Dad sewed it while Mom picked out accessories that would cover his hasty repair job.

It all makes me yearn for someone to talk to. I whip out my phone and call my mom as I walk down the sidewalk to the subway. This feels like something one should be able to talk to one's mother about. The phone rings six times against my cheek before she picks up.

"Hi, *chérie*," Mom says in her new affected accent when she picks up. "How's Brooklyn? You must be glad to be back."

I stare at the ground, where I'm scuffing the toe of my shoe against the sidewalk. "Yeah. It's good. I wanted to ask you about—"

"I miss you so much already," Mom says, flattening the rest of my sentence.

No one made you leave me behind, I want to tell her. *You're the one who left me here.*

Instead I release my tongue and say, "Yeah."

"Oh, Paul wants to say hello," Mom says, and I sigh. The last thing I want to do right now is talk to my stepdad.

"I'm about to get on the subway," I say, even though the entrance is still three blocks away. The largely empty street, lined with trees and curved brownstones, stretches in front of me. "I wanted to call and say hi."

"It was so nice to hear from you," Mom says. "I love you."

"You too," I mutter, and smash my finger on the end-call button. So much for that.

It's fine. I don't need to talk to my mom about Emma. I don't need to talk to anyone about Emma. There's nothing to talk about. I don't love her.

CHAPTER ELEVEN

Emma
• •

I groan as we trudge away from the Flatiron, the weight of the camera settling into my already sore muscles. After we'd left the house this morning and I'd carried Uncle Eduardo's camera for a block, I almost regretted asking if we could borrow some of his equipment, but after seeing the look on Sophia's face, I'm glad I did. It's worth the burn searing my incredibly non-muscular arms right now.

"Let's head to the public library," I say. It's not too much of a walk from where we are, and we can get some footage of the city on the way. Plus, those lion statues in the front are iconic.

We cut through the park, which is bustling with activity from picnickers and dog walkers. I shift the weight of the camera bag on my shoulder, grinning as I remember Sophia's tiny equipment. With my free hand, I pull out my phone.

EMMA: So sorry about your camera . . .

As soon as the text is sent, my stomach twists into itself. Is that too friendly? Too flirty?

Myrah bounces ahead, practically skipping even though she's weighed down with the audio equipment. She skids to a stop at the crosswalk in time to avoid an untimely run-in with a bus.

"Someone's happy," Kate says with a sly grin, her dimples creasing her cheeks.

Myrah's face lights up with a smile that warms the whole street. "I can't stop thinking about Peter. He took me to see this super-cheesy movie, and I completely missed the whole second half because he was holding my hand, and then afterward he kissed me."

I screech and grab her hands as she launches into a detailed description of how soft his lips are, but the back of my neck grows hot, and I'm painfully aware, as I always am in moments like these, that I'm the only one of the three of us who's never been kissed.

"I think this might *finally* be it," Myrah says, her eyes shining as she speaks. "I'm trying to play it cool, but I'm hopeful. He could be my first real boyfriend."

I sigh wistfully right along with her.

"When do we get to meet him officially?" Kate asks.

The last of the cars pass through the intersection, and we charge across the crosswalk before the light changes. The sunlight has drawn everyone outdoors, so we have to maneuver through the crowds on our way up to Thirty-Ninth Street.

Myrah looks down at her pink-polished nails. "When things are serious. I don't want to get my hopes up too high. It's never worked out before."

My phone buzzes, and I snatch it out of my pocket.

SOPHIA: Size doesn't matter, Emma. It's how you use it that counts.

I chuckle at the memory of her tiny video camera, then bite down hard on my lip. I can't tell if we're fighting or flirting anymore.

I shouldn't be doing either. I should be focusing on the movie. I should put my phone in my tote bag and get to the camera.

My fingers fly across my phone screen instead.

EMMA: Maybe so. But using nicer toys never hurt anybody.

A dark blush creeps down my neck when I hit send, and I chuckle.

Because that counts as flirting, right? I can't help but smile at the thought. What does that mean? I'm not actually into Sophia.

Am I?

"What's so funny?" Myrah asks.

Before I can answer, she lunges forward, reaching for my phone. I fling my hand out of the way so fast, the phone slips out of my fingers and clatters against the sidewalk. I bolt for it, but Myrah beats me to it. She snatches it, and I can see that the screen is lit up with another text from Sophia.

"Jesus, do you and Sophia ever give it a rest?" she says, tossing the phone to me.

I look down at the mercifully uncracked screen, my heart clawing its way up my throat.

SOPHIA: *You're ridiculous.*

I clench my jaw as I read the same two words over and over again. Did I take it too far? Did I misread her text?

Why do I even care?

I scroll up through our texts. There aren't many. I force myself to close the screen and put the phone into my pocket.

A second later, I take the phone out again.

EMMA: *So are you.*

We reach the library, and I lay the tripod down below the white lion statue standing guard on the side of the staircase. This is the perfect setting for Myrah and Kate's first date, I decide as I frame the shot. Every great love story in the world is housed beyond the building's doors.

The whole time, I keep an eye on my phone, just in case, but Sophia doesn't text back.

When I get to my apartment, Dad's messing around in the kitchen. The tangy smell of mangoes fills the room.

"I thought you were going out tonight," he says.

"I am in a bit," I say as I kick off my shoes to join him in the kitchen. My socks slip against the newly Swiffered tile floor. I hop up to sit on the countertop, and lean over to stay out of the way of Dad's chopping. I sigh. I've been dying to confide in my parents about everything that's going on, but I have no idea how to do so when a pretty big part of the issue is the potential for romance between me and another girl.

They won't get it if I can't admit there's a possibility that I like her back.

Not that I do. But I *could,* and they don't know that, and I can't tell them yet. So.

I clear my throat. "Have you ever found out a friend has a crush on you?"

I try to sound casual, and even though Dad's eyebrows shoot up to his hairline despite how much it's receding, he doesn't tease.

"Last time that happened, I ended up marrying the friend," he says.

I sigh. Mom and Dad's love story has been etched into the lines of my heart for years. They became friends after they found out that the other was leading the rival faction in the prank war they'd started in their freshman dorm. And then they fell in love. It was everything I've ever wanted for myself.

But I'm not about to marry Sophia.

Obviously.

"So is one of your friends in love with you, or are you in love with one of your friends?" Dad asks, taking in my expression.

"It's not that."

"What is it, then?" he asks, shifting his gaze to the stew.

"I guess it kind of is like that," I mutter.

Dad chuckles as he scrapes the sliced fruit into a salad bowl. "Do you like him back?"

I swallow. I know I've given him no reason to believe that I'd be into anyone but a him, but the choice of pronoun still stings a little.

As does the question. Because, if I'm being honest, I have no idea how to answer it.

CHAPTER TWELVE

SOPHIA

· ·

I stumble onto our designated patch of grass, clutching my stomach. It feels like a tornado has gone off in my intestines, scrambling my insides into a whirlwind of displaced, churning motion. It's felt like this since the shoot earlier.

"You okay?" Tom asks, concern etched across his face as he lays out our blanket.

"I think I'm dying." I scoot so that I'm sitting on the blanket, protecting my skirt from the damp grass. We're gathered in Bryant Park for the outdoor movie series they do every summer. It's crowded already, but not as crowded as it'll get closer to showtime. I let my purse drop a little to the side to mark our territory, then flop onto the blanket, staring up at the hazy sky. I slowly inhale the smell of freshly cut grass and halal food from the nearby street carts, and exhale all at once.

"What?" Matt asks from the corner of the blanket, where he's sorting through the snacks we brought.

"I'm all . . ." Words failing me, I wring my hands together and squiggle my fingers, interlocking them and then breaking them apart.

"You have butterflies?" Tom asks.

"What? No," I mutter. Butterflies are for people in love. A group I most definitely do not belong to. Just because I thought about Emma all the way here doesn't mean I'm in *love*. I'm worried about her, is all. I rub my fingertips against my chest, inhaling hard. "My chest hurts. My heart's been pounding all the way here."

Tom blinks at me. "So you have butterflies, and your heart literally hurts?"

I ignore him, fanning my face with my hand. "Is it hot out here?"

"Not particularly," Tom says.

There's a pleasant breeze cooling the night air, but I still feel all flushed. I fan myself with more vigor, my carefully manicured nails flashing as I wave my hand over my face. "I'm dying."

"The girls are almost here," Tom says with a glance at his phone.

I smack my lips together to even out my red lipstick. "Emma's coming, right?"

"Yeah," Tom says. "She's on her way with Kate and Myrah right now."

"Why do you even care?" Matt asks as he readjusts the way his T-shirt hangs off his broad frame.

Before I can respond, the aforementioned Kate, Myrah,

and Emma walk up to us, bearing more blankets. Emma's holding a Tupperware of chocolate chip cookies.

"My mom said she made cookies if we wanted," she says, holding the plate up to Tom. "I took the liberty of saying we wanted."

I take one. "A wise decision." I take a bite, but my stomach tightens as I try to swallow, and I cough. Crumbs spray onto my face.

Emma stares at me. "Hot."

I blush, wiping my face with the back of my hand. My forehead feels warm. I knew I was sick.

Kate sets up another blanket while Emma passes the cookies around. Myrah snags two. I sit up, taking my usual spot next to Tom, but he shoves me away.

"That's Kate's spot now," he says.

I slide to the edge of the blanket, grinding my teeth at this latest reminder of how many spots I've lost in his heart. I land next to Emma, and tilt my head back to give Tom a nasty look. Though, if I have been demoted, at least I'm next to Emma. The girl I'm *not* in love with.

We snack while we wait for the movie to start. It's too dark to tell, but I could swear I see Kate wink at Myrah at one point.

The movie starts up, illuminating the crowd on the grass. Everyone else is looking up at the screen, necks craned toward the light, but in the semi-dark, it's easier to steal glances at Emma. Out of the corner of my eye, I watch her more than the movie, which is so far super cute. Much like Emma. Not that I think she's cute or anything. Even though I've noticed that her nose wrinkles when she laughs, a realization that is doing strange things to the inside of my chest. She keeps missing moments and joining in the chuckles and nose-breath laughs a second too late, so I think she's aware of my gaze. I drop my eyes.

But as soon as I do, I can feel her looking at me. My cheek tingles under the weight of her eyes on me. I turn to meet her eyes. For a moment, my cheeks burn as we hold each other's gazes, but then she looks down at the container of cookies, like that's what she was looking for all along. I see right through that, and she must know it, but she commits and grabs a cookie anyway. She takes a bite, and a stray strand of melted chocolate flicks across her lip.

I sneak a glance over my shoulder to make sure no one's watching. When I turn around to check, they're all absorbed in the movie. So I turn to Emma.

"You have a . . . ," I whisper, gesturing to her mouth. The movie soundtrack swells over my words. "Here, let me."

I dab a finger across her lip to get the chocolate, and she blushes almost as red as I've seen Kate go. I always assumed that was a special Kate thing, but I guess it's a family trait. I've never seen anyone make Emma blush before. The idea that it's because of me makes my insides strangely warm. For someone who's not in love and all.

"I'm cold," Kate says, even though the evening air is still plenty warm. "Do we have any extra blankets?"

"Uh, yeah," Tom says. He reaches over Kate to grab his tote bag, and pulls out a blanket. After glancing at Kate, he grabs a second one and throws it to Emma and me.

"I only have two," he says. "So you guys have to share."

I'm not cold at all, but I find myself throwing the blanket over the two of us. It's smaller than I expected, so I scoot closer to Emma. Our hips touch under the blanket, and I hear her inhale sharply.

"This movie is so beautiful," Emma sighs.

"Yeah," I murmur, but I'm not really watching.

She looks up when she hears me. Her cheeks, still pink from the earlier blush, redden again. She's glowing in the moonlight, and it's making my heart do this flip-floppy thing that doesn't feel as unpleasant as I always imagined it would when I read about it in books.

Now that we're wrapped in the blanket, it feels like we're in our own special bubble, tucked away from everyone else. The movie, which I haven't been paying attention to at all, must be reaching the end, because the music underscoring the animated antics is swelling, and my breath is peaking right along with it. It makes my hands shake. I stretch my fingers under the blanket, a vain attempt to stop the nervous trembling.

And that's when my fingers brush against Emma's.

I freeze, my eyes darting to the screen. Emma looks away too, but her hand moves closer, and I open my palm, unfurling my fingers to make room for hers. My breath catches for a moment as fear shoots through me, fear that I've read the moment wrong, that she only touched me by accident, that she's going to snap her hands away and taunt me, in front of everyone, about how I tried to hold her hand under the blanket.

Then her hand closes around mine, and I forget how to inhale. I sit there, staring at the screen without taking anything in except how cold her fingers are against my skin, and how unbelievably nice it feels to be the one to warm them.

My mind is racing so fast, I need a moment to catch my breath. What is happening? What does it mean? What do I want it to mean? None of this feels like me. I'm the one who hates love, who pushes it away any chance I get because I know how much it hurts when it inevitably fails you. So why am I letting my heart jump wildly in my chest because Emma's fingers are tucked between mine?

I don't know the answer to any of these questions. All I know is that I love the way Emma's hand feels against mine. All I know is that I'm not sure anymore why I've been fighting with Emma all week. Now, in the warm embrace of the night sky and the blanket hiding us from the rest of the world, all I want to be is soft with her.

What is *happening* to me?

"I'm cold too," Matt says suddenly.

Scooting forward on the blanket, he slides in between Emma and me. I'm forced to the side, with half my butt hanging out from underneath the blanket. I try to glance at Emma, but all I can see is the back of her frizzy ponytail now that Matt's hulking shoulders are in the way.

I give myself a little shake and turn to the movie. Love always ends in tears, I remind myself. This road starts with hand-holding and excessive eye contact and blushing, and ends in disaster. I cannot allow myself to go down it.

This camera has become my worst enemy. We've spent all of Sunday reshooting everything we lost yesterday, and every time we wrap up at a location, I make us stop to back up the footage from the SD card to my laptop. It takes forever, each time, but we can't risk losing another day's work. We already lost a day, which is almost 7 percent of the time between now and the deadline. We don't have time to muck around.

"Don't look so glum," I tell Tom, even though his face, flushed even redder than usual in the afternoon heat, perfectly mirrors my own feelings. "We're going to shoot in the Met now. They'll have AC there."

We walk to the steps, past the massive pillars lining the outer walls of the Met. Matt speeds up, taking the steps ahead of us two at a time with his freakishly long legs. I teeter behind him on the smooth stone, careful not to slip and break the camera. By the time we join him inside the museum, he's already in a full argument with the security guard.

"You can't bring that in here," the guard says, pointing again to the mic Matt is holding.

"Can we leave it at the coat check?" I ask. "The camera has an internal mic. We can—"

"No video camera inside either," the security guard says when he sees my bag. "It's too big. And coat check can't be responsible for items of that value."

"But—" I start to argue. The art was such an integral part of the scene. I was going to walk around the sculptures and look at them so pensively that the Academy Awards themselves would have to come calling.

"No exceptions." The guard points to the door and then turns away from us to argue with a young woman about her ukulele.

We trudge outside. Tom groans when we step out of the turning door, the heat hitting us like a brick wall.

"I guess we can shoot the scene on the steps," I say, pointing to a less crowded spot toward the bottom of the massive staircase. We unfold the tripod legs and set up the camera. I make sure to include the fountains rushing in the background of the shot.

"Ready?" I ask, and Tom nods. "Action."

I step into the frame, fiddling with the detailing on my lace summer dress. I look behind me at the Met steps towering above me, so wide that they encompass the whole shot, and then down at the spattering fountain. This will all look great with the music I've picked out to underscore this first sequence of me looking tragic in the city.

Even though I'm surrounded by the hubbub of voices and car honks and by the greasy smell from the hot dog carts that line the front of the steps, I feel completely alone. Maybe it's because I know I framed the shot so that it looks like I'm by myself, or maybe it's because I can't stop thinking about how cold Emma's fingers are, even now that they're not wrapped around mine. And about why I held her hand in the first place. All of it is worming its way through my brain, pressing into its folds until tears spring into my eyes.

It's not just Emma. It's Dad's new apartment and the void between me and my mom, and my text chain with Julianne, which dried up after she got a girlfriend and every interaction

I've had with Tom since I got back. And my refusal to believe in love, after everything that life has shown me about it. I was so sure it wasn't real. But now, what does that mean for Emma and me? Is there an Emma and me? How can there be?

I've never felt so alone.

My shoulders heave as sobs tear my throat. I drop my face into my palms in time to catch the onslaught of sudden tears that pour from my eyes.

Footsteps clatter up to me. "Are you okay?" Tom asks.

I lift my head, dabbing my face so that there's only the redness of my eyes to betray my emotion. "Of course. I'm fine. The art got to me."

Tom stares at me. "What?"

"It's a good sign," I say. I swallow and force a smile before I go on. "I think what we're doing is meaningful."

After all, I tell myself, that was the point of making this movie, to find the message I want to convey. This is proof that I'm succeeding. My life is fine.

He nods slowly. "Are you sure you're okay? You can talk to me."

"There's nothing to talk about. I think we should hold a casting session, though, really get this story going." I give him a thumbs-up.

His thin shoulders drop, and he nods before walking to the camera, and with every step he takes away from me, I'm afraid I'll never be able to call him back.

CHAPTER THIRTEEN

Emma

. . . .

I stare at Myrah on the camera screen as she adjusts her bra strap and widens her teeth at the camera. She's sitting on a park bench, and I'm supposed to be framing the shot.

"I'm ready for my close-up," she says with a wink.

I don't answer. Setting up shots has become my favorite part of our shooting days, but today I can't get myself to focus. Instead I trace a finger along my palm, the same palm Sophia held under the blanket last night. I bite my lip as I remember the heat of her skin against mine.

"Emma?" Kate says, touching my shoulder. "Are you okay?"

I blink, focusing on the camera. "Yeah. Yeah. Are you guys ready?"

Myrah gives me a thumbs-up.

I peer at the camera to check my framing. Myrah's script revisions were sharp and funny. I want the film to look beautiful to match her words. We're shooting in Washington Square Park, and even though it's so hot that I'm going to melt any second, it's worth braving the heat in order to be here. The greenery in the background of the shot captures the liveliness around us, which will create the perfect setting for the girls as they first acknowledge that they're in love.

Plus, we have to pitch our project at the competition's networking gala next weekend, and there's a big Most Anticipated Film award. I did some poking around on the film festival's online forums, and it turns out that, like, 85 percent of the time, the team that wins Most Anticipated Film ends up winning the whole contest. So this has to be perfect. I need to get us to that premiere in LA.

After glancing between Myrah and the camera screen, I give a satisfied nod.

"Okay." I start the camera and the mic, and gesture to Kate to slate. "Action."

Myrah angles her round face toward the camera and starts the scene. It's from the middle of the story, where Kate's character realizes that she has feelings for Myrah. The two of them giggle their way through the scene, and Myrah keeps touching Kate's arm when she laughs, like it comes easily for the two of them, like falling in love is simple.

Except, for some reason, it doesn't feel right.

"Cut." I stop before the scene ends.

Myrah groans, fanning her shirt around her torso. "What's wrong?"

I run my hand across my face and step away from behind the camera to join them on the park bench where I marked them.

"That was good," I say. "I like that you guys are bringing out the flirtiness of the scene. But I think there's more than that going on here. It's not that easy, you know, to fall in love?"

Kate shrugs. "It was for me."

Myrah squeals and hugs her. This happens every time Kate mentions Tom, no matter how sticky with sweat we all are.

"Well, that's not how it goes for most people," I say, crossing my arms. "It's complicated, and I want to see that in this scene."

After holding hands with Sophia, of all people, how could I think that love is anything but complicated? I have no idea how to make any sense of the way I'm feeling, and neither should the characters. It'll be more real this way.

"I think the best declarations of love are matter-of-fact," Kate says. "It doesn't have to be complicated."

I grit my teeth together, my jaw tightening. "It's not always like that. Besides, big sweeping romances are always complicated."

Kate opens her mouth, but hesitates for a moment, then nods.

I call action again. This time, Myrah and Kate balance the flirtiness with some heavier silences, and their gazes meet a few times as the moment becomes too much for words. It's still not enough.

"Cut," I call again. Myrah glares at me. Kate takes the opportunity to run off and take a picture of a dog so she can keep her snap streak with Tom alive. Apparently they have a thing going where they send dogs back and forth, and it's almost as cute as the dogs themselves.

"Sorry," I say, lowering my gaze to ponder my notes. Kate comes back, beaming at us. "Maybe we could add some dialogue in, something that captures the anxiety of the moment."

Kate tips her head to one side. "I thought you wanted this to be light and cute?"

"I do," I say. "I want it to be balanced."

Myrah gives me a sly look. "If we're adding in some angst and drama, we could go back to working with Sophia's group. That's what she's all about."

I shudder. "Hah. No way."

"You're the one being all angsty about love all of a sudden," Myrah says. "What happened to the cuteness?"

"I told you, big epic romances always have drama," I say.

"Drama isn't romantic," Myrah mumbles. "Relationships that have a ton of drama usually aren't great to be in."

"Let's try this one more time so we can finish," I say, ignoring her.

I jog to the camera. Myrah's words stick, though. Should this all be easier than I'm making it out to be?

I shake the thought off as I call action. I've always known what I want my love life to look like, and there's no room for matter-of-fact in a great romance story.

I tumble through my front door, sighing with relief as the blast of AC hits me. I stretch my muscles as the sickly feeling of sweat dries off my skin.

"How was the shoot?" Mom asks.

I kick off my flats, jump onto the couch, and fold myself around a pillow.

"It was fun," I say, picking up Lady Catulet and holding her to my chest. She squirms, so I rock her in my arms like she's a newborn until she settles down. "I think I'm getting at some cool things about these characters that we hadn't thought about when we were writing."

I'm cautious, as always, to use gender-neutral language. I'm not about to tell them how gay the movie is, after my dad commented the other day "everything has to have a gay character these days."

The rest of what I said is true, though. Myrah and Kate finally nailed the angst I was looking for. We lost a lot of the flirtiness, but it's okay. There will still be a happy ending eventually.

That's the great thing about sweeping love stories.

"Can we see any of it?" Dad asks, joining me on the couch.

Mom's whole face lights up. "Oh, yes, please. I'd love to see what you're working on."

I squirm against the couch pillows. Normally I wouldn't even wait for them to ask. If I were making anything else, I'd have loaded it up on the TV already, and we'd be busy taking it apart like an episode of *Cake Boss*.

But this?

I can't fill our TV with the image of two girls falling in love. I have no idea what my parents will think. What if they hate it? How could I ever finish the movie, then?

How could I ever pluck up the courage to come out to them if they dismiss this movie?

Wanting romance is such a big part of my life, and they know that, but they don't know anything about the kind of romance I might find.

Should I show them this part of myself?

I fiddle with the flap above the SD card slot in the camera. Everything I want to tell them about myself is in there, woven into a story about two girls falling in love.

I snap the flap shut.

"It's not ready yet," I say, the half lie sticking in my throat. It congeals there, hardening into a lump that brings tears into my eyes. I take a shaky breath to steady myself so they don't notice anything is wrong.

And they don't, which breaks my heart even more.

Maybe it's because, hours later, I'm still thinking about coming out, or maybe I'm just growing soft in my old age, but when I'm going through the footage we got today, I find myself texting Sophia.

EMMA: if I beat you with such a superior camera, I don't think it would really count as a win . . .

For some reason, my heart rate picks up as I set my phone down. Every second she doesn't answer feels like an eon. Three eons later, my phone buzzes, and I leap to grab it.

SOPHIA: idk I think it's evening the playing field

EMMA: here I am trying to help you and you decide to be stone cold

My fingers are shaking a little as I type. I swallow past the anxiety building in my chest. Why does this feel so high stakes? It's just Sophia.

Sophia who's in love with me.

SOPHIA: how are you helping?!

I smile as I type, lying on my bed with my phone held above my face.

EMMA: well, I already have the insurance on the equipment, and we're not shooting tomorrow . . . I may be willing to let you use it in exchange for baked goods.

SOPHIA: omg!!! Are you serious? Yes please!!

I start at her enthusiasm, and my phone falls onto my face. Groaning, I toss the phone aside.

And that's how, instead of shooting the next day, I find myself splitting a croissant with Sophia in Battery Park. She tears it in half in a puff of buttery flakes, and hands me one end. I bite into it happily, staring out at the river. Sunlight jumps off the water, and I squint, looking away. We keep walking down the path, weaving our way around little kids whizzing by on scooters, and dogs straining against their leashes.

"So is this what every morning was like in Paris?" I ask through another bite of croissant.

She laughs. "No. For starters, French girls don't talk with their mouths full."

I flip her off as I swallow.

"They definitely do that in France," she adds.

I've handed the camera bag off to her in exchange for my half of the croissant, and she adjusts the strap. The weight of it leaves a red mark on her shoulder.

"Heavier than you're used to?" I ask with a teasing grin.

She groans her assent. "Not sure this was worth it."

"It was for me," I say, popping the rest of the croissant into my mouth.

"Same," she says, and when I look up at her, I catch the softness in her eyes. I match her gaze, and for a wild moment, I wonder what would happen if I reached up on tiptoe and kissed her.

The thought terrifies me. Instead I look away, turning toward the water. I get an eyeful of reflected sunlight for my trouble. Blinking the spots out of my vision, I crumple the now tragically empty pastry bag and drop it into the next trash can at the edge of the park strip.

We round a corner, and I stop in my tracks. "Is that a carousel?"

Sophia laughs. "Yeah, that's the SeaGlass Carousel."

It's a merry-go-round, but without the traditional horses moving in a circle. Instead a myriad of fish whirl gracefully around each other on turntables, accompanied by gentle music. The colors—sparkling blues and pinks—catch in the sunlight, a glowing re-creation of a sun-dappled underwater space.

I turn to Sophia, and she laughs when she sees my expression.

"Fine," she says, leading me to the line. "But only because I still owe you for the camera."

I hop into the line. We're the only ones here not accompanied by little kids, but I'm just not the type of person who can refuse a pretty carousel on a beautiful day. The attendant takes our five dollars, and I scurry onto the carousel, claiming an angelfish. The ride is crowded, so Sophia scoots onto the seat next to me even though it is decisively not big enough for two adult humans. Our thighs are pressed together, my torso squished between her arm and the cool metal wall of the angelfish interior.

I don't mind.

The song "Beyond the Sea" starts up, and our fish jolts into motion. I lean over to stick my hand out of the opening next to me, laughing as we swirl among the other fish. The other glassy fish around us bop in and out of our sight, moving in unpredictable patterns on their turntables. I grin at Sophia, and when she turns to smile back, our faces are so close together that I can feel her minty breath against my lips.

It would be so easy to lean in.

I blink, pulling away. She does the same thing, but she doesn't have room to move, and she sways precariously toward the opening behind her. I wrap my arm around her, pull her closer by the waist.

"Thanks," she says, laughing. She's in no danger of falling onto the carousel floor anymore, but I leave my arm around her for a moment longer before dropping my hand on my lap. I turn to watch the pattern of the fish, suddenly unable to meet her eye as I can feel my cheeks redden.

We move to a gentle stop as the song comes to an end, and

Sophia helps me out of our angelfish. I take her hand as I jump down, and our palms linger against each other for a moment too long. I look everywhere but in her eyes as we walk out of the park.

"Well, thanks for the camera," Sophia says, hoisting the bag higher on her shoulder as we reach the subway. "At least part of the movie will look good."

I nod awkwardly. I don't want this moment with her to be over, but I can't think of an excuse to keep it going. I don't know what I expected would happen. That we would hold hands again?

I glance down at her fingers. "I'm sure it'll all look good."

"I hope so," Sophia says, glancing down at the subway steps. "We're doing auditions tomorrow for the mom character. Can I give this back to you after that?"

I nod. "Well, I'm going into Brooklyn."

"See you later," she says with a smile, and it feels like a promise I can't stop thinking about the whole way home.

I THINK I LOVE YOU—Scene Breakdown

Emma Hansen

Scene 1: INT — Myrah's apartment

Scene 2: EXT — Park — Washington Square Park

Scene 3: INT — Myrah's apartment

Scene 4: EXT — Park — Battery Park? Can we shoot in the SeaGlass Carousel? It's so pretty.

Scene 5: INT — Kate's apartment

Scene 6: INT — Flatiron

Scene 7: INT — Teen center

Scene 8: EXT — Park — Washington Square Park

CHAPTER FOURTEEN

SOPHIA

. . . .

I run my fingertips around the edge of the sleeve on my now empty Starbucks cup, staring at the chair and trying to catch my breath. It's one thing to pretend to know what I'm doing in front of Tom and Matt, but now we're auditioning professional actors. What if they see right through me?

It doesn't help that I can't stop thinking about Emma's hand, her cold fingers pressed against mine. And then the way she wrapped her arm around me on the carousel. It's all enough to make me never inhale again. My head spins.

I glance at the camera to cover my agitation. The room we rented for two hours to hold our auditions is more of a box than a room, with beige walls and a beige carpet. I can't quite tell if the carpet started out beige or if it got that way from years of coffee spills. The only window is so small that it doesn't let in much light. All in all, it's not making us look super professional. At least we have Emma's fancy camera to add some pizzazz to the situation.

My phone vibrates, sliding on the plastic fold-up table we're sitting behind, and I reach over to stop it. When I read Emma's name on the screen, my breath catches.

EMMA: How's casting going?

SOPHIA: trning to beat out the competition?

*SOPHIA: *trying*

My hands are shaking so much, I correct four typos before I hit send, and one still makes it through.

"Should I bring in the first person?" Tom asks.

I nod shakily.

"It's gonna be fine," he says. "They're all more nervous than you are."

I swallow. "This has to go well."

"It's going to be great," Tom says. He smiles at me, rubbing the back of his neck.

"I'm worried she'll think we're babies," I say, twisting my fingers together. What if she doesn't take us seriously?

"Nice to know that's how you see us," Tom says.

"I didn't mean—"

"Sorry we're not as cool as your French film friends," he mutters.

I swallow. No matter how hard I try, I always end up on the outside with him nowadays.

"Sorry. I didn't mean it like that."

"It's okay," Tom says.

"Well, go tell"—I glance at our spreadsheet of appointments— "Amanda Fales that she can come in."

Matt jogs out of the room, and I check my phone as soon as the door swings shut behind him. My phone lights up again, and I snatch it.

EMMA: well, I was going to sabotage you, but now that I know you can't even spell trying, I feel like I don't have to.

I grin, the way I always do these days when Emma's name lights up my phone screen, but before I can text her back, Matt returns with a thirtysomething woman who might be playing the mom in my script, which is less a script and more a vague outline that has left lots of room for improvisation. I lean into my chair, one hand still resting lightly around my coffee, like I've done this a million times. Like I'm not feeling pinpricks up and down my whole body.

"Hi, Amanda," I say. Tom shoots me a look, and I realize that I've put on a light French accent. I clear my throat, but it feels like it's too late to lose it now. "I'm Sophia. I'll be reading with you. Whenever you're ready."

She rattles off the first line without looking down at the printout in front of her, and I scramble through my papers to read the rest of the scene with her. She's pretty good, even if she's not playing the mom character quite mean enough.

"Thank you so much for coming in," I say as she packs up her things, but my mind is a million miles away.

Well, technically, it's about half a mile away in Battery Park, where I last got to hold Emma's hand. The memory flushes me with warmth.

My phone buzzes against the table, and I reach for it, half hoping that Emma's name will pop up.

It doesn't. I read the text four times, my eyes moving too fast for me to catch its meaning.

JULIANNE: Hey! How's New York? Everyone here misses you. I know I do.

My heart feels like it's going to fall out of my butt. I stare at my phone screen, blinking. My thumbs hover urgently over the keyboard, but I have no idea how to respond. Why would she text me now, out of the blue? I haven't seen her in months. She hasn't spoken to me since she started dating someone else.

Does this mean they're not dating anymore?

My stomach lurches. How could she do that to me? She has no right to reinsert herself into my life after she stopped being friends with me, right when things with Emma are—

I mean, I don't know what things with Emma are. But still.

Seeing my expression, Tom glances down at my screen. "Who's Julianne?"

"Just a friend from France," I say, laying the phone face-down on the table, like it doesn't matter. Like my heartbeat isn't thundering in my fingertips.

Tom nods without looking at me. "Nice to see you can keep in touch with some of your friends, despite the distance."

"No," I say, sweeping my phone into my bag without texting her back. "I barely knew her."

Tom eyes me, taking in my twisted expression. "You sure about that?"

"Yeah," I say, too fast.

Seeing Julianne's name reminded me where love ends: in tears and ruined friendships. The memory of holding Emma's hand recedes into the back of my mind. It was a stupid fairy-tale fantasy anyway. I need to snap myself into the real world, where I know love can never last.

"It's hard to understand where you're coming from when I don't know anything about what your life was like there, I guess," Tom mutters.

I clear my throat. "Is the next appointment here?"

"Should be," Matt says. He gets up to go check, and passes Kate on his way out as she swings in, clutching a Starbucks tray and pastry bags.

"I brought you guys coffee," she says, beaming at us.

I groan, stretching as she passes me one. I wrap my hands around the sleeve, the warmth rushing into my palms.

"Another one?" Tom asks, elbowing me.

"Listen," I say, jabbing my finger into his chest. "I have been awake since eight in the morning on a Tuesday. During summer vacation. I will have as much caffeine as I possibly can. Thank you, Kate. You're a star."

Plus, my emotions bottomed out with one text.

Kate smiles even wider, which is truly impressive when you consider how wide she was smiling to begin with. She drops the pastry bags onto the table, leans over to kiss Tom, and waves goodbye on her way out.

As she leaves, my phone buzzes against the table. I pick it up, my chest clenching in anticipation of a double text from Julianne, but it's from an unknown number.

9175553420: Why would you cancel the auditions so last minute? Having that girl tell us at the venue is beyond unprofessional. You could've at least emailed us ahead of time so we didn't all come all the way down here.

My chair clatters to the floor as I jump up, my knees buckling against the edge of the seat. I rush to the door and throw it open to reveal a poorly lit, completely empty hallway. Matt stands at the end of it, talking to a short girl with red hair. She glances up and, when she sees me, turns and runs down the hall.

"Wasn't that one of the actresses who was supposed to audition?" I ask when Matt turns around.

"No, someone who works here," he says quickly. "Someone told all our appointments to leave. No one's here."

"What?" I ask hoarsely, looking back down at my phone. What girl told everyone to leave?

"There's no one left."

I clap my hand to my mouth. How can this be happening? First the disappearing footage, and now this?

"So we have no one to audition?" I ask.

Matt winces. "It would appear not."

I drop my head into my hands. "How are we supposed to make a movie with no actors?"

I stumble back into the audition room, Matt behind me.

"We have Amanda," Tom says. "I'm sure she was super impressed by how French you are."

I look up at him. "Seriously? That's what we're going to focus on now?"

"That's all we ever focus on," Tom says, slamming his chair against the floor as he gets up. "'In France we do this.' 'In France we think that.' 'In France I ditched all my friends and lost my whole personality.'"

160

All the air that once resided in my lungs crashes out of my mouth in one fell swoop. "Are you serious right now?"

"Sophia," Tom says, leaning to rest his palms against the table as he stares me down, "I don't know what happened to you, but you totally forgot about us when you were gone, and you came back acting like nothing has changed, but you've become a completely different person. A person who's kind of a pretentious asshole all the time."

My eyes widen as I struggle to take in his words. Tom's expression flashes with anger, and he's dangerously close to shouting, and the worst part is, he's not entirely wrong.

"Sorry for having an experience without you," I say instead of apologizing. Tears sting my eyes.

Tom shakes his head. "That's not the issue, and you know it."

I drop my gaze. The only thing left to do at this point is apologize. I shove my trembling fingers into my pockets, shrinking under his steely look. All I need to do to make that anger in his eyes go away is apologize. I should. Now that he's said it, I get why he's mad.

But if I try to explain, I'll have to tell him about everything that happened in Paris. I can't open those floodgates. So instead I hang my head, letting the silence weigh down between us until it pushes him away at last. He storms out of the room, his gangly arms swinging wildly by his sides as he goes. Matt stares at me for a moment, the silence hanging heavy in the room, before he follows. I let them go without a word.

CHAPTER FIFTEEN

Emma

. . . .

I smooth the sides of my dress, which whips around my ankles as I walk. For the fifth time since we left the subway station, I fish through my purse until I can feel the edges of the notecards I wrote my speech on.

The six of us decided to go to the student contest mixer together, even though this is the first night that we're officially facing off as competitors. As always, seeing Kate and Tom hold hands as they walk in front of me makes me smile, but this time my smile is a bit pinched. The sight reminds me of Sophia's hand, now hanging limply by her side as she walks next to me, not entwined with mine.

I look away from her. I need to focus tonight. I have to win that Most Anticipated Film award. I mentally run through my speech one more time, twisting my ring on and off my finger as I do.

Myrah glances at me, taking in the anxious motion. "You'll be fine."

I nod, not entirely trusting myself to speak. Besides, she might look calm, but the intricate braids she had done must've taken ages, and her soft pink eye shadow matches the flowers on her dress. She's as nervous as I am.

We reach the Corner Cinema Hotel, tucked away in a rainy corner of SoHo, and hurry inside. We cross the threshold, jostle through the crowd milling in the lobby, and reach the registration table.

"Are you here for the Emerging Filmmakers Mixer?" the receptionist, a short girl with bangs, asks us.

She hands me a roll of name tags when I nod. I take one and pass the rest on before scribbling my name on mine and sticking it to my chest. It rumples over the dress, and I poke at it to straighten it out.

Sophia leans over me to grab a spare name tag, edging away from Tom. I glance at the two of them, frowning. They haven't spoken all evening.

"You look nice," Sophia says.

I look down at my dress to hide the heat creeping into my face. "I, uh, got the dress on Rent the Runway. It's cool. It's this subscription service where you can rent clothes." I'm painfully aware of how fast I'm talking, yet unable to stop myself. "You can rent by the item or get a monthly subscription, and then you can have a certain amount of items out at a—"

Sophia laughs. "I know what Rent the Runway is. Please breathe."

I stop talking long enough to inhale. Our name tags on, we walk past the desk into the reception room. It's a small space with arched stone walls framing little candlelit tables. I inhale sharply as we cross the room. I can't believe that I have to pitch my movie in such a fancy place tonight.

"'Thanks, Sophia; you look nice too' would've been fine," she says.

I glance down at her outfit, which is indeed lovely. She's curled her hair, like she did for the dance, and it makes her look older, in a good way, like she's actually put together. It doesn't hurt that she put on gently sparkling eye shadow and a light blush that highlights her cheekbones. And given that they do a pretty good job of highlighting themselves day to day, it's . . . well, it's a lot to handle.

I grin, my nerves disappearing for a moment. "You know I can't handle compliments."

"All I know is that you're apparently a paid spokesperson for Rent the Runway," Sophia says, but she's still smiling. I shove her bony shoulder in response.

"Let's go find seats and forget this ever happened," I say.

Sophia shakes her head, but follows me to the theater anyway. The seats are big and plush and comfy, wrapping around a massive screen mounted at the front of the room. Myrah and Kate have already found seats near the front, and Kate waves at us when we walk in. Myrah's blushing at her phone, a special expression that I've come to privately call her Peter Smile.

"Are you ready for your speech?" Kate asks when we reach them.

I shake my head, then nod, then shake it again.

"You're having a day, huh?" Sophia says. She glances down

the row of seats, then takes the one farthest away from Tom. They rigidly avoid each other's eyes.

Before I can ask what that's about, she goes on. "Don't worry. I'm sure you'll get loads of people to subscribe to Rent the Runway. Your practice pitch was super convincing."

Kate gives me a quizzical look. She's wearing perfectly pointed winged eyeliner and a red dress she made herself, and she looks incredible.

"Sophia is, as per usual, being an asshole," I tell her.

It's Sophia's turn to give me a shove. Grinning teasingly at her, I take my seat between her and Kate, before double-checking my purse again to make sure the notecards are still inside. I press my thumbs against the edges, forcing myself to breathe as I slump back into the seat. It's cushy and soft, but it's impossible for me to relax into it.

"How are you not nervous?" I ask Sophia.

She shrugs. "In French schools, they make you recite in front of the class more often. It was . . ."

She trails off, glancing at Tom again. Around us, the theater is filling with more and more people, which is making the whole breathing thing hard. In a few minutes, I'll have to get up in front of everyone and talk to all of them about my movie.

My head gets woozy just thinking about it.

Matt finds us as the lights start to dim. A short man in a suit jogs out in front of the screen, and we burst into applause.

"Welcome, wonderful young filmmakers," he says into a microphone, and we cheer again. "I'm Alan Gonall, the director of the festival, and I'm so excited to get to know you and all

165

your incredible projects this evening. We're going to start with speeches from our directors, and then we'll move the party back on out to the atrium for some mingling and voting. And snacks, of course."

The promise of snacks is met with more hearty applause. My hands are slick with sweat as I slap them together.

"Let's start with our first group," Alan says, pausing to peer down at his own set of notecards. "First up is Andrea Cooper, presenting her team's short film, *Escape*."

We applaud again as Andrea reaches the front of the room and starts talking about her movie. I half listen, but my mind is caught up on my speech. I murmur my introduction under my breath. I'm so caught up in the practice that I don't notice Andrea's finished her speech until applause breaks out around me. I join in as Andrea hands Alan the mic back and returns to her seat. Alan scans his page, then looks up at us. "Next up is Emma Hansen, presenting her team's film, *I Think I Love You*."

I join in the applause with everyone else before Kate pokes my shoulder. I almost jump out of my skin. How am I up already?

Legs shaking, I push myself out of my seat and stumble toward the front of the theater. Alan, smiling wide at me, holds out the microphone, and I take it, realizing too late that I've forgotten my notecards in my purse.

Staring out at the audience—rows of faces that seem to stretch for a thousand miles in front of me, even though I know that realistically it's probably about a few hundred people—my head swims.

"Hi, everyone," I say, my voice small even with the mic's help. "I'm the director of *I Think I Love You*, starring Myrah Evans and Katerina Perez."

There's a lump in my throat, and tears threaten to tumble out of my eyes any second. I force myself to swallow, but my lungs feel like they're closing in on themselves. I can't even talk to my parents about my sexuality. What made me think I could get up in front of a room full of strangers and spill my guts? I stumble over my next words as I scan the rows for Kate.

Instead my eyes land on Sophia. She gives me a small thumbs-up, and the tension in my shoulders eases.

"Our film is a lighthearted romantic comedy," I say, more energy in my voice as I start pacing in front of the screen, working myself up for the words that come next. "A rom-com might sound cliché, but as a bisexual girl, I have yet to see myself represented well. I've seen myself represented as the quirky girl who doesn't like labels, as the tragic girl who dies at the end, as the cheater who breaks the protagonist's heart.

"But I've never seen a bisexual love story that ends with a happily ever after. And, almost more importantly, neither has my family. When I come out to them, I want them to know that bisexuality is valid, and I want them to know that bisexual love stories are as possible and beautiful and lovely as any other." I take a deep breath. "And that starts with us, the storytellers in this room, showing them the possibilities."

There's a pause, a dreadful second that lasts an eternity as the fear of being booed sweeps over me. Then the audience breaks out into applause. There's even a few cheers scattered throughout the room as I hand the mic back to Alan. My limbs are lead as I stumble back to my seat.

Sophia shifts in her seat to give me room to pass her. "You'll find your love story," she whispers as I climb over her to take my seat.

Her voice is so quiet, I'm sure I've misheard. "What?"

She looks up at me. "I know how hard it is to never see that story, but you're telling it now, and that's awesome. And it'll happen for real one day too."

The tears that threatened to make an appearance during my speech fill my eyes now. I land back in my seat, and Kate pulls me into a congratulatory hug while Myrah tears herself away from her nonstop texting with Peter to squeeze my hand. I hug Kate, but I'm looking back at Sophia, and I can't look anywhere but into her eyes and wonder what she means and if she sees herself in that story as much as I'm starting to.

The speeches end with Sophia, whose movie is as angsty and over-the-top dramatic and French and pretentious as I thought it would be. I find myself cheering louder than anyone else when she hands the mic back to Alan.

"Thanks for the support," she says with a wink at me when she sits back down.

"And now, the moment you've all been waiting for," Alan says as he reclaims his microphone. "We're going to pass around the voting basket. Please write down the film you're most anticipating—aside from your own, of course—on the slips of paper under your seats, and then place them in the basket as it gets to you."

I scribble Sophia's movie on my voting slip, cupping my hand around the paper, and quickly fold it as soon as I'm done writing, so she won't see. Kate climbs over me to go to the bathroom. Matt takes her folded slip to put in the basket for her when it reaches our row.

Once the basket has been passed around the room, Alan hands it off to a group of ushers who quietly tabulate the votes in a corner of the stage. We're supposed to start making our way to the atrium, where the snacks have been laid out for us, but most of us stay in our seats, waiting for the announcement.

At last, the ushers take the basket up to Alan, who reads their calculations before smiling at us.

"And, by popular vote, the Most Anticipated Film of this year's NYC–LA Film Festival is," he says, and then he pauses dramatically, ". . . *I Think I Love You!*"

I gasp. Kate throws her arms around my neck as the auditorium bursts into polite applause. I glance at Sophia, who's smiling and applauding with the rest of the crowd, but there's a tightness in her eyes, and it occurs to me for the first time that I don't want this competition to come between us.

CHAPTER SIXTEEN

SOPHIA

· ·

We've all moved to the lobby space after the announcement that Emma won the vote, and I've already stuffed my face with five mini-quiches.

"They're not as good as the ones in France," I tell Emma. My teeth land hard on my bottom lip as soon as the words slip out, like I can take them back. This is exactly the kind of shit Tom was talking about.

"When will you give it a rest?" Emma says, but unlike Tom, she's smiling at me.

I give her a sarcastic curtsy. "Oh, so sorry, Mademoiselle Most Anticipated."

She shakes her head, and I hold her gaze for a moment. Her cheeks redden, and she wraps her arms around herself. "I'm gonna go get some air."

Now it's my face that's getting hot. I didn't mean to make her feel bad. "I'll come with you," I say, and without waiting for her response, I lead her outside.

When I open the door for her, a cool breeze greets us. I inhale, enjoying the rare respite from the inescapable summer trash smell. It's late enough that the road passing in front of us is quiet. Only four cars idle at the red light.

I turn to Emma, who's stretching her arms out, also enjoying the breeze. She stares up at the sky. We're in a dark corner of the city, and I can make out a few stars overhead.

"I liked your pitch," she says. "Very angsty. Very French."

I give her a small smile, but it falls off my lips. The traffic lights change in front of us, and the cars sweep past.

"How's your mom doing?" she asks gently.

I grind my teeth. I was kind of hoping we could veer into more romantic territory, the kind I started after her speech, but now we're talking about my mother, so that's great.

"Fine," I say, turning away from her.

"She got remarried, right?" Emma asks.

I falter. She knows that. Why is she asking?

But then I notice the way her lips are pinched with concern, and I realize she's trying to figure out what's on my mind.

"Yep," I say. "That's why I had to spend last year with her. To 'get to know' my stepfather better."

Emma laughs. "And are you perchance bitter about it?"

"What gave it away?" I ask with a smile.

She chuckles again, but when she looks up at me, there's seriousness in her eyes. I've never seen her look at anyone like that except Kate. Like she's not trying to make a joke out of whatever I say next.

"Actually, though . . . ," she says, tilting her head back a little to look up at me.

I'm not sure what to say. I'm not sure how far I can trust Emma with this.

"Well, yeah. I'm bitter." I kick at the sidewalk, but all I accomplish is a stubbed toe. Wincing, I look down at Emma. "A second wedding loses some of its power, you know? I mean, the vows sound a lot less impressive when you also said the same thing to another dude you then left in Brooklyn with your kid."

I swallow. I do sound bitter. Emma lets the silence fall between us. I stare out into the street at the lamp on the opposite sidewalk. It's bathing the street below in a yellow glow.

I look back down, and we make eye contact. Instead of dropping it, I keep looking straight at her. She does as well. Then, predictably, she laughs.

"What?" I ask.

"I just realized," she says, tapping her fingers against her lips. "This is totally why you're so anti-relationship all the time, isn't it? I can't believe I'm hearing the tragic backstory behind all the angst."

I shake my head. She's got me figured out.

"Fair enough," I said, throwing my hands up as I take the hit.

"I'm sorry," Emma whispers. Then she blinks and looks up at me again. "You know that doesn't mean all love is dead forever, right?"

I stare at her. "I didn't say that."

"You say it all the time," she says. "I've spent all summer so far arguing with you about it. I can't believe you. You're so confident and together and amazing—"

"Are you complimenting me?"

"—and shit happens with your family, so you let the whole world fall apart around you." Emma shakes her head at me. "Conflict is part of every great love story."

"I know that," I mutter. "It's so lonely all the time now. My family used to do everything together. This one time, we had an extra day off school for some reason and my mom wanted to go to the Met, and I was so mad because I didn't want to spend my day off doing learning things."

Emma laughs, and I elbow her. "I was little, okay?"

She shakes her head, motioning for me to go on with the story.

"So, anyway, I didn't want to go, but my dad said that we had to because it would make my mom happy. We ended up playing hide-and-seek in the ancient-Greece wing."

I smile at the memory of crouching behind a marble statue, fully believing my parents as they pretended to look for me, even though I'm sure they could see me. They were looking for me together, and I tried my best to stifle my giggles as they walked right past my statue, looking pointedly in the other direction. I took it for granted when they kissed in front of a painting; I even thought it was gross.

"But now my family is completely disintegrated. Do you know how many dates my dad has been on since I've gotten back?"

I haven't told anyone this, not even Tom. But Emma's looking at me like she cares about what's coming out of my mouth, like she wants to take care of the feelings behind the words. She's never looked at me like that before. I'm not sure anyone has.

173

Emma laughs, but there's a weird edge to it. "See? Love is alive and well. You can stop killing it."

"I don't want to kill it anymore," I say, my eyes locked with Emma's. She stares back at me, and though I've come to love the laughter that lives in the brown depths of her eyes, it's been replaced with something else now. Something deeper, as though she's searching the air between us.

"No?"

"No."

The space between our lips surges with electricity, and I yearn to close the gap.

I back away from it instead. "What about yours?"

"My what?" Emma asks.

"Your tragic backstory," I say.

She shrugs, but her face falls a little. She moves past me to sit on the raised steps outside the theater, and her feet rest on the sidewalk below.

"I don't have a tragic backstory," she says, facing the empty street with her back to me.

I snort. "She said, moving away to sit dramatically on the sidewalk and stare pensively out into the dark and desolate street."

She turns to look over her shoulder at me, and sticks out her tongue. Actually. Sticks out her tongue.

"Shut up," she says.

I sit next to her. "You can talk to me."

She chuckles. "Historically speaking, that is not the case."

This time, I don't laugh along. "What about now?"

"Now?" Emma's voice breaks.

I'm terrified of where this moment is leading, but I don't break eye contact with her. "Not history. Now. You could talk to me. Now."

She looks at me for a moment, then nods. Just once, just slightly. But it sends a wave of relief washing over me. The acknowledgment, no matter how small, that things have changed between us.

"I don't know. I don't have a tragic backstory." She turns to face the street again. "I grew up relatively well-off in a nice area with nice, still-married parents who would probably accept me if I ever get up the courage to come out, even if they're not the most socially aware people in the world. And I still turned out a generally garbage person. So." She shrugs, her shoulders heaving. "Poor me, I guess."

Without stopping to think, I reach over to take her hand. She lets her fingers interlace with mine. We both stare at them in silence for a minute. My heart flutters every time her fingers move. I have no idea what she's thinking.

"You're not a garbage person," I whisper.

She laughs quietly. "You sure know how to compliment a lady."

I squeeze her hand. My breath catches. I can't believe I'm holding her hand again, out in the open this time. I can't believe we're both letting this happen.

"You think you are because it's a tragic side effect of being in the closet, and you've also put Kate up on a divine pedestal that you're constantly measuring yourself against. But just because Kate's a great person doesn't mean you're a bad one."

Emma looks away from me. She doesn't move her hand away from mine, though. "I guess. I don't know. I feel like a selfish shit a lot of the time. But then I try to do something about it and . . . Then I'm making everything about me again, and it confirms that I'm a selfish shit."

She throws her free hand up.

"In any case," I tell her, "I think you're great."

She meets my eye, one brow raised. "Really? Because I seem to remember you calling me Activia."

"That's because you were very annoying back then," I say. "And. I mean. You still are."

She laughs. "Says Little Miss France."

I swallow, Tom's words echoing in my head, and take a deep breath. "Tom and I had a fight about that."

"What happened?" Emma asks.

I glance at the hotel that houses the theater. No one's come outside to check on us. There's nothing outside the hotel except its thick black awning, the solitary car waiting for the light to turn green, and probably some rats loitering around the garbage cans.

"I guess I've been kind of an asshole," I say. "I was miserable when I was in France. I spent the whole time lying around in my room and eating my feelings. And France is a good place to do that."

Emma laughs, but she squeezes my hand as she does. My heart skips a beat, and I push myself to keep going. It feels good, finally saying all of this out loud. Even if it is to Emma. Or maybe especially because it's her.

"And then I got back here, and I wanted everything to be

the same as it was before I left," I go on. "But my dad had this whole new apartment and this whole new life, and it's not bad, objectively, I guess, but it's not . . . mine."

Emma nods but doesn't say anything. She stares at our intertwined fingers. I take in her face, the little furrow in her brow, the way her lips have twisted, and I drop my gaze. I've said too much; I've driven her away. I should've kept my mouth shut and stuck with my French phrases until graduation.

"You should talk to Tom," she says at last, looking up at me. "He's your best friend." With a wry twist of her lips, she adds, "For some reason."

I laugh, leaning over to nudge her shoulder with mine.

"Seriously, though," she says. "I take it he's upset because you haven't been talking to him. So, maybe talking to him might fix it?"

I laugh. "You're a genius."

"This is true," she says with a smile.

Our eyes are still locked, but we've stopped talking. Everything that's left unsaid—everything about the way we truly feel about each other now—electrifies the air between us. The hair on the back of my neck stands on end, and I'm hyper-aware of her thin fingers pressing against mine, her eyes blinking slowly without looking away from me, the way her shoulders have relaxed even as the tension between us mounts.

Without thinking, I lean forward. She mirrors me, moving closer until our lips are about to touch. Her warm breath fans across my face. I inhale, tilting my face toward hers, and it all hits me at once.

I'm about to kiss Emma Hansen.

And then, as if it's the easiest thing in the world, I do.

My lips meet hers, and her touch is so soft, it overwhelms me. I'm reeling in the impossibility of the moment, in how surprised I am despite how much I expected it, in how soft she is despite how hard she was, in the fact that this is happening at all.

And then she sinks into me, and my hand is in her hair, pulling her closer, as though she could never be close enough. I move my other hand up her arm, hold her to me because I want this moment to last forever. Her lips move against mine, and I can't believe the simplicity of it, the ease with which I've kissed this girl whom I didn't realize until now I've always wanted to kiss.

Eventually we part. My lips still tingle with the energy of hers.

"That happened," she whispers.

"Yup," I whisper back, afraid that speaking aloud will ruin this moment between us.

Our fingers are still entwined. She stares down at them.

"What does this mean for us?" she asks.

I know what I want it to mean. But I also know, despite all the pretty words we might say to each other here, that it's not possible. Love doesn't work like that. It always ends in heartbreak.

"I'm not sure," I tell her.

"Me neither. Maybe we should . . . not tell anyone? Until we do know?"

"Yeah," I whisper. "Yeah, I agree."

I don't know what to do next, but she lowers her head onto my shoulder, and we sit there, our hands together, my head on hers, as if we are the only two people in the world.

I stare at the camera to avoid meeting Tom's eye. Also to try to figure out how this shit works. For all my blustering about French cinematography, I have no idea how to make this shot look good. I can't even tell if it does look good, or if the framing is a flaming pile of garbage. Which would be quite a feat, considering that we're shooting in Dumbo by the water, in what is probably the most picturesque part of Brooklyn. The river flows wide ahead of us, the bridge looming over the water, and the sun makes all of it sparkle. Much like my heart, which glows every time I remember what happened between me and Emma last night.

"Are we ready?" Tom asks.

I fidget with the lens cap. Emma's words echo in my mind. Swallowing, I look up at Tom.

"No," I say. "Can I talk to you?"

Tom scuffs his shoe against the little park path we're on. "Sure."

I nod to Matt, who takes the script over to Amanda to go over the scene we're mostly improvising today. When they're busy with their conversation, I pull Tom aside. We walk farther down the path, rounding a row of trees shading the side of the park. I don't want Amanda to realize that we've been arguing.

Bad enough that we're a bunch of kids paying her in copy, credit, and a twenty-dollar Starbucks gift card. If we throw high school drama into the mix, she'll run away screaming.

"What's up?" Tom asks. His hands are tucked into his pockets, his shoulders hunched over. He stares at the spot of dirt on the ground between my shoes.

"I, um." I clear my throat. "I'm sorry. You were right the other day, about how I've been an asshole. To be honest, the past year has been hard for me, with my parents divorcing and my mom moving away and everything, and I felt alone."

Tom nods at the ground. "I would've been there for you if you told me."

I blink. I should've told him all of this right when I got back. No, I should've stayed in touch with him when I was away, instead of wallowing the whole time I was gone.

"I think I had to tell myself first," I say. I shift my weight so that I'm standing in a sunnier patch of grass, where the light makes it through the tree branches above us, and I let it warm my face. "I was scared to admit how much my parents' divorce affected me."

"I get that," Tom says. "I guess I should have realized. It seemed like you went to France and came back thinking you were too good for me."

My throat twists as tears spring into my eyes. "Of course not. You're my best friend. I love you," I say, blinking back the tears. "Or whatever."

Tom laughs. "I love you too, friend. Sorry I yelled at you. I should've realized what was actually happening."

I shake my head. "Are we okay?"

"Yeah," Tom says. And before I can turn back to our tiny set, he pulls me into a hug. I waver for a moment, then wrap my arms around his lanky torso, resting my head against his shoulder. He smells like that stupid sandalwood stuff the marketing powers that be have decided is a manly smell. I'm glad for his arms around me anyway.

We break apart and smile sheepishly at each other.

"Let's literally never fight again," I say.

Tom laughs. "Do they not do that in France?"

I slap his shoulder. "I hate you."

I lead him back to the set, where Matt and Amanda are still huddled together, examining the script. I run my thumb over my lips as I walk back around the camera. I've been doing it all morning, every time I think about how Emma's lips felt against mine. Which has been often.

"We're all set to go," I tell them.

Matt looks up at me, and his whole face clouds over when we make eye contact.

"You okay?" I ask.

"Yeah," he says, but his face stays all pinched together, like he's stuck on a thought he'd rather not have. It's not his most convincing performance, but I can't needle him more in front of Amanda about whatever's on his mind.

I flip through the pages of my script, lingering on the lines we're shooting today. This is supposed to be an argument scene between my character and her mom, but I'm not sure it's landing. It's starting to feel like drama for the sake of drama. I turn the pages back and forth, as if rereading it will make the words on the page click. But despite my repeated attempts, nothing is clicking except the loud rumble of the Q train passing over the bridge behind us.

"What's wrong?" Tom asks, taking in the turned-down corners of my lips.

"It's so . . ." I trail off as Emma's voice bounces through my memory. "Angsty."

"I thought that was the point," Tom says.

"I guess," I say, shrugging. "I feel like it's missing something."

Matt crosses his arms. "If it is, can we figure it out inside? There's a Starbucks right there, where they have AC and seating areas and cookies."

I ignore him, Emma's face flashing through my mind again. Her cold fingers in mine. The softness of her lips. "Maybe there should be more of a sense of . . . love."

Tom laughs as soon as the whispered word comes out of my mouth, and I regret speaking.

"Maybe we should join Emma's group again," he says.

I fake laugh at him. "Very funny."

In truth, it sounds kind of nice. Maybe I'd get to kiss her again. But I can't go back now. Death before dishonor, as they say.

"I meant family love, anyway," I add. "Maybe this thing has a happy ending."

"What should we do?" Tom asks.

"End early so I can think it over," I say.

I turn to Amanda to thank her for the shoot and send her

home. She bustles out of the park. I turn back to our equipment, break down the rickety little tripod we've been using, while Tom puts away the camera. Matt watches us with his hands buried in his pockets and a cloud over his face.

"Seriously, what's wrong?" I ask again, looking up at him.

He rocks between his heels and toes, staring at the cracks in the concrete. "I—"

"What happened?" Tom asks.

Matt looks up at him, wincing. "I'm so sorry, man. It's Kate."

The camera bag tumbles off Tom's shoulder and slides down his arm to the ground. He stares at Matt, who stares back with a look in his eyes like he's the messenger who's afraid of being shot.

"Seriously, what happened?" Tom asks again.

"She cheated on the vote last night," Matt says, his gaze fixed on his Converse. "And I think she's the one who's been sabotaging us."

I frown. Kate is the sweetest person I've ever met. "That doesn't sound right."

"I know," Matt says, finally lifting his chin so he can meet my eye. "But who else could it be? She's the only one who was there every time. She was fiddling with our camera before the footage disappeared. And the actor who texted you said that a girl told him to leave right after she stopped by. You know she'd do anything for Emma."

Tom and I exchange glances. This sounds too far-fetched to be believable. Emma gave a great speech. She deserved to win that vote. And for the rest of it? Cameras malfunction, miscommunications happen. It doesn't mean Kate is an evil mastermind.

Matt shifts his weight. He pulls a wad of folded papers out of his jacket pocket—the things men's clothes have room for in the pockets is unbelievable—and hands them to Tom.

"She left during the vote, remember?" Matt says as Tom flips through the papers, eyes widening. "I found these in the basket later."

I pluck some of the papers from Tom's hands, and look down to see voting slips from last night. All filled out in Kate's loopy handwriting. All voting for Emma's movie.

My jaw drops so hard, I'm afraid it'll unhinge. "Kate? Not possible."

"But what about me?" Tom's voice trembles as he speaks.

I echo him in my thoughts. Because if Kate did this, Emma must've been in on it too. How could she kiss me, knowing that she had taken this opportunity away from me?

"She knows how much this competition means to me," he says, rage flashing in his eyes. "That tuition assistance could—if my parents knew I had—it would make all the difference."

I lay a hand on his shoulder. "I know."

After all, it means a lot to me too. My parents aren't going to let me invest in film school if I'm not sure it's what I want, and this movie is a great way to show them that I am.

Tom whips out his phone, pounds against the screen. "I'm going to tell her exactly what I think."

I throw out a hand to stop him. "No, wait."

His phone already buzzes with an answer from Kate. He lifts it, ready to keep texting, but I push his hands back down.

184

"This is a conversation you should have in person."

He falters for a moment, staring at me with eyes so hot, I wither under his gaze. "You're right," he says at last. "I'll go talk to her in person."

"She's at work now, right?" I ask. "Shouldn't we wait until later?"

"I can't wait. I can't pretend like everything's fine," Tom says. "I can't believe she'd do this to me. She knows what this contest means. And she knows—"

He stops talking, but Matt and I exchange looks, knowing what he was about to say. He got cheated on, he gave love another shot, and he got burned with lies. Again.

The memory of Emma's lips fades and is replaced by a heavy, cold dread hardening in my lungs as I struggle to take a breath.

How could they do this to us?

CHAPTER SEVENTEEN

Emma

- -

Waiting to meet Kate late Monday morning, I'm bursting to tell her about Sophia. I can't, because Sophia and I agreed to keep it a secret, but I still feel like I'm walking on air the whole time I spend getting ready this morning.

My first kiss finally happened.

Yes, it was with the devil, but you know what? The devil is pretty cute, and she's a hell of a good kisser.

In exchange for the use of their multipurpose room as a shooting space, I agreed to help out at the teen center this afternoon. I'm pretty excited. Sitting at reception all day sounds way more fun than working retail. But when Kate finally meets me, five minutes late even though she's the most punctual person I know, her face wipes out all my happiness. Her eyes are clouded over with anxiety, and her lips are pressed into the tightest line I've ever seen them form.

She spends the whole subway ride staring at her reflection in the dark train window and ignoring my questions, which means that I spend the afternoon sick with worry about her. She's accompanying one of the day-camp counselors on a field trip to a local Y pool with a gang of preteens, so I take her spinny chair at reception. I spend the morning staring into space, kicking myself off one side of the desk so I can roll to the other.

Kate is the bubbliest person I know. If she has retreated into herself like this, something awful must have happened. I can't get the anxious look in Kate's eyes out of my head, and the numbing repetition of "Good afternoon. This is the Park Slope Teen Center. How may I help you?" doesn't provide nearly as much distraction as I thought it would.

By the time the preteens return, smelling like chlorine, with water dripping from their hair down the backs of their blue PSTC T-shirts, I'm ready to jump out of my skin with stress.

It only gets worse when I see Kate. Her shoulders are crumpled inward, and her face, usually exuberant, is pinched and pale. I throw myself out of my chair and rush to her side, even though Kate gave me warnings about leaving the phone, warnings that made *The Devil Wears Prada* feel like kindergarten.

"Kate," I say, folding my arms around her shoulders as soon as I reach her. "What's wrong?"

She shrugs away from me, which she never does, her eyes downcast. "I don't know. I haven't eaten today. I should probably do that. I'm sure I'm making a big deal about nothing."

"Well, yeah, please don't faint." I guide her to the reception chair so she can sit. "What's the nothing you're making a big deal of, then?"

Kate glances over the desk at the preteens. Their guidance

counselor, a college kid, has them under control. Fiddling with her earring, she digs into her backpack with her other hand for her phone. Silently she unlocks it and passes it to me. I stare at the screen, which blinks brightly with a text chain.

TOM: *We need to talk.*

KATE: *What's up?*

KATE: *Tom?*

KATE: *Is everything okay?*

KATE: *Did I do something wrong?*

KATE: *Tom???*

I slide the texts over to see the time stamps. Tom texted her hours ago, and ignored all of Kate's responses. I hand back the phone, steadying the sudden shake in my fingers so she doesn't see my worry. I ache to soothe the worry boiling in her eyes, but I have no calming interpretations of these texts. Other than that Tom is clearly being a douche nozzle.

And I set her up with him. I all but forced them together, and now he's responsible for the tightness in her eyes.

"I'm sure he got busy," I say. "You obviously didn't do anything wrong, and—"

Kate shushes me imploringly. I glance up, but no one is paying attention to us. Besides, it's way too loud in here for anyone to overhear us. The basketball bros have just come downstairs from the gym on the second floor, bouncing the ball between them as their sneakers squeak against the floor, and some of the group coming out of a morning painting class are playing illicit music on their phones.

I turn back to Kate. "I'm sure everything will be f—"

The doors slam open before she can finish, and Tom strides in, followed by Sophia. Tears fill his eyes, but they're still burning with the kind of anger that makes my knees shake.

And he's aiming it all at Kate.

All my alarm bells are going off. I want to step between them, to stop him from getting to her, but before I can do anything, he closes the distance between us, Sophia behind him. I search her angular face for clues—what could Tom be this mad about? —but her face is frozen, unreadable.

"Hey," Kate says, looking up at him, tilting her head to one side in confusion. "What are you doing here? What's wrong?"

"What do you think is wrong?" he spits at her.

I jerk forward, a fist still balled up. I know I'm the tiniest person in our friend group, but Tom is about as built as a soggy stick. I can take him.

Kate gets up and places a hand in front of me, and I stop at her touch. I'm still ready to hit him, though. I stare him down, but he ignores me.

Sophia towers behind him, her arms folded, and I gape at her. Who are the two of them to gang up on Kate like this?

"I don—I don't know," Kate says. Her eyelids flutter as Tom gets louder.

"You've been sabotaging our movie," Tom says, his voice breaking. "Lying to me. And you know what both of those things mean to me."

The kids closest to us have turned down their music, and even some of the basketball groupies are dividing their attention between the flash of the ball tossed around and Tom's growing anger.

Kate shakes her head, reaching up to touch his arm, but Tom takes the tiniest step backward. She drops her hand, swaying.

"No," she whispers. "What?"

"How could you?" Tom says, his voice wavering.

The music around us cuts out altogether as people stop trying to cover for their eavesdropping. As Tom's voice rises, the hush starts to spread throughout the room. The back of my neck burns when I realize how many eyes are on us.

Tom, however, doesn't notice. Or doesn't care. He's staring Kate down, eyes narrowed. "You're so sweet all the time. Is that some act?"

I look over my shoulder. Everyone is watching. The kids not staring at us are staring too intently at their phones, their ears obviously pricked in our direction. I want to shrink back into the wheely chair and disappear into the crowd, but I can't leave Kate standing here on her own. I force myself to square my shoulders.

Behind Tom, Sophia stares blankly ahead. I try to catch her eye, raising a questioning eyebrow, but she ignores me.

"You want everyone to think you're some sweet perfect angel," Tom shouts, jabbing a finger at her. "I don't know who you are, but you're definitely no angel."

He points at me, and I frown at him, opening my mouth to retort. Who is he to say that about me?

And who is Sophia to stand by while he does it?

I can't believe this is our first post-kiss interaction.

Someone drops their phone, and it bounces off the floor with a clatter, breaking the silence that spread throughout the room. Sophia starts. She looks around us, taking in all the eyes tracking us.

"Tom." She pulls at his baggy sleeve. "Tom, that's enough. This is—"

He shakes her off, still staring at Kate.

"I thought I could trust you," he says, looking her up and down.

His darkened expression alone has me ready to punch him in the face. The most beautiful girl, inside and out, stands before him, and he has the nerve to look at her like she's lower than the dirt scuffing his ratty Converse.

"I guess I misjudged the kind of person you are," he says, his voice low.

"Yeah, well, same here, pal," I say, jabbing a finger in his direction. Not my best work, but my whole body is shaking in anger. I can't think straight.

"Tom," Sophia says again, her tone more urgent. She pulls at his sleeve again.

I step forward, placing myself firmly between him and Kate. "I think you should leave."

Tom sneers at me. "Of course you take her side. God forbid anyone call your precious cousin out on her bullshit."

I reach back to grab Kate's hand, squeeze tightly. Her fingers are as cold as ice against my palm.

"You're being an asshole," I say, my voice low in what I hope is a dangerous-sounding way. "And you need to go. Now."

Tom shakes his head at Kate one more time and stalks off without looking back. I stare at him leave, and glance over at Sophia. Seeing her there, standing by Tom while he yelled at Kate, made my skin crawl. I can't believe I let her touch me, let her become my first kiss. How could she do this?

Everyone watches him go, and conversations return, first a low buzz but clamoring higher and higher as everyone tries to figure out what Kate did. The news that it has something to do with the movie competition starts with the people closest to us, who heard everything from the beginning, but I have no doubt it will spread throughout the room in a matter of seconds.

I also have no doubt that it's completely unfounded. Whatever Tom thinks—there's no way it actually happened.

Sophia gives me an apologetic look, but I turn away from her, letting a distance grow between us that I don't think we can ever repair.

And I don't want to. Kate is more important than any first kiss.

I reach out to Kate, but before I can say anything, her body loosens. Her eyes blank, she falls backward in a dead faint. I jump toward her, but it's Sophia who whirls around and reaches out in time to catch her.

"Oh my God," Sophia whispers, lowering Kate onto the floor. She keeps her hands cupped around the back of Kate's head.

I stare at Kate's body, my mind frantic. What am I supposed to do?

Everyone is already so caught up in the drama, no one except the people next to us notice that it's still unfolding.

"Someone get the nurse," I yell.

Before anyone can move, Kate stirs.

"Oh, thank God," I whisper.

I help Kate stand, wrapping an arm around her torso for support. Sophia jumps up, grabbing Kate from the other side. We turn her toward the hall.

"No. I have to go," Kate says, fighting against us to move the other way. Her whole body is still trembling, so her flailing doesn't exactly stop me from manhandling her to the nurse's office.

"He's the one who should be coming after you to apologize," I say, tightening my grip on her midsection as I cut her off. "Coming to your job to scream at you? Nah. You're not the one who's gonna apologize today."

"But—" Kate protests again.

I shake my head. "Nope. Nurse. Come on."

I can tell she doesn't agree, but Kate shuffles along with us. I shoot Sophia a grateful glance. I need someone to keep Kate away from Tom right now. Between us, Kate lowers her head as a hundred gazes follow us out of the reception area.

"Can you believe that?"

"What do you think she did?"

"It must've been awful for that guy to do that."

The kids' voices swirl around us as we make our way out of the reception area. I glance at Kate, praying that she can't hear them, but her face is bright red and she's staring fixedly ahead.

I tighten my grip on her and turn to stare down the group closest to us. The middle schoolers have the decency to drop their gazes and busy themselves with their phones, but I know the second we move on, they'll be right back to the gossip.

It's a relief when we step into the hallway, away from their prying eyes, even if it means that they've been freed to speculate. At least I got Kate away from their toxic tongues.

I clutch Kate tightly as we bring her to the nurse. She's still pale when we reach the office. I rub her shoulders while we wait for the nurse to finish putting a Band-Aid on a weepy middle schooler still in his basketball outfit. Kate doesn't say anything, just lowers her head to bury her face in her hands, as if she can't bear to look at anyone, not even me. She keeps it there until the nurse is ready for her, even though the harsh fluorescent lighting lining the hallway ceiling makes it impossible to hide anything. Her bright red face still glows between her fingers.

Once the kid goes, the nurse waves Kate into the office, leaving Sophia and me alone in the hallway. I slouch down on the wooden bench outside her door. The bench digs into my spine, but I don't have the strength to prop myself up right now. I let it keep poking at me, and I stare at the posters of health tips and hand-washing instructions that line the white wall opposite.

I'm so wrapped up in my own thoughts and fury at Tom that it takes me a minute, but I eventually remember that Sophia is sitting next to me. As soon as I do, I'm overly aware of her, like the air is alive between us, pulling me closer.

"Can you believe him?" I spit to break the silence.

"He definitely didn't handle it the right way," Sophia says quietly.

I turn to look at her, hoping my gaze will burn a hole into her face. She doesn't return my look. She keeps her eyes fixed on the spot where the wall opposite us meets the floor.

"You think?" I say. "Besides, whatever he thinks Kate did, he's wrong."

"He's not, though," she whispers without looking up. "I was there. She's been . . ." She swallows before pressing on, like she knows that what she has to say is going to piss me off. "She's been sabotaging us all along. She deleted our footage, and canceled our auditions, and she rigged the vote."

My brow furrows. There's no way. No matter what Sophia thinks, that absolutely did not happen. Kate would never do something like that.

At the very least, she would have told me about something like that.

"How do you know?" I ask, trying to keep the anger out of my voice. And failing.

Sophia stares at the backs of her hands. "Matt found the extra voting slips she put into the basket."

I bite my lower lip. Matt might have found "evidence," but Kate is too sweet to contemplate sabotage, let alone actually go through with it. I can't even entertain the possibility.

"This is Kate we're talking about," I say firmly, as if that settles it.

Because it does.

And Tom had the nerve to scream at her in front of everyone at work, leaving her to shrink and wilt in the nurse's office when he's supposed to be the one building her up.

I let my head drop into my hands, and I sigh into my palms. My warm breath drifts back up over my face, but I don't move.

"Hey, you okay?" Sophia asks. The concern in her voice sounds genuine.

So I'm honest. "No."

I lift my head to meet her eyes, and she reaches over to give my hand a sympathetic squeeze. It lasts about a second. Then she drops it like my skin burned her.

"It'll work out," she says.

"I hope so," I murmur.

Because I'm really not okay. And I know it's selfish, to make this thing that happened to Kate be about me. But I'm overcome with worry for her. When she comes back out of the nurse's office, I'll make it all about her and I'll do whatever she wants, whatever she needs to feel better.

If only I had any kind of ability to process real emotion. I want to make a joke of it. I want to laugh at the guilt coursing through my veins, because I'm the one who got them together; or the anger pounding against my skull, because Tom is such an asshole that I could wring his neck with my two bare hands; or the sadness pressing in my throat, because Kate is sad, and that's the saddest thing that could ever happen.

I can laugh off all of my own emotions to avoid feeling them. I laughed when Sophia came back, when Matt asked me out, whenever Kate and Myrah show the slightest bit of worry about me. But this isn't about me; it's about Kate.

I can't laugh now.

Now I want murder.

"You gonna be okay?" Sophia asks again.

"Yeah," I say, my voice low. "I'm worried about her. Stuff like this . . . The people she loves matter so much to her. She gives everything she has to them. And she's such an exceptional person that I worry she sees too much good in everyone else, and then she takes it so hard when they turn out to be low-key terrible. Or high-key terrible," I add, remembering how dark Tom's eyes were and how loud he yelled. "She's too good for this world, and I see that, and I'd do anything to make her happy."

I look up to see Sophia staring at me with something indecipherable glowing in her eyes. I blink, realizing I've never been this honest with her.

"I thought Tom felt the same way," I finish, shrugging.

I dab at my eye bags with my knuckle to catch the tears before they fall, and force myself to swallow. I can't let Sophia see me cry, and as I saw with Kate, this fluorescent block of hallway leaves no place to hide.

"He did," Sophia says softly. "He does. But you know how much this film competition means to him."

"The teen center is her *work*. It means so much to her, almost as much as design."

"The film competition is Tom's work," she argues. "And after what happened with his ex-girlfriend, he takes lying—"

I wave a hand at her to shut her up. The last thing I want to hear right now is a defense of Tom. She must see that he was a huge dick.

"That doesn't mean he gets to scream at her in front of everyone," I say, and Sophia nods. I slump back into the bench. "I want to help her. But I'm not . . ."

I have no idea how to finish the sentence, to confess to Sophia that I'm in no way good enough to care for someone like Kate. But she looks at my face, and somehow intuits what I'm about to say.

"I told you this already," she says, the first time either of us has even hinted at what happened after the party. The memory makes my head spin. I can't think about that right now. I have other things to focus on. Still, Sophia presses on. "We all love you as much as we love Kate."

I gape at her, so she grins and says, "For some reason."

"Did you just compliment me?" I ask.

She laughs. "I've been trying to for a while, but thanks for finally noticing. You're just as wonderful as Kate."

"Well, you're painfully wrong," I say. If she's caught on, I might as well admit that I'm an insecure wreck. Besides, at least when it comes to this, I've become a master at joking about myself. "But I appreciate the sentiment."

"I'm never wrong," Sophia says, her eyes widening innocently.

I snort. "I think every conversation we've ever had proves that you are, yet again, wrong."

"When have I ever been wrong?" Sophia protests.

I give her a look, but she frowns at me. So I take a deep breath.

"Well, there was the time you said you have to hold down

both shift buttons to capitalize a letter," I start. Sophia opens her mouth to argue, but I'm nowhere near done. "There was the time you said that there's milk in brownie recipes, the time you tried to convince us you have to put two spaces after a period, and, of course, let us not forget the great *Is that sweater black or navy* incident of freshman year."

I'm ready to keep going, but Sophia's wheezing, so I stop.

"Well, when you put it like that . . . ," she says, wiping tears of laughter from the corners of her eyes.

"You admit you're wrong yet again?" I ask.

"I can't believe I was trying to compliment you," she says, pursing her lips. "I take it back. Everyone hates you."

"Yeah, well," I say. "Everyone thinks you're a solipsistic asshole."

"That's not true," Sophia says, too quickly. I glance up at her, see the pinched look in her eyes. Is that how she thinks everyone sees her?

I shake my head. "Of course it's not. You should've heard them all babbling on about how excited they were when you came back."

She did compliment me earlier. It's only fair to return one. Even if I do make it clear how bitter I am about it.

Besides, her face lights up for a moment, so much that she rivals the bright lights beaming down on us, and that almost makes it worth it. Almost.

"I guess we'll have to live with the fact that we have friends who love us," she says.

I scratch the back of my neck. It's like we're talking around the subject of our feelings for each other. It makes me want to tell her I overheard Matt and Tom talking about how she likes me. It makes me want to ask if it's true.

Instead I glance at the nurse's closed door.

"He definitely overreacted," Sophia says, following my gaze. "I'll talk to him."

"I refuse to believe for even a second that she sabotaged you guys," I say, looking back down at my hands.

Sophia coughs. "Okay. But. Emma, Matt found the forged voting slips."

I wave a hand. "Details. Something else is going on. Besides, that doesn't justify how Tom reacted."

Sophia doesn't say anything to that, just smiles at me sadly. I settle back into the bench. At least she agrees with me on that.

Silence settles between us again, with only the faint buzz of the lightbulbs and the smell of iodine between us, but it's comfortable. There's never been much room for silence between the two of us, what with our constant battle to get the last word. But now it's nice. Like I can relax into it without worrying about what, if anything, to say next.

I turn to look at Sophia, and she smiles. It reaches her eyes, wrinkling their edges. Before either of us can say anything, the nurse opens her office door, leading Kate out.

"Okay, honey, go home." She leans around Kate to look at me. "Can you take her? I called your aunt; she says it's okay. Kate, you're excused for the afternoon. You need the rest."

I jump to my feet and wrap my arms around Kate's

shoulders. She hugs me back, her arms tight around my waist, and we shuffle into the hall.

"What happened?" I ask. I keep my tone gentle, but Kate's face crumples all the same.

"I don't know," she says. "I don't know how to fix this."

"It's not yours to fix. He's totally in the wrong here, and you are not to go crawling over to try and placate him. If anything, he's going to come crawling back to you. Preferably with lots of tears and begging."

"I don't think he's in a pleading and begging kind of mood," Sophia says, pursing her lips.

I clench my teeth, remembering the way his voice broke as he yelled. "Yeah, I noticed. I guess we'll have to force his hand."

"How?" Sophia and Kate ask at the same time.

I start a little. I never thought Kate, a literal pure cinnamon roll, and Sophia, the literal devil incarnate, would ever say the same thing at the same time.

Then again, Sophia's been growing on me these days. Maybe she's not the devil herself. Just, like, a demon henchman or something.

A demon henchman who happens to be a great kisser.

"Can you tell him that Kate was so embarrassed by what he did to her that she died?" I ask.

Sophia stares at me. "That's the most ridiculous thing I've ever heard in my entire life. And that includes the time you thought cells weren't made of atoms."

I narrow my eyes at her. "You've had that locked and loaded since before, haven't you?"

She purses her lips at me, and I sigh.

"Fine, that's insane. Don't do that. But twist the knife, okay? He should know that what he did was awful," I say. Sophia opens her mouth to argue, but she must realize where that would get her, and closes it again. I turn back to Kate. "And you are not to text him under any circumstances. Okay?"

She nods weakly.

"Let's get you home. I'll text Myrah to bring brownies."

She's still pale, but some of the color has returned to her cheeks. I have to make this work out.

For Kate.

CHAPTER EIGHTEEN

SOPHIA
· ·

I unzip the camera bag and pull out the little camera I've had to go back to after returning Emma's equipment. Ever since we lost the vote to Emma, which I'm *not* bitter about because I'm *happy for her* and *whatever,* I've been stressing about our subpar equipment.

Especially now that we're doing a nighttime shoot in Washington Square Park.

"Guys," I say from behind the camera, through which I can only see a black square. "I can see literally nothing."

A grainy white light pierces through the otherwise pitch-black shot, and I look up to see Tom standing on a park bench, holding his phone over his head with the flashlight pointed at the ground in front of me.

I grin at him. "Thanks. Now it looks like the Holy Ghost is making a cameo."

"Here, what if we move to the benches by the streetlamp?"

Matt asks, pointing to the little round plaza in the middle of the park that houses the fountain and several tall black lamps.

I trot down the path to the large circular fountain, and unfold the tripod next to the new bench. It's more crowded in this corner. Music from three different musicians clashes over the sound of the water slapping against the walls of the fountain. It's also a bit brighter, but not much. I'll still look like a dark shape in front of the camera, especially since the giant arch that oversees the park will be behind me, ensuring that I'm backlit no matter where I stand.

Maybe I can pretend this was on purpose. The character's emotions are dark, she's plunged into despair, the truth is hidden in mystery. It's all very thematic. Poorly shot, but thematic.

I peer through the viewfinder long enough to set up the shot, then glance at Tom. He's busy with the mic setup, whistling as he fiddles with the audio recorder, and it grinds my gears to see him like that. Like he didn't make his girlfriend faint in the middle of her workplace mere hours ago. I mean, I know she lied, and I know I tried to defend him to Emma, but . . . it wasn't cool.

I step away from the camera. "Hey, Matt, would you mind going to that Duane Reade we walked past and seeing if they have any flashlights or anything?"

I fish a wrinkled twenty-dollar bill from my pocket, and he jogs back toward Broadway, leaving me to face Tom alone.

"Are you okay?" I ask, even though he obviously is, which is the whole problem.

But then, to my surprise, his whole body deflates, like I've pricked him with a needle, letting all the cheer seep out of him and into the warm night air. "No. I can't believe Kate would do that to me. I know she loves Emma, but I thought she loved me too. And instead she was lying to me the whole time we were together, like . . ." He swallows, and I grimace at the memory of the funk he fell into after Kendra Lyman cheated on him. "It's like she used me to win this stupid movie competition that she didn't even want to enter in the first place."

"That's not true. She loves you a lot."

He half turns away from me, his footfall echoing against the concrete path.

"If that's true, then it clearly means nothing to her, because she still did this to me," he says, throwing his hands up. "I don't know which is worse, that she never loved me, or that she did and it didn't matter."

I nod at the ground. "I get that. But then again, you love her."

"Yeah," he says, frowning at me. "That's why I didn't lie to her."

I shuffle my feet. "Yeah," I say, drawing out the word. I don't want to say the next ones, but I know I have to. "But you did go to her workplace to yell at her."

"Our whole relationship was a lie," Tom says.

"She fainted."

"She lied."

"She fainted because of what you did." I take a breath to steady the anger thrumming in my rib cage. The hazelnut smell of Nutella from the nearby crepe cart is comforting, but not enough. How can he not see that what he did was wrong? How can he keep justifying it?

"She was lying the whole time we were together," he says again, folding his arms in a tight ball across his chest.

Emma wants me to twist the knife of his guilt. It should be easy. He was awful.

But then I remember that, no matter how badly Tom handled it, we have proof Kate lied. And if Kate lied, Emma was probably in on it. Is she still in on it now?

"I didn't know what to do," he whispers, so low that I barely catch it. "She turned us into a lie."

"And you turned that *us*," I say, putting air quotes around it, "into a humiliating public spectacle. At her *job*. You could've gotten her fired."

"She could've cost me the film competition," Tom points out, but the bravado is leaking out of his tone. His shoulders slump forward. "You're right. I didn't handle it well."

He pulls his phone out of his pocket, casting his eyes around the park. He aims it at a passing cocker spaniel and snaps a picture, then starts typing. "I'll apologize."

I nod. "Thank you."

He hits send, and I reach out quickly for a hug, clutching his gawky frame in relief that our spat is over. I can't stand the thought of allowing the cracks in our friendship to come back. After our rocky reunion, they might never close again.

CHAPTER NINETEEN

Emma

. . . .

This time I make Myrah carry the camera when we get off the subway at Eighth Street.

"You're the one who made me leave Kate," I say when she groans. "You carry the camera."

This is not technically true. Kate told us both to leave her alone because she wanted "time to process what happened." I wanted to stay anyway, but Myrah insisted on doing as Kate had asked.

"You're the one who wanted to use this fancy garbage," she mumbles. "You carry it."

I fold my arms so she can't hand it off to me, and she settles for laying it on the sidewalk at my feet. I narrow my eyes at her, but she shrugs and flounces on ahead of me to the park. I bend over to carry the camera the rest of the way. The well-lit arch that looms over Washington Square Park has never looked so far away, now that I'm bent over from the weight of this giant lens.

I should hit the gym more often.

"I still can't believe," I say, gasping for air as we reach the edge of the park, which is lined with a short black iron fence, "that we left Kate alone after what Tom did to her."

Myrah looks over her shoulder at me. "She wanted to be alone."

"Still." I bend over to put the camera down, then hunch over with my hands on my knees, wheezing.

"Christ," Myrah says, looking at me with her hands on her hips. "You should work out with me."

I'm too out of breath to come up with a witty retort, so I settle for giving her the finger. She flicks my fingertip, and I straighten to slap her shoulder.

Ah, friendship.

I scan the street around us. Even bustling with summer night activity, Washington Square Park is the perfect place for a moody aesthetic. It's dark and cut off from the busy street, and the few streetlights scattered throughout the park cast a grim white light that only seems to make it feel darker.

"Let's start here," I say, laying the tripod bag at my feet. "We can start with you walking down this street, and then move over to get you going under the arch and into the park."

Myrah nods. "Okay. And this is insert for the sad girl-loses-girl montage, right?"

I tug at the end of my loose braid, taking in the scenery. Everything, from the spiky tree branches to the harsh lighting on the looming arch, makes me feel tiny, and I'm filled with the sudden urge to assert myself in this place, like I need to prove to the park that I belong in it. "Maybe we can do something more with it."

"Well," Myrah says, "we have no other actors available."

"A phone call." I bite my lower lip, lost in thought for a moment. I've been saying all along that this movie is missing something, some deeper emotion that hasn't come to the surface yet. But what is it?

And then I remember my parents, the people I love most but who I can never show this movie to.

"I think we should try to work in a coming-out scene," I say.

"At this point in the movie?" Myrah scrunches her face. "I don't know if that'll match the mood."

"Let's try it." I mount the camera to the tripod and work through the settings to adjust for the darkness.

"I haven't written anything for that, and I'm not sure it works with this moment in the movie. Or any point in the movie," she adds. "You said you wanted a cute rom-com."

"Improvise a bit—you know the character," I tell her.

Myrah sighs, but pulls out her phone. I smile.

"Action," I say after hitting record on the camera and mic.

Myrah takes a step forward, her phone lifted to her ear.

"Hi, Mom," she says into it, crossing her legs as she comes to a standstill by the black fence that lines the outside of the park. She rests her hand on one of its spikes and gazes out at the trees. "No, yeah, everything's fine. I wanted to tell you something." She drops her chin, staring at her shoes. "I'm . . . bisexual."

My stomach bottoms out. I stare at her, ignoring the

camera, transfixed by her performance, the fear in her words and her halting movements. I can't take my eyes off her as she nods, listening to the other side of an imaginary conversation. I can always add in a voice-over in post, edit it so that it sounds like it's her mom's voice coming through the receiver.

But even as I plan my editing strategy, I can't help but wonder what Myrah's fake mom is saying right now. Is she surprised? Confused? Angry?

I read her face, trying to figure it out, and my stomach tightens into a billion knots. I'll never be able to untangle them all.

My breath catches as I wait for what feels like an eternity, and then Myrah reaches up and wipes a tear from the corner of her eye, and I realize my hands are shaking.

"I love you too, Mom," Myrah whispers. "Yeah. That means the world to me. Okay."

She lowers the phone, stares at the screen for a moment, then pockets it and turns back to the park with a small smile. She lingers there for a moment, letting the feeling hang in the warm air around her. The hope and acceptance of the scene should stop the tremor in my fingers, but it doesn't. Instead heat floods the backs of my eyeballs, and I have to look down at the camera and play with the settings so I don't cry.

Myrah blinks and walks down the street. I wait until she's out of frame before calling cut.

"That was amazing," I say when she circles back.

"Eh," Myrah says. "Clearly I'm a natural actress-slash-improviser, but I don't think it works with the movie. She's supposed to be thinking about Kate's character in this moment. I don't see how this fits into the arc."

I stare back at the camera. That scene was perfect. How can I ever make Myrah understand that not only does it fit in, but it's impossible to disentangle it from the rest of the plot?

"I liked it," I say. "I bet I can work it into the movie in editing."

Myrah tips her head to one side. "Why are you so hung up on this?"

I'm not sure, but Myrah's performance was so good, and the scene felt so real. It has to be in the movie.

It belongs there, because for some of us, coming out in some way is an inescapable part of falling in love.

Yet another reason why love will never happen for me.

I take a deep breath, ignoring the stench of weed coming from the north side of the park.

"Let's move on for now," I say. I have the footage, and I'm in charge of editing. I'll find a way to work this in. "Should we go set up by the arch?"

Myrah nods, and helps me carry the tripod. When we round the arch, I spot another camera setup across the fountain.

"Tom and Sophia are here too," I tell Myrah, pointing. And it looks like they're fighting, which fills me with vicious pleasure. Tom deserves to be yelled at after what he pulled today.

But then, instead, Sophia pulls him into a hug.

That doesn't look like the interaction I asked her to have, in which she drags Tom for what he did.

But maybe she already did that.

"Hold on a sec," I tell Myrah, and before she can stop me, I cross the fountain to join them.

Sophia starts when she sees me, and Tom won't look me in the eye.

"Can I talk to you?" I ask her, ignoring Tom. I don't want to meet his eye either. Not after how he talked to Kate today.

Sophia nods, and follows me past the drug dealer/chess player sitting at one of the tables in a dark corner of the park.

"How did he take it?" I ask her.

"Really well," she says, smiling. "He texted Kate to apologize."

I raise any eyebrow. "Wow, a whole text."

"He's sorry about how he handled it," Sophia says, folding her spindly arms across her chest. "What more do you want?"

I huff. "I want him to put as much energy into apologizing as he did into yelling at her in the first place."

"That's not fair," Sophia says, glaring at me. "She lied to him. She's been sabotaging us."

I gape at her. I can't believe, just a day ago, I was confessing all my insecurities to this absolute demon and listening to her stupid emotions. I let her kiss me. I let her be my *first kiss*.

And now she has the nerve to treat Tom like he's still a friend. Instead of the giant asshole pariah he should be. She's acting like we should all move on. Kate's the only one who has to swallow the aftermath while everyone gossips about her and gives Tom a free pass. Even though it was 100 percent his actions today, he's passed all the consequences to her. And Sophia let him. And now she has the gall to stand in front of me and blame Kate for the way Tom acted?

I turn on my heel and storm toward the street.

I have nothing more to say here.

"Wait, please," she calls after me. "Please don't do this. We were . . . Things were different."

A shudder passes up my spine despite the heat lingering in the air. I can't believe I let her touch me. I need to flush away that moment, at any price.

"Until you decided to be all buddy-buddy with Tom again. You're automatically forgiving the guy who humiliated my cousin, aka the sweetest girl to ever walk this damn planet?" I yell at her. Even the drug dealer is staring at me. "Yeah, I'm fucking upset, Sophia. I tell you about how much she means to me, and then you—"

"I want to help," Sophia says.

I narrow my eyes at her. "By forgiving him because he knows how to send a text?"

Sophia throws up her hands. "I'm sorry." She pauses, staring at me with those hazelnut eyes I thought I'd grown to love. "I don't think that's what this is about, though."

I take a step toward her. "Oh? And what, pray tell, is your psychoanalysis, O wise one?"

"You're . . . scared of this." She gestures in the air between us. "You've wanted a big sweeping romance your whole life, and now that it might happen, you can't run away fast enough."

I laugh, but it doesn't sound like my voice. It's a cold, metallic burst that doesn't suit me at all. But I can't seem to stop myself. I'm angry at everything: Tom, for being so cruel; the teen center kids, for spitting his cruelty back into Kate's face; Sophia, for not caring. And me. For never being able to admit that I care so much about all of it that it might consume me.

It all comes out in a rage of words I barely process, or even hear as I say them.

"You think *this* is a great sweeping romance?" I ask. There's so much mocking in my tone, I startle myself with it. "This is nothing."

"It could be something," Sophia says. "And that scares you, but—"

I'm not *scared*, I tell myself. I'm angry. I can tear this whole thing apart if I want to, never face it again.

So I do.

"Says the girl who spends her life tearing down the idea of relationships because her mommy got remarried."

As soon as the words are out of my mouth, I regret them. I stand there, breathing hard, sweating like I've run a marathon. But I haven't. All I've done is run my mouth.

Sophia takes a step back, reeling. Her eyes bore into mine, but not with the same intensity we shared before. It's a disbelief so powerful, I almost cry.

"Well," she says after a moment. "You sure showed me."

She stands there. She's waiting for me to apologize, and I am too.

But I can't. I can't do anything except let her leave, because if she does, if she chooses to leave me standing here, then I never have to revisit the moment after we kissed. I can let myself choose to be not worthy. And right now, that sounds a lot safer.

So I hold my breath, and choke down how sorry I am, and wait in silence long enough to watch her shake her head at me and spin on her heel. She retreats to the fountain and the light of the arch and Tom, the heels of her boots clicking against the pavement with every step, leaving me to stand alone in the darkness under the trees.

As soon as I land on Kate's bed, I burst into tears. I bury my face in one of her pillows to muffle the sobs, because even through the dense fog of my own emotions, I'm keenly aware that I'm being extra.

Behind me, I hear Myrah tell Kate what happened in a hushed whisper. She leaves out how we were fighting about Tom, for which I'm grateful. The last thing I want right now is for Kate to blame herself for my stupidity.

It's not her fault I decided to trust Sophia.

Because it was me who chose to sit there with her on the stupid sidewalk outside the Corner Cinema Hotel, blithering on about things I've never told anyone else before. Like she's someone I can trust. Someone I can talk to. Someone I'd want to talk to.

The thought makes me cry harder into the pillow.

Kate reaches over to stroke my hair, which has come undone from its braid. It hangs over my shoulders, shaking as I sob. Her touch is comforting, but it also reminds me that I'm supposed to be there for her. I'm failing her, yet again. I have no idea what happened between her and Tom, and instead of trying to find out or take care of her, I'm soaking her pillow with my own stupid drama.

With friends like me looking out for her, it's no wonder Tom managed to pull that crap off today.

I roll over. My eyes feel puffy and achy, and I'm sure they're red to match. I turn my head sideways, pressing my cheek against the pillow, and stare at Myrah.

"I told you I should've stayed home."

"I thought you'd enjoy the shoot."

"What a brilliant insight that turned out to be," I mutter.

Kate scoots closer to me and lies down to rest her head against my shoulder. I scoot up to rest my head on top of hers and wrap my arms around her shoulders.

"What happened?" she asks.

I shrug, jostling her head as I move. "I got into a fight with Sophia."

"Yeah, but," she says, propping herself up on her elbows to stare at me from above, "what else is new?"

I've never heard her speak so bluntly, without any of her usual sweetness sugaring her words.

"What was different this time?" she presses.

I pause. I don't want Kate—or anyone else—to know about the competition event and the talk and the kiss, and I want even less for her to know that she came up in our fight.

It's not like we could ever be a couple, I remind myself. I'm so deep in the closet, I've made the overflowing laundry hamper my permanent address.

At the thought, I remember the scene I made Myrah shoot. Watching her character come out to her fake mom has lodged a seed of doubt in my gut, and as much as I try to shake it off, it's already grown roots.

But that doesn't mean *I* should come out. Does it? That's not what this movie was supposed to be.

Besides, I don't even want Sophia, I remind myself more forcefully. My eyes well up again, and I blink a bunch to dissipate the tears. I'm not about to cry again. I've been extra enough today.

"I don't know," I say. I don't know how to answer her question without telling the truth. I pin down the most honest answer I can muster without mentioning the kiss. "It was real this time. Before, it's just been disagreeing about the movie. This time it was an actual fight."

Kate lets herself slip back into the pillows. She stares at the ceiling for a while.

"But I thought you didn't like her anyway," she says without taking her eyes off the ceiling. "Why do you care what she thinks?"

I tap my feet together. My heels roll against the duvet. She makes a good point. Why do I care?

"I don't know," I say, admitting it to myself and to them. "I don't know how I feel about her."

I flop my head back, joining Kate in staring at the ceiling. Without moving my neck, I shift my gaze to look at her out of the corner of my eye.

"What about you?" I ask.

She bites her lip. "I'm sorry."

I open my mouth to tell her she has nothing to apologize for, but she keeps going.

"I don't want to work on the movie anymore," she says quietly.

I stare at her soft face, suddenly dizzy. It's too late to recast now. If Kate quits, there's no movie.

If Kate quits, I lose everything. The festival, LA, putting bi romance out there for the world to see, all slipping right out of my fingers when I was on the verge of having it all.

"I didn't text Tom back, like you said. But with what happened today, it's poisoned everything," she whispers. "How can I face it now . . . ?" She trails off, her eyes scanning my face. "Is that okay?"

I deflate. It is, objectively speaking, not okay. It's too late to recast, and we don't have nearly all the footage we need. If Kate drops out now, the movie is over, and all my dreams are dead.

But then I look at her, and the devastation all over her face, and I say the only thing I can.

"Of course it is," I say, squeezing her hand. "Let's stop talking about our very depressing love lives and order pizza instead. You deserve it. I'm proud of you for not answering Tom's text. I know it's hard. But he doesn't deserve your forgiveness just because he took a grainy picture of a dog."

Kate grins and moves to order the food.

I fill my cheeks with air and let it all burst out at once. Sophia and Tom wormed their way into our lives to ruin them, it seems.

And the worst part is, they don't care. They waltz into our hearts and break them from the inside out without caring at all.

CHAPTER TWENTY

SOPHIA

. . . .

My heart is officially broken.

It's been smashed into itty-bitty little pieces. It's been torn apart, and the splinters are gouging into each other, a constant digging pain.

Tom lies on his bed, his face in the pillows. I'm slumped at his desk chair, bathed in the synthetic glow of his laptop screen, my head in my hands. We haven't said anything in a while. Occasionally one of us groans.

Matt stares at us. "You guys are pathetic."

"I'm in mourning," Tom says. His voice is muffled because he's speaking into a pillow. Kate still hasn't answered his text.

"Same," I say, staring at the void between me and the bean-bag chair across the room. Emma's face stares back, the anger in her eyes threatening to swallow me whole. I can't stop re-playing how she spat back everything I ever confided to her.

Matt looks between the two of us and rolls his eyes. "You're both going to have to move on at some point. Snap out of this moping."

I don't look at him. I keep staring into space. I'm wrapped up in the memory of Emma's voice, low and scornfully teasing as she shattered everything we'd built. Her words reverberate in my ears, turning everything I've felt into a mockery.

"She turned everything against me," I say. My head gets heavier in my hand.

Tom flings himself onto his back and groans at the ceiling.

"I can't believe she lied to me."

I frown at his words. I can't really believe it either. But not in the way he means it, that he's shocked. I'm shocked too, but there's also a gnawing doubt worming its way through my gut. I saw the proof with my own two eyes, but it's still so unbelievable.

I mean, Emma might've been horrible tonight, but she makes a point. Kate Perez? Sabotage? It's unimaginable.

"Me neither," I mutter.

"You were right, Sophia. I was such an asshole," Tom moans.

"Hmm?" I'm barely listening at this point. His words pass through my ears without my brain processing their meaning.

"I shouldn't have yelled at her like that. I was so . . ." Words failing, he lifts his hands to the ceiling, flailing his fingers in anger. "And she was sitting there all . . ." More hand-flinging. "And I got so mad, and I shouldn't have."

Emma was so mad too. I can't escape her anger.

"She lied to you," Matt says, seething. "She's been messing with us this whole time."

"Yeah, but still," Tom says. "I should've talked to—"

A surge of anger rises through me, left over from watching Emma foaming at the mouth at me. I force myself to sit up and look at him.

"It's no use lying there expressing your regrets to the ceiling," I point out.

Tom shoots me a look. "Says the one sitting there expressing her regrets to the floor."

It's my turn to groan. How can I face Emma again?

Tom looks back to the ceiling. "I can't believe she sabotaged us."

Matt stands up and strides toward the bed.

"It happened. You need to move on," he says. Turning to look at me, he adds, "You both do. We should separate ourselves from the rest of them. They're toxic bitches anyway."

I squirm at his language. I might be annoyed, but that doesn't mean I'm magically down for misogynistic garbage. "Doesn't make it cool for you to call them bitches."

Matt rolls his eyes. "Tom deserves a clean break."

I close my eyes, taking a deep breath. The only thing worse than the thought of seeing Emma again is the thought of not seeing her, or of seeing her and not talking to her. How am I supposed to deal with this?

My phone rings when I get home. I roll my eyes preemptively before picking up.

"Hi, Mom," I say dully when I answer.

"Hello, *chérie*," Mom says.

I grit my teeth. *You aren't French*, I want to snap at her, my stomach sinking as I realize that this is how I've made Tom feel since I got back. Instead I force some pep into my voice. "How are you?"

I cross the living room to my bedroom as she answers. Dad isn't home—the apartment is empty, per usual—but I still don't want him to walk in on me talking to Mom. After the divorce, talking to one in front of the other feels a little like being caught cheating.

"I miss you," she says.

"I miss you too," I say, surprised by the earnestness in my voice.

It's true, though. I miss Brooklyn Mom, who lived in the same house as me and believed in our family and didn't pepper random French vocabulary into our conversations. France Mom, who won't shut up about *Paul* and *croissants* and *the day trip we took to the museum was* divine, *mon amour; there's so much* culture *here* . . . not so much.

Especially since the first thing France Mom did was leave me.

"This distance is so hard," she murmurs.

The tension floods back into my jaw. "Maybe you shouldn't have left, then."

A hard silence follows my words. I've surprised myself again, though this time it's not the sentiment itself that's shocking so much as the fact that I've voiced it.

"You know why I left," she says after a long moment, her voice low. "I wasn't happy in Brooklyn."

Memories of her lying in bed for days float into my mind. I knew she wasn't happy here. It never occurred to me that she had to get so far away from me to find happiness.

"So you moved to France," I say flatly. "Without me. You only brought me with you long enough to *get to know Paul,* and then you sent me right back to Brooklyn."

I land on the edge of my bed and kick at the floor with my toes. I still haven't decorated anything in here, and the barrenness of the room feels suffocating. Though not as suffocating as the forced decor of the living room.

"Did you want to stay here?" Mom says after a moment.

I pause. The answer is, of course, an emphatic *no.*

"You never asked," I say, not wanting to hand her the win. Because that's not the point. The point is and always has been that she abandoned me and destroyed our family and moved away to start a brand-new one that I wasn't invited to be a part of.

"I didn't think I had to," Mom says. "You know how much I want you here. But you made a point of being miserable the whole time you were here. Now you're saying you wanted to stay with me. I don't know how to respond to this."

"I didn't want you to leave," I say.

Mom sighs. It makes the receiver crackle.

"I know," she says. "But something had to change."

I twist my fingers through my hair, my blood boiling over. The reasonableness of her tone only makes my own fury swirl further out of control.

"Evidently," I snarl.

"*Chérie,* don't be so angry," Mom says, her tone still even. "I miss you."

"You should've thought of that before," I shout, and slam my finger onto the giant red end-call button on my phone screen.

I run my trembling fingers over my face, trying to steady myself. This whole night has been too much. She shouldn't have called. I shouldn't have picked up the phone. I shouldn't have said those things. But they've been weighing heavily on my heart. And I've been telling people things lately. I might as well keep going.

My phone rings again, and I stare at it. I can picture my mom at the other end, the phone clutched to her ear as she paces the floor, praying I'll answer. I don't reach for my phone. Anger still thrums in my veins, and if I answer, I'll end up regretting what I say. Eventually the phone stops ringing. The call screen disappears, replaced by a text from Tom.

TOM: *I still can't believe she did this to me.*

I stare at it, the little nagging doubts that have been swirling through my mind all day solidifying. I can't believe it either.

I know what I have to do.

Script Supervisor's

DAILY LOG

Title: I THINK I LOVE YOU

Shoot Day #: 3

Director: Emma Hansen

Completed Scenes: 1

SCRIPT PAGE #	SCENE	CAMERA ROLL	SOUND ROLL	SHOT DESCRIPTION
9	9	1	1	WS: MYRAH WALKING DOWN STREET
9	9	1	1	CU: MYRAH ON PHONE
10	9	1	1	WS: MYRAH WALKING INTO PARK
3	2	N/A	N/A	MYRAH AND KATE MEET-CUTE— HOW?

CHAPTER TWENTY-ONE

Emma
. . . .

I stand on the sidewalk, arms folded against the morning air. The temperature will get to the nineties by noon, but it's early enough to be almost chilly. The only other people out and about are a couple and their small dog, who pauses to yip at every tree they pass. I look up at Matt's wide town house. He's the one who found evidence against Kate, so if I'm going to figure out what happened, this is the place to start.

I left Myrah's this morning, where we were supposed to be editing around the fact that we can't shoot any more scenes with Kate, but now that I'm here, I have no idea what to do.

I bounce on the tips of my toes, my sneakers squeaking as I try to work up the courage to go knock. I need to see that evidence. For Kate. I need to know what happened so I can help her.

As soon as I take a step toward the building, I spot someone running around the street corner. I start, ready to bolt and pretend like I was never here. But then I recognize the tall, slender frame.

Sophia.

"What are you doing here?" I ask.

I want to yell at her some more, but if Matt hears and comes out, I'll lose the element of surprise, which is the only thing I have going for me and my whole plan would be ruined.

"Nothing. Thought . . . ," she wheezes, struggling to catch her breath.

I stare at her, biting my lip to stop myself from laughing. Nothing about this is remotely funny, but I still can't help it.

"Breathe," I tell her.

She drops her hands to her knees, staring at the ground and wheezing. "Sorry. Saw you. On Subway. Ran. Catch up."

I can't stop the giggle that escapes my lips, but by the time she looks up at me, I've fixed my face. I glare down at her as sternly as I can. "You should consider going to the gym once in a while."

She straightens, stretching her back. "You're one to talk."

I pinch my lips at her. "Ooooh, witty."

Sophia closes her eyes and sighs. "Look, I'm sorry. I thought a lot about what you said, and you're right. Tom was an asshole, and he totally deserves to be called on it. I'm sorry I didn't do that right away." She pauses, rubbing the back of her neck. "But he does regret the way he reacted."

"Good," I say, surprised at my own viciousness.

"And I also realized that there's no way Kate would cheat on anything, let alone something that would hurt Tom. So I wanted to find out what really happened," she says. I stare at her as she gestures to the front door. "Want to come ask Matt with me?"

I purse my lips.

"Come on," Sophia says, jabbing my shoulder. "I apologized. Which," she adds with an arched eyebrow, "is more than you did."

I exhale. She's right. "I am sorry. I was as soon as I said it. I don't know. You're right. I was scared. I shouldn't have taken it out on you."

"You were right too," Sophia says. "I shouldn't have let Tom off the hook so easy. Let's investigate together."

I struggle not to smile, but it's tugging at the corner of my lips without my consent.

"What would we even ask him?" I gesture to Matt's place. "I came here without a plan, and I still haven't come up with one."

"We could take a break and prepare interrogation questions," she says temptingly. "We could go on a stakeout and look for clues."

"Fine," I say, breaking. "But on one condition."

"Yes?" Sophia says with a sigh.

I look up at her, still smiling.

"I still say you asked me on a date," Sophia says.

I drop the mixing bowl onto the counter, shaking my head.

At my insistence that she owed me apology food, Sophia brought me back to her apartment to bake the one thing she knows how to make: lemon squares.

"Demanding apology snacks is not asking someone out," I say, reaching into one of her cabinets to hunt for sugar.

Sophia shrugs with a smirk. "Whatever you say."

I straighten, glaring at her, but I can't stop the smile from spreading across my face. This has to be flirting, right?

Whatever it is, I like it.

"If you've learned anything over the past few days, it should be that I'm always right and you should listen to me more often," I say.

Sophia's gaze softens. "I'd certainly like to."

I bite down on the straw hanging between my lips, choking on my surprise. To steady my breath, I take another sip of the Coke that Sophia gave me.

"Don't be smart with me," I say, sliding a lemon across the counter to her. "I haven't forgiven you yet."

Sophia groans as she cuts it in two. "You know, your thing was bad too. When will you forgive me, then?"

"When I get my lemon squares," I say. "And I know. I'm sorry."

The lemons cut, Sophia squeezes them above the mixing bowl. A few drops of the juice trickle down her palms. I reach over to wipe the residue from her wrist. She looks down at me, catching my eye, and I snap my hand away.

"So what should we do about Matt?" Sophia says. "Do you think the evidence he found is real?"

I measure the required cups of sugar and dump them in with the lemon juice. "I was thinking about that. I don't think he'd fake evidence, though. Why would he mess with Kate?"

Sophia taps her lips with her finger, her eyes all squinted in concentration. "Definitely a lack of motive."

"You're having way too much fun with this."

"And you," she says, jabbing a flour-covered spatula in my direction, "are not having nearly enough." She slouches over the counter, crossing her arms. "So, Detective Hansen, do you have any hunches?"

The spatula movement sprayed me with flour. Sophia brushes a few flecks of it off my cheeks, and I try (and fail) not to blush at her touch.

"Well, Detective Kingsley," I say, playing along when she goes back to mixing, "I believe it must have been someone on an opposing team who wanted to get us disqualified by framing Kate. We did, after all, win the Most Anticipated Film award."

Sophia traces a fingertip along her chin, stroking an imaginary beard in thought. "An interesting theory. But the victims experienced sabotage before the vote, and before any interaction with other teams aside from Kate's."

My lip twitches at this. After all, there was no evidence of other sabotage.

"Has it occurred to you, Detective Kingsley," I say, "that perhaps the team in question was not being sabotaged but is in fact a bunch of dumbasses?"

Sophia smacks my arm.

I shake my head. "So unprofessional. I'll report you to the CO later."

"It was definitely sabotage," Sophia says. "But we should probably consider all angles."

"I'll have my team investigate your dumbassery right away."

She drops her head into her hands. "I meant about looking at people from other teams," she says into her palms.

I drain my Coke, and reach across the counter to grab Sophia's untouched glass. She slaps my hand.

"Excuse?"

"Mine's done," I say, gesturing to my empty soda. "And this is my apology meal."

"One sip," she says, holding up a single stern finger. I waterfall way more than a sip's worth of her drink into my mouth, and she shakes her head at me.

"We need to figure out who's been messing with us all along." Sophia pauses as she scoops our lemony mixture into the baking tray over the crust and slides it into the oven. "You know . . . I saw Matt talking to someone after all our auditions were canceled. I thought it was someone who was supposed to audition for us, but he said it wasn't. Do you think he was lying?"

"All I know is that whoever is responsible for my cousin's unhappiness, I will rip him apart limb from limb," I say, setting Sophia's Coke back on the counter.

Sophia laughs. "Again with the violence."

"I have a lot of hate," I mutter.

"Oh, no, I know. I've borne the brunt of it for many years now," Sophia says with a smile. "But you gotta keep the threats within the realm of possibility, or they're not scary."

I flex my biceps. Even I have to admit it's a pitiful show.

Not that I'll admit anything out loud.

"I'm terrifying," I say, deepening my voice.

Sophia stares at me. "Thanks, Batman. I'm sure you'll scare the information right out of Matt."

Fanning herself with one hand, she moves away from the oven. I follow her out of the kitchen and through the living room.

"We have no other leads," I say. "So we should start with him. If he was lying, maybe he was the one who sabotaged you."

Sophia pushes her bedroom door open, and I gasp when I see it. This is the most depressing room I've ever set foot in. The walls are white and bare, her bed is tightly made, and the only thing on her plain nightstand is a phone charger.

"I see you made yourself right at home," I say.

She glances over at me. "I just got back."

"Ages ago," I argue. I'm about to tease her for her utter lack of wall decorations when I see the pinched look on her face. I let it drop.

I sit on the edge of her bed, and we watch a show on her laptop while we wait for the oven timer to go off. I barely register what we're watching. I'm too aware of her body, so close to mine that I can feel the heat radiating off her. The fact that we're literally Netflix-and-chilling doesn't help.

It's a relief when the oven timer goes off and Sophia runs back to the kitchen. We continue our show until the pastries have cooled. She packs the squares into a Tupperware, and we head to Matt's place for our stakeout.

On the way, we pass a little furniture boutique, and I pause.

"I still owe you an apology," I say. "I can't let you beat me with these squares. Wait here."

Leaving her to sweat it out on the sidewalk, I run into the shop. I don't know what I'm looking for, exactly, but I find it when I spot a sequined throw pillow with the Eiffel Tower on one side and the Empire State Building on the other. I pay, run back outside, and present her with the bag. She laughs when she sees the pillow, her eyes lighting up.

"Your room needs *something*, Kingsley," I tell her.

"It does," she agrees. "This is perfect. Thank you."

I smile as she keeps walking, the bag swinging at her fingertips. I'm glad we're even now, but more than that, the thought of something I gave her living in her room makes me feel like floating all the way to Matt's place.

CHAPTER TWENTY-TWO

SOPHIA

· ·

I tear open my Tupperware as soon as we reach the stoop across the street from Matt's house, and pass Emma a lemon square. The smell of citrus permeates the air around us as soon as I stuff one into my mouth. Powdered sugar sprays onto my lips as I chew.

I settle in on the stoop, which has wide brown steps that are tall enough to make a comfy backrest as I lean back. The street in front of us is lined with parked cars and evenly spaced-out trees.

Emma glances at me. "These are really good."

"Thanks," I say with a smile. "It's the extent of my baking skills."

"So, sabotage aside, did you talk to Tom about your fight?" she asks as she reaches into the Tupperware for another square.

I nod. "Yeah. That was good advice. Or whatever."

She laughs. "So the movie's going better?"

"Yeah. How's yours going, Miss Most Anticipated?"

She nudges me. "It's going okay."

I frown. There's an edge to her tone that contradicts her words.

"You sure about that?"

"I added this scene that Myrah doesn't like," she says, her eyes fixed on the Tupperware between us. "One where the protagonist comes out to her parents."

I look up. The fear lacing her voice is one I'm all too familiar with.

"Is that . . ." I swallow. "Is that something you're thinking about?"

"No," Emma says, too quickly, then pauses. "I don't know. I guess it doesn't feel necessary. Like, I could end up with a boy, and then it wouldn't make any difference."

I look up at her. End up with a boy? I mean, I know that's technically possible, but I'd kind of started having different ideas about who she might end up with.

She must feel my gaze on her face, because she looks up and whispers, "Then again, I might not." She sighs. "And either way, ending up with a boy wouldn't change that this is part of who I am."

I stare at her for a moment. A breeze rustles the tree branches, swirling a few stray leaves across the ground. Emma inches closer to me before it dies down. The day is quickly warming, and I angle myself so that my shadow falls across her face, shielding her from the sun.

"That's true," I say. "You're allowed to have this be important to you, no matter who you date."

She nods at this. "I know it matters. I guess it's always been easier to pretend it doesn't. But now, making this movie and everything, I'm realizing it does."

"It does," I agree.

"Not sure that means I'll do anything about it, though. I don't want to ruin what I have with my parents."

"I get that," I say. "But letting them get to know you better should never ruin anything."

She gives me a look, and I acknowledge her unspoken point. "*Should* being the operative word, I know. But your parents are great. I'm sure they'll be cool about it."

Emma turns back to Matt's building, a tall and beautiful brownstone with wide even windows draped in flowery blue curtains. "So what's our strategy here?"

I crane my neck to examine Matt's building. The curtains are drawn, and I can't see anything inside. The building, like the street, remains still and quiet.

"We should call the festival," I say, slapping Emma's hand, "and see if anyone's reported any vote rigging. If Matt noticed, maybe someone else did too."

She winces as I slap her hand again enthusiastically.

"It's a fine idea," she says, "but why do I have to be abused?"

I pull my hand back. "Sorry. I got excited. Here," I say, pulling out my phone and pushing it into her palm, "pretend to be a journalist."

"Why do I have to call?" she asks.

I shrug. "My mouth is full."

And before she can point out that it's not, I bite into my lemon bar. She looks up the number and dials it, shaking her head at me as it rings.

"Hello," she says when the person answers. She pinches the top of her nose, and her voice comes out high-pitched with a nasally edge. "This is Brenda LaCroix from the *Tribune*. I was calling to follow up on the election rigging claims we discussed."

I choke on the lemon. "*LaCroix?*"

It's her turn to slap my hand now.

"I spoke with Alan," she says in the same nasal drone. "Is he there? . . . I see. Well, can you let me know if there have been any updates in the investigation into the matter?"

She pauses again, her head tilting. I tap my fingers against my knee, waiting for her to finish listening to the woman on the other end.

"Well, I heard reports that the Most Anticipated Film vote was rigged this year. I wanted to include it in the arti— I see." She pauses. "Well, that's a relief. . . . Yes. Of course. Bye-bye, now."

She ends the call and hands back the phone.

"Abby in reception says no one reported anything," she says.

I stare at the street in thought. "Why would someone frame Kate for rigging the vote, but then not report it? It's sort of an essential part of framing someone for something."

Emma glances at Matt's front door. She stares at it for a

moment, then shrugs. I have no idea how this stakeout is going to help us figure out what happened to Kate, but I have no idea what else to do. Kate won't talk, the festival won't talk, and Emma won't stop talking, so this is all a recipe for disaster.

Emma cracks her knuckles, which snap startlingly loud, considering how tiny she is. "I hope he comes out soon," she says.

I glance at her, then her fist. "Why?"

"We're here to beat the answers out of him, right?"

I'm not sure she's kidding, but I laugh anyway. If it's not a joke, I'll turn it into one.

"Have you looked in the mirror lately?" I ask.

She glares at me. "Why?"

"Because you keep threatening violence," I say. "I'm wondering if you know you're about as tall and terrifying as a marshmallow."

Emma folds her arms and straightens her back so that she almost reaches my shoulder, because that's where she ends up at her fullest height. "Yeah, if the marshmallow was on fire."

I blink. "What?"

"I don't know." She flings her hands up. "I thought, like, s'mores. Sometimes the marshmallow . . . No?"

I shake my head, grinning. She's so dumb. It's so cute.

"Fine," she says with a humph. "What are we hoping for, exactly?"

I turn back to my examination of the building across the quiet street. Privately I'm kind of hoping that, with all this apologizing, we'll end up forgetting about Matt and making

238

out on this stoop, but that's the kind of thing that'll never happen if I say that's what I'm hoping for. So I settle for shrugging.

"I don't know. For him to come out and do something incriminating, I guess? I mean, he's still our only lead."

She frowns. "Why don't we go interrogate him?"

"And say what?" I ask, digging my phone back out of my purse.

"Something accusatory," she says. She's still staring down his front door. "I want him to come out. Maybe we can startle him enough that he tells us what happened. It's not him, but it's probably the easiest way to get him to tell us everything he knows."

"I have an idea." I stare at my phone screen, fingers hovering over the keyboard in hesitation.

SOPHIA: The festival called . . . they said we're disqualified.

I show the text to Emma, who nods her approval. I hit send.

The typing bubbles pop up immediately. I raise the phone between us, and the two of us lean in to wait for his reply. I can smell the lavender in her hair, and for a moment, I forget what we're doing here. Then my phone buzzes with Matt's response.

MATT: WHAT? Why?

SOPHIA: They said our team reported falsified evidence incriminating another team. Did you report Kate?

Emma and I exchange looks. A few minutes later, Matt bursts out his front door. Frantically doing the last of his shirt buttons, he rushes down the street.

Emma and I glance at each other, locking eyes for a moment, before we tear off after him. In an instant, we're scrambling across the road, our feet pounding against the concrete, and onto the sidewalk in front of him. He screeches to a halt when he sees us, his chest rising and falling from his hurry.

"What are you doing here?" he asks.

"Where you off to in such a rush?" Emma asks, hands on her hips. Matt shrinks under her gaze even though he's about three times her size. A marshmallow on fire after all.

"To . . . meet Tom . . . ," he mutters.

"That's not true. Tom's still asleep." I don't know this for sure, but it's probably true.

"Off to talk to Abby in reception?" Emma asks, taking one neat step toward him.

"Who?" Matt says, but his voice is all squeaky. He must've called the festival office too. And why would he do that if he wasn't guilty?

Emma lunges at him, a hand outstretched, and for a second I think she might kill him. Even though she has absolutely no muscle. And her nails are trimmed so short that they couldn't do any damage. I reach out to stop her anyway, and she lands against my arm with a thud.

"I know you had something to do with framing Kate," she shouts.

Her voice echoes down the street. Matt glances over his shoulder. His face is turning red, probably from a combination of high-key lying and embarrassment, even though there's no one around to watch our confrontation.

"I have no idea what you're talking about," he says. "I found all her fake voting slips." He looks at me. "You were there; you saw it. Call off the witch hunt. We already found the witch." He turns back to Emma, scorn in his eyes. "Right in your family."

I brace my muscles against Emma in anticipation of her lunging at him again. She feels it, and it's enough to keep her from beating his brains out. Though at this point, I kind of wish she would.

I stare at Matt. Something about his words sticks. I *was* there. I saw the whole thing.

"You're the one who said the footage was deleted," I say slowly. Emma turns to look at me, frowning, but the pieces of it are starting to come together. "You're the one who found the slips. And the one who went out of the room during casting. It's you, isn't it?"

Matt's gaze falters, and before he can say anything in his defense, I know I'm right.

"I don't know what you're talking about," he spits, but it's too late. I know he's lying. Next to me, Emma's shaking.

"You saw the slips," he says, but his voice falters.

"I also saw you take Kate's slip to put in the voting basket for her," I say. "Did you put it in for her, or did you keep it and make a bunch of photocopies?"

Matt stares at me, totally frozen.

"Why would you frame Kate?" I ask. "Is it because Tom wouldn't help you with Emma?"

She jumps at the mention of her name, and turns to me with her face flaming, but I keep my eyes on Matt.

"That's so petty." My eyes are burning, but I don't blink. I keep staring him down until he withers.

"You think that's petty?" he says. "You're the one who needed help with Emma, in the end."

I frown. "What are you talking about?"

"You two," he says, shaking his head. "I can't believe you fell for it."

I drop my arm, and Emma steps away from me. Suddenly I can't bear to touch her in front of him, like he's been watching us all along and laughing at what he sees.

"Fell for what?" she asks, her voice shaking like she already knows.

"Oh, you mean you don't know?" he says, sneering. "You really think she's in love with you?"

He nods to me, and I blush, startled. I'm not the one who caught feelings first. Unless . . .

Matt turns to me. "Oh, and I bet you heard that she's in love with you, huh?"

Emma and I look at each other. She pushes past me, taking another step toward Matt, but all the bravado has withered from her frame.

"They set you up," Matt says, laughing cruelly. "Your so-called friends. They staged all those conversations you overheard. They thought if they tricked you into believing you were in love with each other, they'd get you guys to merge the two groups back together." He looks between the two of us. "I can't believe it worked. You two are stupider than their dumb plan was."

I blink. For a moment, his words don't make sense. But then I start to process it all. That's why Kate and Myrah never looked my way, even though the bookshelf wasn't exactly the best hiding spot. That's why Kate disentangled herself from Tom to be in that room at the same time as me. Come to think of it, they were probably being so over-the-top at reception that day to drive me away, so that I'd be alone in the room, an audience to their lies. And why Emma and I ended up alone in the coffee shop half an hour early.

Emma stares at him for a moment. I can't rip my eyes off the back of her head, as though it will help me read her mood right now. All I can do is pray, in that instant that seems to last a lifetime, that this won't change anything. That we can keep holding hands under blankets, and maybe even on top of them one day, out in the open, where everyone can see.

I mean, sure. It's not what I was expecting. I never thought Tom and Kate would mastermind a matchmaking coup with this level of trickery, but . . . Matt isn't wrong. It's working. Maybe it can keep working. After all, that kiss meant something. The laughter we shared over those stupid lemon bars not moments ago on the stoop across the street, it all meant something.

The thought of it all slipping away because of something so far beyond my control makes my whole body seize, fear climbing my throat. This doesn't have to be the end, I tell myself. Just because they lied to us doesn't mean our feelings haven't been honest.

But as soon as Emma turns around, I know that it's over.

Her eyes are already reddened, as if anticipating tears, and the laughter that lit up her eyes throughout our day together has gone. I can see it written all over her face, all over the onslaught of tears building under her eyelashes.

I take a step backward, stumbling as though I've been shoved, which I basically have. Every emotion on Emma's face has pushed me backward, smashed through my rib cage to crush my heart. I can feel her pulling away from me, and now it's my turn to blink back tears as the realization strikes me.

Everything between us is all over.

CHAPTER TWENTY-THREE

Emma

• •

When Matt's words hit me, my stomach bottoms out. Heat creeps up my neck and takes over my face. I turn away from Sophia. Her arms drop from me like my skin has burned her.

I can't believe it was all a lie. Every laugh we've shared since I heard Tom and Matt's lie didn't have any extra special meaning. Her hand holding mine at movie night probably meant nothing to her. Our kiss—the one that was so special to me, not just because it was my first but because it was with her— might've been nothing more to her than a mistaken peck on the lips.

I've been looking at everything through the lenses Tom and Matt gave me when I overheard their staged conversation at the restaurant, and now the glass has been smashed and I can see the truth through the cracks. Sophia never loved me at all.

Maybe she was right. At the dance. About me and my chances of ever finding love.

Maybe romance really is never meant to happen for me.

Whatever. It's not like it's everything I've ever wanted.

Tearing myself away from her, I run down the smooth sidewalk, away from Matt. It's sloping down toward the road, and I stumble over my feet as I pick up involuntary speed. I skid around the corner, dash past rows of cute storefronts and hipster coffee shops toward the subway entrance.

I don't know where I'm going, exactly, only that I need to get away from Matt's laughter and Sophia.

Footsteps clap down the sidewalk behind me. I glance over my shoulder to see Sophia running after me, tottering on her heels, but I turn away from her and quicken my pace as I near the subway. Her footsteps slow as I outrun her, barreling down the stairs, through the turnstile, and into the R train as it pulls into the station, for once, right on time.

My blood pumps fast through my body. I can hear it rushing against my ears. My head spins from the weight of it. All along, I thought she loved me. They said she loved me.

And like an idiot, I believed them.

I lean against the pole, which is discomfitingly warm, and watch the subway stops flash by, from Union Street past Atlantic Ave to Jay Street–MetroTech.

I get off the subway and walk slowly up the stairs to the street. The smell of salty pretzels and hot dogs hits me as soon as I reach the sidewalk and round the corner to Myrah's place. She's the last person I want to see right now, but I left my laptop here when we were editing this morning. I storm inside and hit the elevator button six times before it finally reaches me.

Myrah swings open her apartment door after my fifth knock. "What's going . . ."

She trails off when she sees my face, hot with tears and red with anger.

"You lied," I say, shocked by how steady my voice is.

Myrah takes a slow step backward, opening the door wider for me to follow her in, but I don't leave the hallway. "What?"

"Sophia."

It's all I have to say. Her whole face falls.

"Emma . . . ," she says, reaching out to me.

I push past her, slapping her hands out of my way, and barge to her room to snatch the laptop.

"Don't touch me," I say, my voice breaking under the strain of the sob I'm struggling to hold back.

She's my best friend. She and Kate. They've meant everything to me since I was fucking born.

Even though there's no one around to hide from, I bury my face in my hands. Heat from my cheeks burns into my palms.

"Emma, wait," Myrah pleads.

I don't stop for her. Without so much as a glance back, I turn away from her and storm right back out of the apartment, ripping my phone out of my pocket to call a Lyft. I have to get away from here fast. Running downstairs while frantically ordering a car is apparently a death wish, though, and I stumble on the last few steps, crashing against the hard-tiled floor. My phone clatters onto the floor next to me. Stinging pain shoots into the heels of my palms.

Rolling my wrist as I stand and pocket my phone again, I look up to see Myrah rushing toward me.

"Are you okay?" she gasps.

"Physically, yes," I snarl, rubbing my wrist with my other hand.

I'm still trying to catch my breath from all the running and falling. My chest heaves as I pant, staring Myrah down.

"Was it all fake?" I ask, breathing hard.

Myrah stares at me, and even though it takes her a while to say anything, I know from the way her face twists that they lied about everything. She wrings her hands, then runs her fingers over her face. My heartbeat pounds in the silence between us.

"Yes and no?" she says at last.

I glare at her, and she squares her shoulders under my look, folding her arms.

"Well, which is it?" I ask.

I'm surprising even myself. I've never spoken to Myrah this harshly before. But then again, she's never mounted a full-scale campaign to humiliate me in front of my rival before.

So it's a bit justified.

"It might have been staged, but what we were saying was tr—" she says, but I cut her off before she can launch into any justifications.

Nothing can justify the burning in my chest. The feel of Sophia's fingers in mine and her lips on mine flashes through my memory, and angry tears well in my eyes. What could prompt someone to do this?

"So, fake," I say over Myrah.

Myrah sighs. "If that's how you want to—"

I shake my head, laughing through my nose. "Cool. Thanks for that."

I turn away from her. My phone pings with my driver's information, and as soon as I leave the building, I see the black car pull up at the corner ahead.

Sliding into the seat and away from Myrah's gaze at last, I let the tears slip from my eyes. They flow down my face easily, but I choke down the accompanying sobs. The last thing I need is for the driver to figure out that I'm crying it up in the back of his car and ask what's wrong. I sit there and pretend that my eyes are watering because of the sickeningly heavy smell of pine tree car freshener.

When he drops me off in front of my building, I stumble up the front steps and drop onto my stoop. That's when I let myself fall apart.

I convulse over myself, sobs racking my body as I shake with tears. After years of reminding myself that I don't deserve love anyway, I let in the possibility of love and got burned immediately.

Goes to show that I was right all along. This will never happen for me.

When I've cried myself out, which takes longer than I'd care to admit, I mop my face on my sleeve. Dried tears stiffen on my cheeks, and I look up to see a couple walk past the stoop and turn into the little bookstore next door.

That's one nice thing about New York. You can cry in public in peace, and no one will bother you.

I stare at the row of garbage bins lined up by the stoop. I'm lost in thought, but there's nothing to daydream about anymore. In truth, there never really was, I admit to myself. Because going out with Sophia would mean coming out to my parents.

And there's no way that's happening.

That realization crashes over me like a blow to the back of the head. It's true, and I can't pretend otherwise even to myself. I can't come out without risking my relationship with my parents, but not coming out effectively destroys any potential at a relationship with Sophia.

Good thing that's already been wrecked before it even started.

It's so unfair. I was a breath away from happiness. And instead of closing the distance and kissing her and living happily ever after, I lost everything because of homophobia at large.

And. Well. If I'm being entirely honest, also because of Kate.

I've never gotten into a fight with her, and even after yelling at Myrah, I balk at the idea of confronting her.

Then again. I let Sophia kiss me because Tom said she was in love with me, and that was all a lie. A lie Kate helped set up. My first kiss, my first potential romance, everything I've ever waited for, and it turned to dust before it even started.

Jumping up on impulse, I push myself off the stairs and run into the building. It's lucky—or maybe not—that Kate lives right next door. It doesn't give me any time to think past the blinding hurt pulsing through my veins.

Especially since Kate swings open her front door before I can knock, clutching her phone.

"Myrah called. She told me what happened," she says, reaching out to grab my hands. "I'm so sor—"

"Save it." I wrench my hands out of her grip.

She lets me go, staring blankly at me. "I was trying to help."

"Help?" I say, my voice breaking into a high-pitched screech.

All of it flashes before my eyes. The way Sophia's skin smells like peaches and her lips twist when she thinks something is funny but doesn't want me to know it. The way she pulled me closer when we kissed, like I was still too far away and she wanted to bridge the distance.

Ruined.

All of it.

Kate looks down, swallowing. "I'm sorry. I thought it would work. It seemed like it was working."

It's my turn to stare at the floor. I count the stains scuffing my sneakers.

She's not wrong. None of it would have happened if I hadn't heard them talking about how much Sophia was allegedly into me. It's the reason why we started happening.

But it's also the reason why nothing can happen now. How can I possibly fall in love with Sophia when I know that she has never and probably will never love me back?

"I can't believe you lied to me," I say, falling back on the truth of my hurt. "And you got everyone in on it. Like I was the butt of some joke you all had."

My face flushes at the thought.

Kate nods. "I'm sorry. I should've been honest with you. Maybe that might've worked."

Even as she says it, I know it wouldn't have, but that doesn't stop the tears from welling in my eyes again. I keep my gaze fixed on the floor so she won't see them.

"I . . ." I shake my head at her feet. "I need time."

It breaks my heart to say it, but there's too much anger thumping against my temples right now, bursting through my veins. If I stay, I'll say something that goes too far. So, for the first time in my life, I tear myself away from Kate and storm back to my apartment.

The front door slams behind me, my thoughts swirling with furious speed. I can't help but linger on how humiliating it was to realize Sophia never loved me, that I acted like she wanted me when really I was so stupid to believe such an obvious lie.

Kate, my favorite person, the best person I know, lied to me.

And even if it hadn't all been a lie, nothing could have happened from there because my parents could never know.

I stand by the door, breathing hard. In the end, what's stopping me? Why do I have to keep hiding?

Sophia's right. My bisexuality matters. It always has, and it always will, no matter who I end up with. There's no point in hiding it anymore.

I take off my shoes and leave them by the door. Dad is sitting on the couch flipping through channels while Mom reads a book next to him. They look so peaceful and perfect, like a painting of what a perfect couple and family should look like.

I stare at them, blood pounding in my temples. I can't stop

now. If I wait, the impulse will wither and die in my veins, and I'll be right back where I started.

I have no movie to show them. No romantic prospects to tell them about. But I have the truth that's been lying heavy against my heart for years.

I force my leaden legs to step forward so I can sit next to my dad on the couch. I face straight forward, not even twisting my shoulders to turn to him. He's focused on *House Hunters*.

The sight of the show makes my stomach flip. Everything is so normal. I could so easily sit on the couch with them, settle into the pillows and watch the show and pretend like nothing is wrong, like I've done every other night of my life.

What if this impulse jeopardizes everything I have with my family?

But I've finally realized that not telling them jeopardizes it way more. I can't keep letting them stand in my way. I can't keep waiting for something else to go wrong so that I don't have to face the possibility that I could be happy.

Besides, I've already destroyed any potential anything with Sophia, and gotten into a fight with my two closest friends. If I'm setting all my relationships on fire today, might as well go for the big one. At least this one will be honest.

"What's up, bug?" Dad asks. He leans over to grab the remote off the coffee table, and hits pause.

Because it's not enough that they watch HGTV when it happens to be on. Oh no. They seek it out.

I shake my head a little, desperate to clear it out. I have no idea what's come over me. Why am I doing this now?

Then I remember Sophia's thin lips smiling at me over her stupid apology lemon bars. I can't exactly go all in with her—or anyone—if I don't go all in with myself.

And I know that looks different for everyone. Not everyone can come out safely. Not everyone needs to. Everyone has their own timeline. But for me, right now, I've finally realized that the only thing holding me back is my own fear of unworthiness.

It's probably time to overcome that.

I squeeze my hands together, trying to calm the shake in my fingers. They tremble against me instead.

"Nothing," I say, my nerves failing at the last moment. I slump back against the couch, disappointed.

Dad pokes my knee. "Seems like something's on your mind."

I shrug, staring at the TV. It's paused on the Realtor's peppy face.

"Just . . ." I trail off, taking a deep breath. The words are right there, stuck against my teeth. I will myself to push them out, to say them aloud. I picture it, what they would sound like, bold and confident out of my mouth.

I can't seem to make it happen.

"Just the movie," I finish lamely, sinking further into the pillows. I wish they would swallow me whole.

Dad tosses the remote between his palms, nodding. "Anything in particular?"

"Just gay," I blurt.

Across the couch, Mom drops her book. She shifts her weight to turn to face me. Dad stares.

"What?" His voice makes it clear that he means it in a confused sense, but I can't help hearing the stern *what*. The what-did-you-just-say *what*. The nothing-will-ever-be-the-same *what*.

I swallow.

"Not gay," I whisper. "Bi."

Why would I ever let it happen like this? The speeches I've practiced late into the night, the fantasies of tears and hugging and immediate acceptance and reassurance. None of that is about to happen. Not least of which because I've said all of five words, and not a complete sentence to string them into.

"Who's bi?" Dad asks, turning back to the TV.

I suppress a groan. He thinks I'm sharing gossip. Which means I have to come out. Again.

And the first time was so exhausting.

"I am," I whisper.

Dad looks back to me. "Oh. Well. Cool."

I swallow, staring back at him. That's it?

"Yeah," I say, voice hard. "Cool."

"That's great, honey," Mom says, smiling encouragingly.

Dad fiddles with the buttons on the remote, staring down at the little knobs. I watch him, knocking my knees together, waiting for one of them to say something else.

I wait for what feels like an eternity.

"Is that it?" I ask, finally breaking the silence myself. "This is a big deal."

"I know," Dad says, patting my knee.

Mom keeps smiling encouragingly. She's thrown in a creepy nod that makes her look like a car windshield bobblehead, devoid of any deeper meaning beyond the motion.

Everything they're saying feels like something they've picked up out of a script, something they know they're supposed to say. But it's clear they think nothing has changed.

I was afraid of something changing, but now that nothing has, the nothing gnaws at my gut. It's one thing to be accepted, but another altogether to be treated like something so huge, so explosive to me, doesn't matter to them at all.

"It matters to me, Dad," I say, painfully aware of the pleading note in my voice. "I'm trying to—"

Dad's face pales. "I didn't mean to—"

"No, no, of course not," I say, waving it off. "It's okay. It doesn't matter."

Dad nods. The silence stretches between us so painfully that my arm hairs stand on end. Eventually he presses play, and the Realtor snaps back to action, pitching the third house to this couple with impossible needs.

I stare at the TV, not processing anything except my own embarrassment. I've made too big a deal out of this, when it was nothing all along. Heat creeps up my neck, setting my cheeks on fire. I'm glued to the couch, no matter how much I might want to escape this moment.

"I'm gonna go to bed," I say.

"Okay." Dad's eyes flick off the TV for a second, but it's long enough that I can see the pink splashing across his face. At least he's as uncomfortable as I am.

But then again, his romantic prospects haven't been totally ruined.

I trudge back to my room, trying not to make too big a deal of it. As I leave, I can hear them whispering. I'm sure it's about me, but I have no idea what they could be saying.

I tumble back onto the bed and punch my pillow as I land.

CHAPTER TWENTY-FOUR

SOPHIA

. . . .

I walk to Tom's, the sound of Emma's footfalls as she ran away from me ringing in my ears. It's an hour-long walk from Park Slope, where Matt lives, to Tom's place in downtown Manhattan, but even the sun beating down on the Manhattan Bridge, sure to leave a sunburn on my collarbones, doesn't faze me.

After what Matt said, nothing can.

Even though he said nothing that I didn't know all along. I might've fallen for what the squad said about Emma loving me, but I always knew love wasn't real.

I walk off the bridge, my skin already prickling with the premonition of sunburn, and cross Chinatown. The smells of fish markets and fried dumplings mingle in the air. I make my way through the crowded streets, which are packed with tourists and market-goers.

I don't care about any of it. I can't stop thinking about Emma. The look in her eyes when she found out. The way she left me behind as soon as she knew the truth.

It's for the best, I tell myself forcefully. It would never have worked out anyway.

I'm so wrapped up in my thoughts that, for a moment, I forget why I've walked all this way. Then I remember I have to go upstairs and explain to Tom that he's a giant asshole who publicly humiliated his girlfriend for no reason.

My lower lip quivers at the thought. He's going to take it so hard.

Then again, so did Kate.

I walk up to the buzzer. He opens the door a second after I ring, his face melting into a smile when he sees me.

I grin back, but I can feel the terse stiffness in my jaw. "Hey."

"What's wrong?" he asks, his eyes darting to the tightness in my lips.

I shift my weight. My whole body is numb. "Can I come in?"

He steps aside in answer, opening the door wider to reveal his living room, which his mom has covered in kitschy tokens, colorful animal statuettes, and a wooden cutout that says *It's 5 O'Clock Somewhere.* I step through, interlacing my fingers as Tom leads me to his room.

I plop down on my usual seat at his desk chair, dabbing the sweat off my forehead, and watch Tom as he settles on the edge of the bed, staring at me. He normally lies back against his pillows and tosses me a video game controller as soon as I'm sitting, but he must have realized something's wrong, because he keeps his toes pressed against the carpet. His eyes are wide behind his glasses.

"What's going on?" he asks.

I clear my throat. "It's about Kate."

Tom stiffens. His anxious stare hardens into more of a glower.

"What about her?" he asks.

I stare at his feet. He's wearing his stupid banana socks. The sight of them makes my gut twist. How can I tell a guy who wears banana socks that he's the world's biggest jerk?

Well, second-biggest, after Matt. But then again, if you can't tell your best friend, who can you tell?

"She didn't sabotage us," I blurt.

Tom opens his mouth, probably to remind me what we saw together, so I push on before he can say anything. "We talked to Matt. He confessed to the whole thing. He was mad that you didn't help set him up with Emma, so he framed Kate to wreck your relationship. He made it look like Kate was sabotaging us, but it was him all along."

I talk fast, getting the whole story out before he can try to argue. He stares back at me, processing my words. He looks like he's been punched in the gut.

"What?" he whispers, hoarse.

"She didn't do anything wrong."

He looks at me. "I'm the asshole here, then."

I stare at him, not able to give him any kind of comforting response. It's true, and we both know it. I scoot the desk chair over, the legs scuffing the carpet, to wrap my arms around him.

"You were upset," I whisper into his chest.

He doesn't return the hug. His arms hang limply by his wiry torso. "That doesn't excuse anything. Even if she had lied to me, it was too much. And now . . ."

He trails off, letting his head hang. He exhales, a rush of air clipping past my ear.

"I have to make it right," he whispers, his breath hot against my cheek. "If she didn't—a text isn't enough."

I nod, getting caught in the fabric of his shirt. "It isn't."

He straightens. "I guess I can start by bowing out of the contest. If that's okay with you. I don't want to be in her way."

"Kate already dropped out of Emma's movie," I murmur.

Tom's face, somehow, falls more. "Because of me?"

He takes my silence as an answer.

"Well, tell Emma that I'm dropping out. Hopefully Kate will feel like she can participate again."

I pause. I know how much this means to him.

"It's the least I can do," he says, and I nod. Kate shouldn't lose out because he made a mistake.

I pull out my phone and type the text to Emma. If Kate enters the contest again, Emma could finish her movie. Her movie should be finished. Her face lights up when she talks about it. I've seen it. I get it now, after hearing her speech and listening to her talk about coming out, how much it means to her. But I falter before hitting send. "We're not exactly on speaking terms, I don't think."

Tom looks up at me. "What happened?"

"Matt told us what you guys did," I say.

Tom nods, dodging my gaze. "Sorry."

I'm not sure how to respond. Should I be mad? He did lie to me. Not any normal lie either—it was more of a giant campaign he recruited all my friends into, so that he could convince me that my rival was in love with me. When I remember the conversation I overheard, staged by Kate and Myrah in the middle of an empty room, it makes the hair on the back of my neck bristle with anger.

But on the other hand . . . if he hadn't said anything, I wouldn't know what it feels like to kiss Emma Hansen. And, contrary to what I might've thought before, kissing Emma Hansen feels pretty nice. If Tom and the rest of them hadn't lied, that would never have happened.

It's too much to figure out now, so I settle for shrugging and saying, "Thanks for apologizing."

I hit send on the text I composed to Emma.

My phone buzzes a moment later, and my heart buzzes with it.

Stop that, I say to myself as I check the screen. No good can come of it now. No good was ever going to come of it, but it's especially not going to happen now.

EMMA: Movie is off anyway. No time to finish. There's no way I can shoot enough footage and edit everything in two days.

I stare at the screen, my heart landing thickly in my stomach. This movie meant so much to her. Whatever's happening between us may be over, shattered with Matt's words, but maybe I can still fix this for her.

My fingers fly over my keyboard again, and I chuckle to myself. I can't believe that, after everything that happened, their stupid plan worked.

We're going to merge the groups again.

CHAPTER TWENTY-FIVE

Emma

I spend half of Wednesday morning in bed. Not out of laziness (well, partially) but because I can't stand the thought of facing my parents. I stay wrapped in my duvet, bundled against the frosty AC unit blasting from my window.

I don't even know what's bugging me so much. They didn't throw me out of the house. They didn't spit homophobic arguments at my face.

It was like they didn't care at all.

I spent so long working myself up to that moment. Months mulling over what I'd say. Countless hours panicking about how they'd react. And, granted, I went in totally blind, blurting out whatever incoherent half sentences I could muster through my own anxious numbness.

They acted like all that was nothing.

In a foolish moment, I wish for Sophia. She'd understand. But it's not like I can ever face her again. Instead I curl up under my duvet, pulling it most of the way over my head, and watch Lady Catulet romp around the mess of dirty laundry on my floor. It's hard to breathe through the thick duvet cover, but at least I'm hidden away.

Even though I'm kind of hoping my parents will try to come find me.

"Emma! You want me to make you breakfast before I go?" Mom yells from the kitchen.

I don't respond, instead listening to their scuffling as they bustle around the house, getting ready to go. Mom yells for me another time, and Dad tries after her.

I breathe against the mattress, not responding. Lady Catulet bounds onto the bed to poke at my feet, and I wiggle my toes for her. She pounces on them, and I bite back my giggle.

"She must be still asleep," Mom says to Dad at last.

Footsteps pound down the hall, and my door creaks open. I squeeze my eyes shut and slow my breathing. After a moment, the door closes again.

"Let her rest," Dad says. "She seems stressed, and I think . . ."

I don't get to hear what he thinks, because they continue their conversation on their way to work, the front door slamming behind them. Silence descends over the house.

I unfurl in the bed, a sudden urge to move pumping through my veins. I stretch my legs against the mattress.

Kicking the blankets off, I jump out of bed and dress, throwing clothes on at random. I glance in the mirror on my way out of the room, cringing at the deep imprints my pillow has left in my cheeks, but there's no time to fix it now.

I slip on my shoes and cross the hall to knock on Kate's door. Aunt Natalie opens it. She's holding a spatula dripping in waffle mix, which makes my stomach rumble. It's not like me to turn down an offer for breakfast.

"Is Kate up yet?" I ask.

"You can check her room," Aunt Natalie says, gesturing with the spatula.

I hustle down the hall, my stomach twisting. We've never had to make up after a fight before, because we've never fought. I have no idea what to say.

I burst into the bedroom, ready to apologize, but when I see her, I stop short. I was expecting her to still be a mess. But she's sitting cross-legged on her neatly made bed, her hair twisted into a loose braid that tumbles past her shoulder, light makeup dabbed across her face. More confusing yet, her bedspread is covered in piles of books. My books.

I blink, taking in the scene. Kate has never been into Shakespeare. She likes YA romances and old rom-coms.

"You okay?" I ask. How can I focus on making up when Kate is clearly in the middle of some kind of nervous breakdown?

"Me? Of course! I've been reading," Kate says. She's talking quickly, the words pouring out in a blur. "So far I've been through *The Taming of the Shrew* and *A Midsummer Night's Dream,* and now I'm onto *Much—*"

"Shakespeare kick?" I ask, taking in the pile.

Kate beams at me, but the cracks show in her smile.

"There's so many classics I've never gotten to, so I raided your room while you were out yesterday," Kate says, smiling, though it almost looks more like a grimace stretched across her face.

She holds up a few books from the stack next to her, as though this is supposed to be evidence of her sanity rather than clear proof she's gone completely off the rails.

"Are you sure you're okay?" I ask again, staring at the books.

"Sure," Kate says, shrugging. "How are you? Are you still mad at me?"

I wince. "Not really. Sorry I yelled at you."

She shakes her head. "Sorry I lied."

Her lower lip is trembling.

"Are you sure you're okay?" I ask again.

"Of course," Kate says. She pauses for a moment, tilting her head. "Well, I am a bit upset."

I take a step toward her, reaching out to hold her.

"Of course you are," I say, my voice breaking. "You still haven't let yourself *feel* anything about what happened with Tom, and—"

Kate waves a hand at me. "I'm upset about *The Taming of the Shrew.* It's so sexist."

I blink. "That's not—"

"We all put Shakespeare up on this pedestal, and tell his stories over and over again like they're so special, but that play is terrible to women," Kate says, not hearing me.

"No arguments here, but—"

"The whole premise is that this girl needs to be 'tamed' so she can be a good wife to this asshole?" Kate says.

I stare at her. I don't think I've ever heard her swear before.

And why is she going on about this? Still in full rant mode, Kate doesn't register my surprise as she presses on.

"What's up with that? What about her? What about how she feels? What about what she wants? What about the fact that she's a good person, and she tries hard to be a good friend and a good girlfriend and she got dumped on for no reason?" Kate's voice is wavering now, and I can tell she's on the edge of tears. "What about how she was humiliated in front of everyone and now she has to hide out while he can go on and pretend like nothing happened when he ruined everything?"

She bursts into tears, the dam finally crumbling under the weight of everything that's gone wrong. I can feel myself almost burst along with her, but I force myself to keep it together. Instead of falling apart, I climb onto the bed, kneeling up so that I'm taller than her, and wrap my arms around her shoulders.

"I'm so sorry, love," I whisper.

Her whole body shakes, racked with sobs. The front of my shirt grows damp, but I don't pull away. It's about time she let herself feel her own feelings, instead of worrying about everyone else's all the time.

"I don't get it," she says, sniffling. "How could he not trust me? I keep replaying all the things he said at the dance, and I don't understand how we went from that"—she stares off into space, her arms hanging limply at her sides—"to this."

I bite my lower lip. "About that . . ."

Kate looks up at me again, and I chew my fingernail. I meant so well, but I did the exact same thing to Kate and Tom that they did to me with Sophia. I guess this whole mess is my fault, after all.

"We . . . I set that up," I say.

"What do you mean?" Kate asks quietly.

"You guys were so obviously into each other, and you were both so painfully shy that we wanted to help, so we . . ." I inhale sharply, the light fragrance of the flowers Kate keeps all over her room calming me before I have to say Matt's name. After what I found out, the fact that he was ever involved makes everything that much more disgusting. "We put Matt in Tom's mask."

Kate stares at me, her eyes watering again. "Oh. Well."

For a moment, I think she might yell at me. That I might get the anger and disdain I deserve. For once.

But then Kate laughs a little. "I guess that makes us even."

I hang my head. "I came to apologize. I had no right to be so mad. Especially when I did the exact same thing."

"I get it, though," Kate says. "It's different, me and Tom, and you with Sophia."

"Exactly," I murmur. "Especially when . . . my parents . . . Well, I came out to them last night."

Kate gasps. "How did it go?"

I shrug. "Okay, I guess. They didn't seem to care."

"I'm sure they do," she says, nudging my shoulder with hers. "They probably don't know how to express it."

"I guess," I mutter.

"Why now?" she asks.

I swallow, staring at the poster of Monet's water lilies that

Kate has on the wall opposite her bed. "I guess . . . I was mad, and I took it out on you. And I'm sorry. Because I was mad at myself. All this time, the biggest thing that's been standing between me and love is . . . me. And that's . . ."

I trail off, and words fail, so I hug her again, because I have no idea what else I can do at this point to thank the girl who's seen me screw up everything and still loves me.

"How could he not trust me?" Kate whispers into my shoulder, her voice small.

"Because he's a huge asshole," I say, as firmly as I can, my hands tight on her back.

We pull apart, and Kate shakes her head at me.

"No, he isn't," she says. "What if I wasn't good enough? What he did was—"

Her words tear through me, pressing like hot needles against my skin. I can't believe Kate feels this way. I grab her shoulders, perhaps a little too hard, because her eyes widen as I give her a little shake.

"Kate. Listen," I say. "That's not true. You're the best person I know." I pause, taking a breath, and shake my head. "Actually, no. You're the best person. No qualifiers."

I take a deep breath, lowering my hands. They slide down her arms.

"Well," Kate says, staring down at her manicured fingernails, "I guess it was pretty terrible."

A bubble of pride swells in my chest. Kate calling someone out on their shittiness? Finally.

"Yes, thank you," I say, beaming.

"And an apology text? That's so not enough," Kate says. "I have to put myself first, I guess. Do what I need to do to be happy."

I reach over to hug her again. "Good. I'm proud of you."

Kate pulls away, scanning my face.

"What about you?"

I shrug. "What about me?"

"You and Sophia?" Kate says.

She looks so hopeful that it crushes my soul to do it, but I shake my head. It's not enough to deter Kate. But when it comes to this, apparently nothing will.

"You sure?" she asks.

"I don't know," I whisper. It's the closest thing to an admission that she'll get from me.

"Maybe she deserves a chance?" Kate asks.

I snort. "Maybe. No. She's Sophia. It would be . . . She's Sophia. And so much has happened. I guess . . . maybe. But the point is irrelevant. She was never in love with me. It was all a lie." I force a laugh. But then I stop myself. It's probably time I let myself feel my feelings, instead of brushing them off all the time. "Are you sure you're okay?"

"I will be," Kate says. "I'm going to focus on me for a bit."

I throw my hands up. "I never thought I'd see the day."

We laugh, and it's carefree for a moment, and nothing has ever felt so good.

"Tom dropped out of Sophia's movie," I tell her. "She told me last night. She wants us to merge the groups so that we can have something to turn in tomorrow."

Kate looks up at me, her eyes wavering, and I cross my fingers in my pocket.

"If Tom isn't part of the contest anymore . . ." Her voice trails off. "And Matt's admitted everything . . ."

"Do you want to join our group again?" I ask.

She nods, and I squeal, hugging her. "We'd better hurry, then. We're meeting at"—I swallow, willing myself to say her name despite the awkward fear clogging in my veins at the thought of seeing her again—"Sophia's place in a bit to see what we need to shoot to put the two movies together. And we have to finish the whole thing today. So."

Kate jumps out of bed, and I follow her, my gut churning. This should be interesting.

For two people who wanted to make such different movies that we needed to split the group over it, Sophia and I sure made similar movies. Not only did we choose the same shooting locations, but her character fits perfectly into my story. She's so angsty and confused that the coming out arc fits into the movie now. Even Myrah's on board. We have to shoot a few extra moments of footage to tie the two movies together, and then it'll be all set.

Maybe then my parents could see that coming out scene, and then they'd understand what last night was *supposed* to look like.

We're starting the day in the Brooklyn Botanic Garden,

which is in full summer bloom. Families mill around us, taking in the summer colors.

"Okay, so we need a scene where Myrah's character talks to yours, and they encourage each other to come out," I say to Sophia, keeping my eyes fixed on the checklist taped to the front of my notebook, rather than looking at her face. Even without making eye contact, my cheeks are burning. I tell myself this is because of the sweltering air around us, and force myself to go on. "And one where you talk to Kate's character about her feelings for Myrah. And maybe one with your character talking about rom—"

"I think I have something that could work for that," Sophia says. She's also keeping her head down, looking through her shot list.

"Okay," I say, clapping my hands together.

I turn away from Sophia, which is a relief, and to the rest of the crew, which pretty much negates the relief. Between Kate, who's playing with her earrings so much that her earlobes are starting to chafe, Myrah, whose eyes are all puffy for a reason she refuses to talk about, and Sophia, who has been going out of her way to not touch me all afternoon, it's not exactly the cheeriest crew.

"So, we're turning our two movies into one angsty rom-com that focuses on a girl struggling to find love even as she's dealing with a toxic relationship with her mom. I think both our films veered from what we'd initially planned tonally," I say, glancing at Sophia, "so this could work."

Sophia looks up at me, and we make eye contact for the

first time all afternoon. Her eyes send a jolt down my spine. *Remember how you thought she loved you?* a little voice cackles in the back of my head. Stupid.

Next to Sophia on the bench, Myrah's wiping her eyes again, and I exchange glances with Kate. She jerks her head over, and I nod in silent agreement.

"Let's take five, and then we'll get started."

Kate jumps up off the bench, and I take Myrah's arm, leading both of them off to the side. We walk down the path, leaving imprints in the grass with every step. We stop by the bright red arch framing the entrance to the Japanese garden. A brook flows by us, lapping over stones on its way under the bridge that leads to the Japanese arch.

"What's going on?" I ask, turning to face Myrah.

Myrah lifts her head to face us, revealing reddened eyelids and smudged mascara. "I think I need to break up with Peter."

"What happened?" I ask, my voice cracking. Hasn't she been through enough with all these breakups? Can't any of us find love and be happy?

"He didn't text me back yesterday," she says, her voice muffled.

I'm about to launch into my usual *You deserve better and all men are trash anyway. Are you sure you're not gay, cuz it's way more fun? No? Okay, well you deserve better anyway* spiel, but Kate coughs quietly.

"Is that it?" she asks gently.

Myrah and I stare at her. For a moment, the only sound that passes between us is the water flowing past us.

"Shouldn't he want to talk to me?" Myrah asks, crossing her arms.

Kate looks down at her fingernails. "He does, though. You guys talk all the time. It's okay to miss an evening. It doesn't mean you have to blow the whole thing up."

"It's not just that," Myrah says quietly. "He's not exactly super romantic. He hasn't done anything big for me, and I'm not gonna sit around waiting for him to create the perfect rom-com moment. Don't I deserve the perfect romance?"

"I don't think that's a thing," Kate says after a pause. "And honestly, I don't think it should be. The best love is matter-of-fact. It doesn't need those big gestures and those big romance moments. Real love comes in the everyday moments, the daily life you share."

I clench my fingers, ready to disagree, but Myrah, to my shock, nods.

"I see what you mean," she says, her voice so low, it's almost lost in the air.

"Maybe it's time to stop letting fear ruin everything before you've given it a chance," Kate says with a wise, teasing grin.

"Look at you," Myrah says. "One relationship, and you're suddenly the expert."

Kate tosses her hair in fake vanity, and we laugh.

We return to our set by the cherry trees. I follow them, trying to keep my face neutral so they don't know how much I disagree with their new supposedly profound thoughts.

I'm never going to give up on romance.

"Here are your new lines," I say, distributing hastily stapled scripts between the three of them. "Courtesy of the lovely and excellent Myrah."

Myrah takes an elaborate bow, and the rest of us burst into applause.

"Let's get going," I say, stepping behind the camera.

Sophia veers off to the side with her script. We agreed that, in the interest of time, we'll shoot each scene once with both cameras, so that we can cut together from both angles without having to do too many takes. The movie's already going to be all over the place in terms of video quality and cinematographic style, so we might as well lean into it. After all, we have to finish today, or else this was all for nothing.

The plan also has the added bonus that I can stand as far away from her as possible. I keep my eyes on my camera the whole time, keenly aware of Sophia doing the same thing a few feet away.

When we finish in the gardens, we're on to a nearby thrift store. The plan was to shoot a cute montage of Kate and Myrah trying on new clothes, but then Sophia dares me to try on these purple leather pants with fringes all down the sides, so obviously I have to make her wear an oversized poncho with a neon zigzag pattern. We end up strutting down the aisles and trying to top each other's finds. I trip over the giant heels she picked out for me, taking a rack down with me. I tumble into a pile of hangers and mismatched clothes.

"Are you okay?" Sophia rushes over to me, and relief floods her face when she sees that I'm laughing.

"Yeah," I say, taking her outstretched arm. She pulls me up, and I teeter in the heels, stumbling forward into her arms. I look up at her. Her face is so close to mine, and the memory of her lips on mine flashes through my mind.

I swallow, and force myself to stand upright and move away from her. *She never loved you,* I remind myself. She was never mine to hope for.

I need to stop hoping for her.

CHAPTER TWENTY-SIX

SOPHIA

. . . .

"Cut," Emma calls.

I don't look at her as I switch off my camera. I don't look at any of them. Kate and Myrah must know that I know about their matchmaking scheme, and Emma's been avoiding me all afternoon. I thought we might have shared a moment when I saved her from falling for a second time, but she's back to staring too hard at her camera to avoid looking at me. I'm ready for the tacky store carpeting to swallow me whole.

"I think that's everything," I say, handing my camera to Emma.

She takes it without looking at me, and tucks it into her camera bag. "Guess that means it's time for me to disappear into my editing cave. I have about"—she checks her phone—"six hours before the deadline, which is not enough time, but we're going to make this work."

Myrah cheers as Emma dashes off to the subway with the SD cards, leaving the rest of us to pack up the equipment.

Because that's what I needed this afternoon. Some alone time with Emma's best friends. I keep a laser focus on the tripod I'm disassembling to avoid looking at them, but I can still sense them exchanging glances as we work.

"I'm sorry," Kate says as I kneel to unscrew the lower half of the tripod legs. "About the lying."

My fingers stumble on the screws. I know Kate technically participated, but she's not the one I feel betrayed by. Tom's the one who's been my best friend since forever. "It's okay. I get why you guys did it. Is Emma okay?" I ask without looking up at her. "I know she was upset when Matt—"

Kate bobbles her head from side to side. "She's been better. She, uh, came out to her parents."

The tripod slips out of my hands entirely. It clatters against the carpeted floor, and I scramble to pick it up.

I know that fear, the kind that settled so deep into my bones that it's still a part of me, even though I've been out for ages. Before I told my parents that I'm a lesbian, the fact that they didn't know was all I could think about. I had to question everything I said to them, double-checking every thought before I said it aloud, so afraid of outing myself by accident. I spent every conversation bitter that I had to filter myself, and simultaneously afraid that I hadn't filtered enough. Knowing that Emma has gone through it all on her own, when I could have helped her, breaks my heart all over again.

"What?" Myrah gasps. "And they were totally understanding and she hyped it all up for nothing, right?"

"Not exactly," Kate whispers. "They kind of brushed it off.

She's pretty upset about it. I think she wanted it to be a bigger deal."

I fold the disassembled tripod into the bag and zip it up. I'm the only one of us who can understand what she's been through, who could truly be there for her. Maybe I should go to her. I could be there for her now in a way that none of the others can.

But then I remember the way she ran away from me, after Matt told us what happened, and I realize that's not true.

I'm the only one who can't be there at all.

When I get home, I dial my mom's number, praying even as I lift my phone to my ear that she doesn't pick up.

She does.

"Hi, Mom," I murmur into the receiver.

Her voice crackles with surprise on the other end. "Hi, honey. Is everything okay?"

"Yeah," I say, leaning back into my pillows. "I wanted to see how you were doing."

"That's nice, hon," she says. "I was worried. You don't normally call."

I swallow. There's the side of guilt. Why does it have to come with every interaction we have?

"I miss you," I say, my voice cracking. It's true. I miss the days we used to spend getting manicures and gossiping, without Paris sprawled around us like so much not-home.

"I miss you too, love," she says. I wonder if she means it at all the same way I do, or if she means that it's been a while since we've seen each other. Maybe a little bit of both? I hope so.

"How's Paul?" I ask, struggling to keep the bitterness in my voice at bay. I don't know why I called, but it definitely wasn't to have a fight.

I get up, pace around the coffee table. I stare at my feet, measuring even steps along the hardwood floors.

"He's good," Mom says. The receiver clicks and crackles as she talks. We're using a free app that makes it easy to set up international calls, so it's worth it, I guess, but it makes her sound even farther away. "We're both good. I had another job interview today."

"Oh yeah? What for?"

"Tour guide for art history walking tours of the city," she says, and I can hear the note of pride in her voice.

"That's great," I say, my voice straining. "Congrats."

"What about you?" Mom asks. "How's New York?"

"Good," I mutter. "Nice to be back."

I realize too late that she'll probably take it as a dig. Before she can layer on another guilt trip, I speak up again.

"Hey, Mom?"

"Yes, honey?"

I pause. I'm not sure what I want to say next. But then I remember what Tom said about me when I got back, and how much unnecessary angst is dripping from every second of the movie I made without Emma. No matter what it is I *want* to say, I know what I *have* to say.

"I'm sorry if I was an asshole in Paris."

Mom doesn't say anything. The awkward sound of her breathing crackles over the line. I'm not even sure what I'm hoping for. For her to say I wasn't? That would be a lie. For her to apologize too? I don't think she'd even know what she's apologizing for.

"I'm sorry too," she says, but her tone makes it clear I was exactly right. She has no idea what to be sorry for. She only knows that I want her to apologize for something. And maybe she's right, and she shouldn't have to apologize to her surly teenage daughter for moving on. But she never even thought about keeping me there with her, and even though I know that she didn't want to uproot me permanently or whatever, it's hard not to let that one sting a little.

Maybe, when she comes to the screening to see the movie, and she sees how hard this whole transition was for me, she'll understand.

"Don't be," I mutter. "I gotta get going. Movie work."

"Sure, hon," she says. "Work hard."

"Bye." I hang up before she can say it back, and toss my phone into my purse. I want to storm straight to my room and throw myself onto my bed and be dramatic about all these feelings I can't identify, but that's when Dad intercepts me on his way in from the kitchen.

"Hi, Sausage," he says when he walks in.

I grin at him, a little guilty. I didn't realize he was home, or I would've tucked myself away in my room to make that call.

"Are you ever mad at Mom?"

He blinks and takes a slow sip of his coffee. "Why would I be?"

"She left us," I point out.

"We got divorced before she left. It's not like I feel abandoned," he says with a smile. It fades after a moment. "Do you?"

I shrug. "I don't know. I guess I feel like love is dead."

"Because it didn't work out with your mom and me?" Dad asks.

I shift on the couch, tucking my foot under my other leg. "Why did you get divorced?"

Dad sits on the couch, balancing his coffee mug on his knee. "Things weren't working anymore."

I stare at him. "Could you be a little more vague? I don't need too many details."

Dad chuckles. The dark liquid swirls in his mug as he moves. "You were there; you saw it. We fought every day. About money, about distribution of household chores, about anything. Were you happy, the last year we were married?"

I look down at the armchair pillow. Before my parents decided to get divorced, I spent a lot of time watching movies in my room, the sound turned all the way up in my earbuds to drown out their yelling.

"No," I whisper. "But I was happy before then. When the three of us did everything together. Why did it ever have to change?"

Dad nods. "I was happy too. But your mom is happy again now, and so am I."

I look around his new IKEA-laden apartment. It's brand-new, a fresh place that hasn't heard any parental screaming.

"And she's found someone new to love," Dad goes on. "And I will too, someday. If this OkCupid thing is all it's cracked up to be. And in the meantime," he adds, looking down at his mug, "I have coffee. Which is the real love story here."

I twist my lip in thought, remembering the way Mom and Paul laughed together at the dinner table, and argued playfully on long metro rides, and always split a dessert. They're good for each other.

And my dad always looks so hopeful when he's getting ready for a first date. Why have I been begrudging them their new happiness?

Maybe love isn't all the way dead. Maybe it didn't die with my family. Maybe my family isn't dead at all. Both my parents are happier now than they were before.

Maybe I can be too.

I laugh. "Hey, Dad? Can we have a family dinner sometime this week? Just the two of us?"

Dad smiles. "Yeah, of course. You pick the day."

"Thursday," I say, getting up, and I bend over and kiss him on the cheek before heading to my room.

Emma must be some kind of editing whiz, because she turns in our movie on time. And, five days later, we get an email inviting all of us to the screening. We made it to the top ten out of over fifty teams. This is everything I've been working for. If I invite my mom to the screening, she could finally understand why I need her to apologize. She could fix things between us.

I'm the only one in the squad who understands what Emma is going through. I'm the only one who can't be there for her. But that doesn't mean I can't do anything.

I close the email app and open my text chain with her.

SOPHIA: My mom can't make it to the screening after all. You should have my plus-one. That way you can take both your parents.

If she says yes, it means I don't get to bring my mom out and show her what a big deal this movie is to me with this screening. I read the text four times before I hit send, fingers shaking, but as soon as the little whoosh sounds, I know I've made the right choice.

CHAPTER TWENTY-SEVEN

Emma

. . . .

I've spent so much time fiddling with the edge of my dress that a little hole has appeared in the lace. I stick my pinkie inside and wiggle it. It tears the lace more.

My parents are by the Corner Hotel bar sipping glasses of wine. They ordered me a Coke. It's sitting untouched by their glasses, but I can't bring myself to join them. Not before the screening starts and they've seen the movie.

At the thought, my fingers go right back to widening the lacy hole in my hem.

"Are you excited?" Kate asks, maneuvering through the crowds to reach my side with a glass of Sprite in one hand. She's gone full movie star in her look tonight, with a floor-length light pink dress she's been working on all month.

"*Excited* is one word for it." I press my palm against my stomach, as though that could steady the butterflies.

Kate takes my hand into both of hers and squeezes it

against her chest. "I'm so proud of you. I know this wasn't easy. I hope it pays off."

Before I can answer, Sophia ducks behind a waiter to join us.

And I forget everything we were talking about. Because she looks like an actual princess. Her hair is too short to do anything fancy, but she's wearing a flowy yellow dress that makes her look like she's floating when she walks.

I catch myself before I let my gaze linger too long on her glossed lips.

"You guys look so nice," I say, looking down at my own outfit choice, a knee-length dress that's too nice to wear to school but that's leaving me feeling way underdressed next to them. "I didn't realize we were going full Hollywood."

Sophia laughs, and the richness of the sound thrums into my chest. I push it out, forcing myself to remember Matt's words. Kiss or no kiss, she never really loved me.

"Any excuse to be fabulous," she says, winking at me.

"Oh? Is that what they say in France?" I poke her in the ribs, and she has the grace to blush.

"As a matter of fact, they do," she says. "I don't know if you've heard, but fashion is kind of a big deal there." She glances at my outfit with a soft smirk. "More than it is here, anyway."

I slap her shoulder with the back of my hand. "Sorry my American style isn't good enough for you."

Her eyes soften as they meet mine. "There's nothing about you that isn't good enough, Hansen."

I open my mouth, but I have no idea how to respond. I

stare at her, keenly aware of Kate standing next to us with her mouth agape. Without looking at Kate, I reach over and lift her chin to close it.

"We should go find seats," Sophia says, breaking the moment.

"Myrah's saving us some," Kate says, and leads us from the lobby into the theater. "You know she brought Peter?"

"Looks like you gave her some good advice," I mutter. Nice to know that giving up on romance works.

The screening is in the same place where the mixer was, but this time our seats are closer to the front, in the contestants' section. We walk down the red carpeted steps, and as soon as we reach our seats, I crane my neck to search for my parents in the crowd. They haven't gotten to their seats yet, but Peter is near the back saving spots for all our plus-ones. As I sit, I angle myself so that I can see him out of the corner of my eye. After all, the whole point of this is that I can watch them watching my movie.

Well, that and finding out if I get to go to LA. My chance at a professional film career rides on how our short does tonight.

I twist the hem of my dress around my fingers as we wait. The lights dim and brighten three times, and the theater becomes much more crowded as everyone hurries in to find their seats. Within a few minutes, Alan strides out in front of the screen.

"Welcome, all, to the final screening of this year's NYC–LA Film Festival. We're so excited about the talented emerging artists who made it to the top ten. Let's give them a hand."

The theater bursts into applause and cheers. I exchange looks with Myrah, who winks at me, and my gut tightens. This is it. Everything I've ever wanted is right at my fingertips.

"Let's get started with the films."

He gestures to the screen, and the lights shut off around us as the screen comes to life with the first movie. It's not mine, and I'm momentarily relieved, until I realize this means I have to wait longer.

As I watch my competitor's work on the screen, I feel Sophia's shoulder shaking against mine. I turn to see her shaking in a fit of silent laughter.

"What?" I whisper.

She presses her knuckles to her lips, suppressing a fit of giggles. "It's so good," she whispers through her fingers. "Ours is trash fire next to this."

I look back up at the screen. The shots are carefully composed, and the camerawork is smooth. It's well-acted—the actress on-screen is delicately tearing up in the last scene, and at least six people in the audience are crying right along with her.

Sophia's right. This looks like an actual movie. And our film, despite our best efforts, was smushed together from two wildly different stories and shot on cameras with aggressively contrasting video quality. The team behind this film clearly spent the past few weeks focusing on their movie. We spent the past few weeks so wrapped up in our own drama, it's a miracle we finished at all.

And then I'm laughing too. Sophia and I lean into each other, tears leaking out of the corners of our eyes as the second movie comes on. It has exquisite cinematography and a well-designed color scheme that probably has deep symbolism. I dab at my eyes as Kate shoots us her best mom look.

It only makes Sophia laugh harder.

The second movie, which followed a woman trying to escape her abusive husband, flickers to an end, and ours takes the screen. Sophia and I exchange looks before turning back to the screen. This is it.

It didn't come out too bad, all things considered. The shots we put together from the two cameras obviously don't match, and there are two little plot holes we didn't have time to fix completely when we combined the two movies. But overall, we created a coherent story that doesn't look half-bad.

I twist in my seat, scanning the crowd for my parents. They're staring at the screen, and they're holding hands. I see my dad whisper something into my mom's ear, and she nods. Her head leans over to rest on his shoulder.

I spend the rest of the movie staring at them. I only duck once, when my dad looks like he's glancing in my direction, but it turned out that he was scratching his nose. I can't tell what they're thinking at all.

What if they hate it? What if they decide to un-accept me after they see it? Is that a thing?

By the time the movie ends, I can barely breathe.

Once all the films have played, the lights flicker back on, and Alan returns to the front of the room, this time holding a big envelope. "We're so proud of all these entries. Let's give it up for our young artists, folks!"

Everyone cheers.

"But now we're ready to announce our winner," Alan says, tapping his finger against the envelope. "The first-place prize includes a scholarship and a premiere party in LA, where the team will have the chance to meet with industry professionals from all over the biz."

Sophia and I glance at each other, and I bite my knuckle to keep from laughing again.

"And the winner is . . ." Alan takes his time opening the envelope. "Rebecca Lim with her film *At the River's Edge!*"

The audience bursts into applause, and I join in enthusiastically. Kate lays a comforting hand on my shoulder, but I shrug at her with a smile. Their movie was good. They deserved to win.

I glance back over at my parents, who exchange disappointed looks as they applaud Rebecca Lim. LA or no LA, I might have gotten what I really needed out of this movie.

"Hey, congrats," Sophia says, nudging me. "I know that wasn't easy for you to make."

"You too," I say.

"True," she says. "But I know it wasn't easy for you to show."

I look back at my parents, who are standing and gathering their stuff. Dad's craning his neck, looking for me.

I turn back to Sophia. "Yeah. Thanks."

She smiles at me for a moment, her eyes meeting mine. I stare back at her, yearning to bridge the space between us, but I know it can never happen. She doesn't love me like that, never has.

"Good luck," she says.

My lower lip trembles for a moment as I waver under the weight of my own indecision, and when we stand, I pull her into a hug. She hums with surprise for a moment, then wraps her arms around my shoulders, crushing me into her bony chest. Her hair smells like peach conditioner, and her skin smells like rose water. I squeeze her for a moment before letting her go.

"I should go see my parents," I tell her.

Kate hugs me from behind, and Myrah gives me a thumbs-up as I wind my way through the crowd to find my parents outside. Dad's already called an Uber for us.

"Congratulations," Mom says, beaming when she sees me.

"Thanks."

Mom pulls me into a hug. "I hope you're not upset you didn't win. Getting here is such a huge honor, and it'll still look great on your college apps. And your movie was so good. Personally, I disagree with their decision."

I giggle. "I'll tell them you said so."

Dad thumps me on the back. "Great job, kiddo. I liked your movie."

We pile into the car. Once sitting, I knock my knees together, not sure what to say. I hoped that, once they saw the movie, they'd bring up my coming out. Instead they spend the car ride chatting about how well my camerawork is coming along, and how great this will look on my college apps.

I hope they're right, but it's not what I want to talk about right now.

The car drops us off in front of our building, and I follow

them into our apartment, chewing my tongue until it's ready to burst. And then, when the door has closed behind us and my parents are settled on the couch, I let it.

"Being bi is a big deal to me," I say as I cross the living room to stand by them. "I spent a lot of time acting like because I could still end up with a boy, it's not a big deal. But it is, and it's a part of me no matter who I date. It took me a long time to work up the courage to tell you, and you can't dismiss it."

The words tumble from my lips, leaving me panting as I stare at my parents, waiting for them to respond.

"I didn't want you to think it changes the way I see you," Mom says. "I'm glad you told us, and I'm glad it's a part of who you are."

Dad nods. "I thought I was supposed to be all . . . cool with it."

"You are," I say, laughing. "Don't play it too cool, though, okay?"

"Fair enough," Dad says with a chuckle.

Mom hugs my waist. "I'm proud of you, sweetie. For telling us. I know it must've been hard. And for making that movie. It was good. I don't care what those snobby festival people think."

"The movie that won was way better," I say.

"But nowhere near as brave." Mom sniffs. "Yours was beautiful. Thank you for sharing it with us."

Behind me, I hear my dad sniffle, and his arms wrap around me and Mom to join the hug. I lower myself to join them on the couch, and we fall into the pillows.

"I get it, honey," he whispers. "It's a big deal to us too. In the best way."

I let my shoulder muscles relax with relief. I was afraid they'd push back or try to lecture me or something.

Instead we end up in a warm pile on the couch, watching HGTV, right where we belong.

I stare at the ceiling, the glow from my phone lighting up the room. I check the time, out of desperation, to see 3:13 a.m. staring back at me. I fall onto the pillow, forcing my eyes shut. But then visions of Sophia's lips moving toward mine flash across my eyelids, and my eyes bounce open again right away. If sheer exhaustion can't glue them shut, I don't know what will. I flip over and pick up my phone again, the light shining over Lady Catulet's eyes as she peers at me from her perch on my pillow.

Kate says I can always talk to her if there's something on my mind. It's 3:15 a.m., and my thoughts are thick with Sophia. The way she laughed during our stakeout. The fierceness with which she helped me confront Matt. The softness of her lips.

I'd say that counts as "on my mind."

EMMA: *I think you're right. I think I do love her. What the hell am I supposed to do with that?!*

CHAPTER TWENTY-EIGHT

SOPHIA

I walk from the Corner Hotel to Tom's place, a goofy smile plastered on my lips the whole time. The look on Emma's face while she was talking to her parents told me everything I needed to know. I did the right thing, giving her my plus-one spot.

Nighttime in New York is the best time to deal with emotions. The sky is pitch dark, but the city is lit up with a thousand streetlights and car headlights and office light pouring out from windows. I match the pace of my fellow New Yorkers clipping down the sidewalk. We get a bad rap for this, but I think it's nice. I like to think that, whatever place we're all in a rush to get to, there are loved ones waiting there for us.

That's certainly the case for me, I think as I reach Tom's corner of the East Village. If our friendship could survive these rocky few weeks, it can survive anything.

My weird euphoria fades when I buzz Tom's apartment. Even if Emma has sorted out her situation with her parents, things between us remain unsettled. What Matt told her ruined any possibility of an "us." But then Tom beams when I reach his bedroom, and I can't help but smile again.

"How was the screening?"

"It was good," I say with a shrug. "We lost."

"Kate must be disappointed," Tom says.

I plop down at his desk chair and spin it around. "You miss her, huh?"

"I want her back," Tom says, his voice cracking.

"I know how you feel."

"What do you mean?"

I sigh, parsing through my thoughts as I struggle to translate the turmoil in my heart into words. "I don't know. It's . . . Well, that trick you guys played on me and Emma threw me for a loop."

"Sorry," Tom says, wincing. His glasses tilt at the movement, and I resist the urge to straighten them for him.

I force a laugh. I didn't come here to fight, and I don't want to.

"It's okay," I say. "It helped me realize how I feel about her. But she thinks it means I never loved her, and that anything I say now is fake."

If only there were some way to show her that wasn't true. How can I make her understand what I've come to realize myself—that our arguing has always been a front for something more?

I bolt upright in my chair. If there's one thing that's always meant the world to Emma, it's Kate. Specifically, a certain plan I refused to be a part of when I first got back.

I turn to Tom, grinning. "We have to come up with a way to get you back with Kate."

"How?" Tom asks. "I was so horrible to her."

I think for a moment, my lips twisting, until the perfect idea comes to me. A chance to go back. A chance to redo it all. To tell Emma the truth this time. To make her see. "I wasn't part of the first matchmaking plan, but I think we can still use it."

Tom squints at me. "Huh?"

I jump up and grab his hand. "We need to go buy some poster board."

He follows me, bemused, as I take the stairs two at a time all the way down. We'll need glitter too.

Once we reach Duane Reade, I stock up on poster board and glitter pens. Tom makes me stop at the bodega on our way home to pick out flowers. We stay up until way too late, circles forming under our eyes as we perfect the drawings on the poster and argue about what songs to add to the playlist, and dig up his mask from the dance. I have to find mine when I get home.

By the time I'm heading home, I'm smiling the whole way. Maybe Kate and Tom have a shot at this love thing after all. And maybe, if this works, and if I turn out to be the luckiest girl in the world, maybe I do too.

When I get home, Dad is still out on his date, the first second date he's been on since the divorce. I take a deep breath as I close the door behind me, letting the silence fall over the apartment. It doesn't feel as heavy on my shoulders as it used to. Sometimes you have to be the loved one that other people rush home to, and I guess that means being okay with sitting in an empty apartment for a while.

I kick my shoes off into the closet and drop down onto the couch. I swing my legs up over the side, which Mom never lets me do, and hook my phone up to the speakers so I can play all the songs Dad doesn't like. I slide my phone onto the coffee table and stare at the ceiling, bouncing my foot along to the rhythm and trying not to think about Emma.

I fail miserably. She's all I can think about. Her laugh, high-pitched in a way that would be kind of melodic if it weren't so loud. The way her lips felt against mine, soft and urgent at the same time. Even the insults she threw at me when I got back are pretty funny, thinking about them now.

After a moment, I grab my phone again, and I pound out a text to Tom. Just because romance didn't work out for my parents doesn't mean it won't work out for me.

SOPHIA: you guys were right. I really like Emma. A lot.

I hit send and wait until my phone says it's been delivered to Tom, then fall onto the couch, taking up all the room, and wait for it to buzz. I have no idea if something with Emma is still possible, but all I can do now is hope it is.

CHAPTER TWENTY-NINE

Emma
· ·

The closer we get to the teen center, the more Kate's hands seem to tremble.

"You ready?" I ask, exaggerating the pep in my voice with an openmouthed smile. I'm here for moral support. It's her first day back since Tom yelled at her last week, and she begged me to come so she wouldn't have to face her coworkers' judgy looks alone.

She looks unsteady on her legs. Looking down at me, she shakes her head. "No."

I put my hands on my hips, tilting my head. "Come on. What happened to the new and improved Katerina Perez, ready to show the world exactly how little she cares what they think?"

She even dressed the part. The dress she picked out for today accentuates all her curves, and she went with a bolder makeup look than usual. Her eyeliner is so sharp, it could kill a man. She looks like a totally gorgeous badass.

But now she's shrinking herself again, her toes scuffing against the pavement. "That was a lot easier the other day, when it was just with you. How can I face everyone else?"

I grab her by the wrist. I'll drag her into the building kicking and screaming if I have to. She can't back out of returning to work now.

"Come on," I say, pulling her by the arm.

"Nope," Kate says, even though she's already trailing after me.

"I'll be with you the whole time," I remind her, looking over my shoulder to give her a thumbs-up.

Kate takes a deep breath to steel herself as we reach the doors. "Fine. Let's do this."

"That you can, love," I tell her.

I pull open the door for her to walk through. I stick up my hand, and she gives me a high five on her way in. She throws her shoulders back as she passes me.

As soon as we cross the threshold, Kate gasps. She stops short, blocking my view of whatever she's looking at.

I walk around her to see a giant poster draped across the staircase wall, reading ROOFTOP DANCE in glittery letters, with an arrow pointing to the elevator. A path of sunflower petals leads us to it.

We hurry into the elevator, exchanging looks, but don't say anything the whole ride up. She steps out as soon as the elevator doors slide open, her mouth ajar when we push open the door leading to the outside.

The whole place is decorated just like for the dance, with

lanterns strung above us and gentle music playing on the breeze. Tom stands between two trees, which he's used to string up a banner that reads I'M SORRY. It flutters in the breeze. He's holding a handful of sunflowers wrapped carefully in pink tissue paper.

Kate walks down the rows of tables to join Tom under the banner. She looks like she's floating, her eyes dazed. Sophia is sitting at a nearby table, chin resting in her cupped hand. I waver for a moment. Should I sit next to her? Will she read into it if I do?

I take a deep breath before crossing over and lowering myself onto the chair next to hers. We're surrounded by groups of people, all busying themselves pretending not to be listening. I glance around the roof, and realize that more than one person is holding a mask, which must have come from the empty box Sophia has on the table behind her.

Tom holds out the flowers to Kate.

"Did you do this?" I whisper.

She nods, looking up to meet my eyes. "I know how much it meant to you. I'm sorry I wasn't part of the plan the first time around, but I'm hoping I can make up for lost time."

"I didn't know how to say I was sorry," Tom says to Kate. "I'm so, so sorry."

"I get why you were upset," Kate says. She's not looking straight at him, but a pink tint is already flowering in her cheeks.

"I could've handled it better," Tom says, in the understatement of the year.

"Well, yeah," Kate says with a smile. "Pretty much any other way would've been better."

Hearing her say that, my chest swells with pride. Look at her go, asserting her own wants and needs. I beam at her.

"I'm sorry," Tom says again. "My text wasn't enough. I wanted everyone who saw my outburst to see my apology, so everyone can see that it wasn't your fault. It was all mine. You're so special, Kate. I'm sorry I did that to you." He gestures to the flowers. "Is it cheesy to say I picked these out because you're such a genuine ray of sunshine, and you bring happiness to everyone you touch?"

"Yes," Kate says. She takes the flowers anyway.

As more people arrive for the day, the crowd of onlookers swells behind us. They're all silent, not even pretending like they're not listening.

Tom gestures to the mask he's wearing. "It wasn't me. At the dance."

Kate shoots me a look before turning to him. "I know."

I glance at Sophia, and she grins. "Thanks for doing this," I whisper to her.

She shrugs. "It's the least I can do. I know how much it means to you."

We turn to the scene unfolding in front of us.

"Well," Tom says with a blush. "I don't know what you thought I said, but I want to tell you the truth now. I think you're beautiful, and sweet, and kind. I think you're the best person I've ever known. And . . . I love you."

The simplicity of his words brings out their truth, and tears spring into my eyes.

Maybe Kate was right. Maybe matter-of-fact love is the truest kind. Because now, listening to Tom, I realize that he doesn't need to say anything else. He's already said everything that matters.

But I guess the moment is too good to last, because Matt pushes through the crowd. The groups of kids and counselors part as he shoves his way to us.

"Re-creating the dance?" he says with a sneer. "Original, Tom. You were quick to forgive, huh?"

I jump out of my seat, ready to hit someone (namely Matt), but Sophia beats me to the punch.

Not literally. She stands up and starts talking before I can jump him.

"Oh, hey, man. The head of the center is looking for you," she says in a would-be casual tone. "Something about bullying and harassing an employee on one of her outside ventures?"

I smirk, and Matt's face falls.

"That's not true," he says, his voice faltering.

Sophia shrugs. "Take it up with him. You might want to come up with a more solid defense, though. I heard him talking about legal action."

I glance at her, and she shrugs. There's probably not much legal action we can take, but it's worth an empty threat to see the fear flash through Matt's eyes.

Kate stares at Matt, her whole face crumpled. I'm jumping for joy, but seeing her hurt breaks my heart. She always wants to see the best in people. Especially the ones she loves.

She walks over to him. "Matt, wait."

Matt turns to her, hopeful. "Come with me? Help me sort this out?" he asks.

In response, Kate slaps him across the face.

I swear. Katerina Perez. Slaps him. Across the face.

Matt screams, hand flying to his cheek in shock. I turn to smile at Sophia, but she has disappeared. I scan the crowd for her, but I can't find her.

"Can I go back to my romantic gesture now?" Tom asks.

Kate laughs. "It's okay. I forgive you. I think we should ease back into it a bit, but—"

Pop music erupts over the speakers, cutting her off. Tom grins, arms stretched out to Kate. She takes his hands, and he spins her into his arms.

Around us, the rooftop has turned into a dance floor. Tom and Kate sway to the music, not taking their eyes off each other. Nearby, Myrah and Peter are twirling around one of the tables. I wave at him, and he spins her in our direction.

I turn to see Sophia making her way to us. She has a huge grin plastered on her face, and I can't help but return it. Even if she's way too pleased with herself for how this came together.

"You did all this for Kate and Tom?" I ask when she reaches us.

"Well," she says, her voice slightly raised so I can hear her over the blaring music and dancing crowd around us, "I guess I also did it for you. I know how much that matchmaking plan meant to you. I wish I'd been a part of it the first time around."

I gaze at her, not sure what to say. Why would she do all of this for me?

"I wish I'd done a lot of things differently," Sophia goes on. "I wish it hadn't taken our friends coming up with a ridiculous plan for me to realize how I feel about you. How I think I've always felt about you. It wasn't them making stuff up. Don't you remember how we danced together?"

I look down. I do remember. There was a moment there, something that passed between us. Before Kate, Tom, and Myrah conspired to make us believe we were in love, something already existed between us.

"They might not have realized it—hell, *I* might not have realized it," she says, taking my hands, "but they were telling the truth."

"What do you mean?" I whisper, looking over my shoulder, where the rest of the squad stands, watching us.

Without a word, Tom hands me his phone. I look down at the screen, bemused, to find a text chain between him and Sophia.

A text chain about me.

Laughing, Kate pulls her phone out of her pocket and, before I can stop her, thrusts it into Sophia's hands.

Sophia and I look at each other, and a smile twists my lips. There's nowhere else to hide. I look down, scrolling through her messages to Tom. I scroll faster and faster until the words blur together, though I'm not sure if it's because of the speed or because my eyes are watering.

When I finally look up, the tension between us has melted away.

There's nowhere left to hide.

"'I feel like my heart is going to burst out of my rib cage,'" Sophia reads. "Real original."

I laugh. "Hey. You wrote that the thought of me makes you want to sing, but also to die. At least I get points for eloquence."

Sophia looks down at my phone, scrolling through it again. "You said that you wish you could go back to the night of the mixer and tell me everything you held back because you were afraid."

"Yeah, well," I say, scrolling through the bits I missed because the tears blurred my vision. "You said that you feel like you can tell me anything."

"Here you wrote, 'I think I love her more than David Tennant,'" Sophia says, smiling triumphantly. "I think I win."

"Damn," I say, but I'm smiling uncontrollably. Losing has never felt quite this good.

I can't look away from her eyes. I forget anyone else is there, even though there's music blaring and the floor is shaking a little from the early-morning rave.

"They didn't lie," Sophia says softly. "I was always in love with you."

I look down at Tom's phone, the one she blew up late into the night, talking about me. About how much she likes me. It terrifies me to my very core, but I believe her.

And not because of this grand gesture she made, re-creating the whole dance. It's because of the way she laughed during our apology meal. The way her eyes softened when I confided in her. The way she's always made me laugh, even when I thought I hated her. All the little everyday moments that have warmed my heart countless times add up to this.

Without saying anything else, I pull her toward me. Our

lips meet, her touch warm and soft against me, and I melt. The insecurity and the fear and everything that stood between us melts with me, until there's nothing left but her skin and her lips pressed against mine.

"I love you," she whispers against my lips.

I blink for a moment. This is everything I've ever wanted, but I always pictured it so differently. I pictured the grand love my parents had, the great speeches at the end of rom-coms, the romantic gestures that never failed to make me cry.

But all of those wild fantasies of what great love should be pale in comparison to what exists now, for real, between me and Sophia and the breath of air between our lips.

So I say the only thing I can, because it's the only thing that needs to be said. "I love you too."

Myrah clears her throat, and we break apart.

"Great. This is great," she says.

Sophia grins, but turns my face with her fingers so that she can kiss me again. And before I can stop myself, we're full-on making out in the middle of the rooftop.

"Oh, gross," Tom mutters. "Was this a bad idea?"

"Probably," Kate says.

I don't take the bait. Sophia is too warm. Eventually, though, we have to come up for air. That's when I realize my face is burning.

"I can't believe that after years of listening to you bitch about how dumb relationships are, I'm going to have to watch you make out all the time," Myrah says, arms folded. Peter wraps his arm around her, and my heart swells.

"Sorry, buddy," Tom says, reaching over to pat her shoulder. "We're too good at matchmaking."

Sophia and I laugh, intertwining our fingers, our lips meeting one more time.

And I guess Tom is right.

For all our faults, we're pretty good matchmakers.

ACKNOWLEDGMENTS

This book couldn't have happened without the support of so many people, and I'm forever grateful to have each of them in my life.

Penny Moore, my wonderful agent, I am beyond grateful for your guidance, wise words, and tireless work for me and this book. You're a superstar, and I can never thank you enough!

I'm eternally grateful to my editor, Kelsey Horton. Thank you for championing this story and helping me find its heart. I *know* I love your vision for Sophia and Emma!

Thank you to Bara MacNeill and Colleen Fellingham, my copyeditors; Jeff Östberg, who designed the most gorgeous cover I could've imagined; and the whole team at Penguin Random House who worked to make this book the best it could be.

To my Pitch Wars mentors, Sonia Hartl and Annette Christie, thank you for seeing the potential in this book way back when it had no plot (and then making me add a plot!) and for your constant support since. And to the entire coven of love—Kelsey Rodkey, Andrea Contos, Rachel Solomon, Susan Lee, and SPJ—thank you for putting up with my constant subway crying. You make my words and my life better.

Thank you to everyone at the New School for inspiring my writing, especially Nadja Tiktinsky, Haley Neil, Victoria Voigt, Annie Fillenwarth, Ashley Mays, Ace Boutin, Finn Moore, and Madison Lewis, for the steady support of emotional and writerly Band-Aids. Special thanks to Professor Caron Levis for making me fall in love with writing all over again. Thanks also to my NYU community, especially the suffer club, my academic soulmate Maggie Iuni, and Professor Pat Crain, for all your support on my thesis.

Thank you to everyone who saw me through this process: Evelyn Luchs, Brooke Holman, Karis Rogerson, Jack Filsinger, Marisa Kanter, Carlyn Greenwald, Dr. Cullen, and Raseel Sharaf—not all heroes wear capes.

And, of course, my eternal thanks to my family. To my mom, for reading to me before I knew how and making me a writer since before I can remember. To my dad, for his constant support (sorry there's no janitor). To my brother, for illustrating the first book I ever wrote and for letting me turn all our Monopoly games into elaborate storytimes. To my aunt, who always believed in me. To my cousin, the very coolest person I know. To my grandparents, for always being there for me. To my stepfamily, for showing me all along what it takes Sophia the whole book to learn. And to Sammy, who sometimes stopped sitting directly on my keyboard long enough for me to get a few words in.

ABOUT THE AUTHOR

AURIANE DESOMBRE is a former English teacher pursuing an MA in English literature at New York University and an MFA in creative writing for children at the New School in New York. *I Think I Love You* is her debut novel.

aurianedesombre.com

GET
Underlined

**A Community of YA Book Nerds
& Aspiring Writers!**

READ

Book recommendations, reading lists, YA news

LIFE

Quizzes, book trailers, author videos

PERKS

Giveaways, merch, sneak peeks

CREATE

Community stories, writing contests and advice

We want to hear YOUR story!
Create an account to write original stories,
connect with fellow book nerds and authors, build
a personal bookshelf, and get access to content
based on your interests!

GetUnderlined.com
@GetUnderlined

Want a chance to be featured? Use #GetUnderlined on social!